BY CAMILLE KELLOGG

Just as You Are

The Next Chapter

THE NEXT CHAPTER

THE NEXT CHAPTER

A NOVEL

CAMILLE KELLOGG

THE DIAL PRESS
NEW YORK

The Dial Press
An imprint of Random House
A division of Penguin Random House LLC
1745 Broadway, New York, NY 10019
randomhousebooks.com
penguinrandomhouse.com

A Dial Press Trade Paperback Original

Copyright © 2025 by Camille Kellogg
Dial Delights Extras copyright © 2025 by Camille Kellogg

Penguin Random House values and supports copyright. Copyright fuels creativity, encourages diverse voices, promotes free speech, and creates a vibrant culture. Thank you for buying an authorized edition of this book and for complying with copyright laws by not reproducing, scanning, or distributing any part of it in any form without permission. You are supporting writers and allowing Penguin Random House to continue to publish books for every reader. Please note that no part of this book may be used or reproduced in any manner for the purpose of training artificial intelligence technologies or systems.

THE DIAL PRESS is a registered trademark and the colophon is a trademark of Penguin Random House LLC.
DIAL DELIGHTS and colophon are trademarks of Penguin Random House LLC.

LIBRARY OF CONGRESS CATALOGING-IN-PUBLICATION DATA
Names: Kellogg, Camille, author.
Title: The next chapter / Camille Kellogg.
Description: New York, NY: The Dial Press, 2025.
Identifiers: LCCN 2025000780 (print) | LCCN 2025000781 (ebook) |
ISBN 9780593730539 (trade paperback; acid-free paper) |
ISBN 9780593730546 (ebook)
Subjects: LCGFT: Romance fiction. | Queer fiction. | Novels.
Classification: LCC PS3611.E4439 N49 2025 (print) | LCC PS3611.E4439 (ebook) |
DDC 813/.6—dc23/eng/20250108
LC record available at https://lccn.loc.gov/2025000780
LC ebook record available at https://lccn.loc.gov/2025000781

Printed in the United States of America on acid-free paper

1st Printing

BOOK TEAM: Production editor: Cara DuBois • Managing editor: Rebecca Berlant • Production manager: Ali Wagner • Copy editor: Mimi Lipson • Proofreaders: Liz Carbonell, Julie Ehlers, Alissa Fitzgerald

Book design by Alexis Flynn

Title-page art: Little Monster 2070/Adobe Stock

The authorized representative in the EU for product safety and compliance is Penguin Random House Ireland, Morrison Chambers, 32 Nassau Street, Dublin D02 YH68, Ireland. https://eu-contact.penguin.ie

To everyone who's still figuring it out.

CONTENT WARNING

This book contains depictions of disordered eating, panic attacks, and the loss of a parent.

THE
NEXT
CHAPTER

CHAPTER 1

JUDE

Jude Thacker was crying at work. Again. Something that her boss had explicitly forbidden her from doing.

Not just because her boss was a heartless, emotion-hating corporate overlord (although he was). The rule was mostly based on the hypothesis that if a customer walks into a bookstore and sees a butch woman sobbing hysterically behind the checkout counter, that person will probably feel uncomfortable and less inclined to linger. Weeping was not good for business—even if it *was* over the new, exquisitely perfect Eileen Styles book.

But Jude couldn't help it. She was a book crier. It was part of who she was, an essential square in the quilt of her personality. The second someone's curmudgeonly but wise grandmother went into the hospital, or a beloved dog died, or a main character fell ill and their love interest canceled everything to care for them—waterworks.

In this case, the book in question wasn't even sad. It was just so *good*, a romance where the characters completely, obviously belonged together but the main character was too stubborn to get over her fear of needing someone else—until her love interest got injured in the curling tournament semifinals and seeing her carried off the ice on a stretcher made the narrator realize that she would do anything to be with this girl. It was beautiful. And also a painful reminder that Jude was extremely, depressingly single.

Thus, the tears. They were sad-happy-depressed-jealous-joyful tears. *Complex* tears. Jude contained multitudes.

She was rereading the final chapter for the fourth time while wiping her eyes with her increasingly soggy sweatshirt sleeve when someone leaned across the checkout counter of the Next Chapter bookstore and asked, in a wary but sympathetic tone, "Are you okay?"

Jude jumped. She hadn't even heard a customer come inside—that was how bad of a bookseller she was being. But in her defense, it was a weekday at 2:30. The lull zone. She'd thought she was safe to cry in peace. Snapping the book shut, she opened her mouth to explain to the customer that, yes, she was okay, she was just an overly emotional sap who got too attached to fictional characters. Then she looked up. And suddenly Jude was not, in fact, okay.

Because across the counter from her sodden self was the most beautiful woman she'd ever seen.

The woman was small—petite and several inches shorter than the average person who leaned across Jude's counter. She had pale skin and dark eyebrows and dark hair that stopped a little above shoulder length. And she was *pretty*, with big brown eyes that looked up at Jude in concern and pale pink lips that were quirked a little with amusement at whatever dumbfounded expression Jude was making. She was wearing a black shirt with a silky red bomber jacket, and she had one hand on the counter as she leaned in, bringing her face only a few inches away from Jude's.

Whatever Jude had been about to say died in her throat.

Why had this customer come in today of all days, a day when Jude had been *crying* and not, say, carrying heavy boxes with her biceps on display?

"Am I okay?" Jude repeated the question, remembering that she had to say *something*. "Unfortunately, no. I just finished Eileen Styles's new rom-com and it has destroyed me emotionally. I may never recover."

"Oh my God, *Curled Around Your Finger*? No spoilers!" The woman's hands shot up to cover her ears. "I haven't read it yet. Actually"—she lowered her hands and glared at Jude suspiciously—"it doesn't even come out until next week. How are you reading it?"

Jude let out a small, guilty laugh, but internally she was fist-pumping. Eileen Styles wrote lesbian love stories. And if this woman was into them enough to know the next publication date—well, Jude's one-in-one-billion odds of having a shot with her had just turned into one-in-one-million. "Bookseller privilege. The boxes arrived this morning, and they're embargoed until Tuesday, buuuuuut I may have opened one box. Just to, you know, check that they were the right book." She made a show of looking around nervously, even though the only other employee working today was in the back doing inventory. "You won't sell me out to my boss, will you?"

"I would never sell out another Eileen stan," the woman said earnestly. She tipped up onto her toes to peer over the counter at the book. Jude could smell a faint waft of perfume—something floral and subtly sweet. "Was it magical?"

"Unbelievably magical. I think it's her best one yet."

"Better than *The Tundras of Your Heart*?" The woman pursed her lips to the side skeptically.

"*Way* better. She's grown so much as a writer since then."

The woman sighed. "Can I hold it?"

Jude passed her the book and watched as the woman stared at it dreamily, tracing a finger across the illustration of two women in curling uniforms, making flirty eye contact over their poised brooms. Then she turned it over to read the back.

"Knowing this book is coming has been the only thing keeping me going this month," she said. "It's silly, but Eileen's books feel like the only thing I can depend on sometimes. No matter how upside-down my life feels, I always know that her books are going to be good."

"That's not silly at all." Jude only hesitated for a moment before adding, "Keep it."

The woman looked up. "Oh, no, I couldn't—won't you get in trouble?"

Jude shrugged nonchalantly. "I won't sell it to you," she said. "It's just a copy that mysteriously went missing." She smiled, and after a beat, the woman smiled back. It was a beautiful smile, open and warm and friendly.

"Thank you." The woman wrapped her arms around the book, hugging it to her chest. "Really. That means a lot to me."

"I'm Jude." Jude didn't normally shake customers' hands, but she held hers out before she could second-guess the gesture. When their hands touched, Jude was glad she had.

"Kat." She looked up at Jude through her eyelashes and then glanced away, the cute gesture making Jude's stomach fizz like a bath bomb.

"Can I help you find anything?" Jude asked, eager to keep the conversation going.

"Well . . ." Kat ran her hand through her hair, just over the left ear, pushing it back. "I actually have a list of books I came for. But while I'm here, do you have any other books like Eileen Styles?"

Jude tried not to let her grin grow too cocky. Recommending books was what Jude did best. It was her passion, her most highly rated skill. If there was an Olympic book rec-ing event, Jude could have snagged the gold.

"We actually have the biggest queer book selection of any store in New York," Jude said with pride, coming out from behind the counter. Now that they were closer, the contrast between their heights was more pronounced, making Jude feel twice as tall as usual. Jude led her over to their queer section: an entire wall of the store, decorated with different pride flags. "Which books have you read already?"

"Um." Kat blushed, her cheeks turning a delicious shade of dark pink. "I've read all of Eileen Styles's books, but not much else. I'd love some more romance novels, but also, maybe . . ." She hesitated again. "Just any queer book recommendations that you have?"

Jude bounced on the balls of her feet. "Well, then, we are going to be here for a long time, because I have millions. But I'll do my best to restrain myself a *little*." She started pulling out titles. "These are probably my top three favorite sapphic romance novels," she said, handing them to Kat. "And these are my favorite queer literary fiction books." She tugged three more books off the shelf in quick succession. She loved flying between the shelves like this—it felt like a dance. She had worked at The Next Chapter since she was fifteen and she knew every inch of every display.

"This one is a memoir about an abusive relationship, just so you're warned," Jude said, tapping *In the Dream House*. "And this one is beautifully written, but also unbelievably sexy." She plopped *Mrs. S* onto the pile. "And *that* one"—she tapped *Mistakes Were Made,* which Kat was already holding—"has finger banging on page seven. And strap-on sex!"

Kat's blush turned even deeper, and Jude wondered if she'd crossed a line. But then Kat let out a little laugh and said, "I'll take it."

Jude grinned, then eyed the growing stack in Kat's arms and rubbed the back of her neck. "I should probably stop."

"No, don't," Kat said. "I really need to read more queer books. I'm a little embarrassed that I haven't already. I randomly found one of Eileen Styles's books in an airport and read everything she wrote, but after that . . . I guess I just didn't really know where to start." She darted a glance at Jude, as if afraid of being judged.

"I totally understand," Jude said. "Queer books have a real visibility issue, so unless you know where to go looking for them, it can feel really intimidating to get started. That's part of why we have such a big queer section here—it helps people realize just how many options are out there."

"That's amazing." Kat surveyed the shelves, shaking her head a little bit. Jude felt a rush of pride. She loved seeing the awed expression in queer people's eyes when they came into the bookstore. They had spent their whole lives being inundated with straight stories; there was something profoundly moving about realizing that you weren't as alone as you'd thought.

Kat set her books on one of the display tables and fidgeted with them, lining up the edges. Jude could tell before she spoke that the question she was about to ask would not be a casual one. "Do you have any, like, guides? Like, how-to books?" She didn't look at Jude as she said it.

Jude felt a sympathetic twinge in her chest. She recognized that feigned nonchalance and could sense the need under it. She could hear the questions Kat wasn't asking, *How do I do this? How do I go about building this life that's so different from the one I grew up expecting?*

"Here." Jude pulled down *This Book Is Gay*. "This book says it's aimed at teens but it's really helpful for everyone. And this one is essays by a woman who came out in her thirties." She placed *Would You Rather?* in Kat's hand.

Kat blinked up at Jude with her big, wide eyes. Jude wanted to hug her. She wanted to wrap her arms around this softhearted, brave, unsure person and tell her that it was all going to be okay, and that no matter how hard figuring all this stuff out was, it was worth it.

But Jude didn't know how to say all that to a stranger without being weird or presumptuous. So instead, Jude gave Kat a small smile and tried to convey it with her eyes.

Kat gave a small smile back. "What if—" She stopped and

cleared her throat a little bit, then continued in a hesitant voice. "I have this friend who . . . doesn't really know what label is right for them? And hasn't really, like, done anything about it? Could that person still call themselves 'queer'?"

"Absolutely," Jude said in a soft voice. "I mean, I'm not the arbiter of what's queer and what isn't. But that's the thing—no one is. You don't need to be one hundred percent sure of your sexuality to call yourself queer. In fact, most people aren't *ever* completely sure. If *queer* feels right to you, you get to call yourself queer. Even if you're worried you might change your mind later. Even if other people try to tell you that you can't." Jude shrugged. "At least that's what I believe. And what most of the queer people I know think, too."

Kat stared at her, and Jude swallowed. Had she said too much, gone on for too long, overstepped a boundary? But then Kat blinked rapidly and looked away, and Jude realized she was trying not to cry.

"I, um," Kat said, her voice a little thick. "Thank you. I needed to— I mean, my friend needed to hear that." She winced. "Will have needed to hear that?" She raised her eyebrows and laughed awkwardly, and Jude laughed, too.

Damn, she was cute with her little self-deprecating grin. Jude had stepped closer when she handed over the last book, and neither of them had moved back. Jude's heart started to race. She could feel every inch between them, excruciatingly aware of how little space separated their bodies.

Kat's dark eyes tugged on Jude like a magnet, making her unable to look away. The collar of her T-shirt felt three times tighter than it had this morning. Jude was aware that it was her turn to say something, but all she could think about was how the air seemed to be growing heavier around them, pressing them toward each other. She couldn't stop herself from taking a small step forward—a tiny step, but one that Kat mirrored immediately. Her perfume smelled like sun-warmed flower petals. Even though they had just met, Jude wanted to kiss her. Admitting that to herself made her already racing heart race even harder, squeezing on each beat like a fist clenching hard.

Clenching very hard. Clenching *too* hard. Each beat so strong it felt like her heart was filling up her throat, squeezing the passageways she needed to breathe.

Oh no. Not here. Not now.

Jude's fingers had gone numb. Her wrists tingled painfully, and she twisted them in tight circles, trying to stop the sensation before it climbed higher up her arms. Trying to stop herself before she went too far.

She could not have a panic attack in front of this woman. She could not start thinking about what had happened the last time she'd asked someone out and what that had led to. But suddenly, that was all Jude could see—Becca, biting her lip by the store's biography section. Looking up at Jude with those regretful, pitying eyes. Saying, "I'm sorry, Jude. It's just better this way," and then walking out, the cheerful shop bell chiming behind her.

Jude's heart became a frantic wingbeat in her chest. Her throat was clogged. Something was blocking it. She couldn't get enough air. What was wrong with her? She just needed to *calm down* and breathe. She was fine. So why wouldn't her body recognize that?

She took a step back from Kat, then another.

"Is there anything else I can help you with today?" Without meaning to, Jude had dropped back into her customer-service self, the words coming out with an impersonal lilt.

Kat stared. "Oh." Her voice sounded confused. "Um, I—" She fumbled in her purse for her phone, then held it out so Jude could see a Notes app list with four titles on it. "Do you have these?"

"Of course. Let me grab them."

Jude's hands shook as she found the books. What was she

doing? Why was she blowing this? But her chest felt squeezed now, in addition to her throat, and black snowflakes had started to fall in the corners of her vision. What if she really couldn't breathe? What if she was having a heart attack? Was she going to collapse right here?

Jude dropped the books on the counter and hurried behind it. The second she did, she felt a little better. Her heart was still thrumming desperately against her too-tight chest, but she could breathe a little more. She knew every inch of this counter. She was safe here.

"Which of these would you like?" she asked, gesturing at the pile of books she'd recommended without looking up.

"All of them, I guess."

"*All* of them?" Jude must have pulled over a dozen books from the shelf. "Are you sure?"

"Yeah." Kat's voice was flat.

Jude wished she could shake off her panic and act normal again, but she couldn't seem to do it—her spine refused to relax, and her eyes wouldn't lift to meet Kat's. She rang up the books in silence. It seemed to take an impossibly long time, the strained silence broken only by the irregular beep as she scanned each title.

"And a tote bag, please," Kat said. Her voice was stiff and formal.

Jude tucked the books into one of their store-branded tote bags and then slid the bag across the counter. This was the last possible moment to ask for Kat's number or invite her for a drink or say *something*. Jude opened her mouth, willing herself to find the courage, willing her throat to find the words.

But what came out instead was "That'll be two hundred and nineteen dollars."

Kat rummaged in her purse, her jaw tight. She didn't look at Jude as she dropped eleven twenties on the counter. Jude reached for the cash register to get her change, but Kat hooked the tote bag over her shoulder and moved away from the counter. With a huge effort, Jude managed to look up and meet her gaze.

"It was really nice to meet you, Jude," Kat said in a quiet voice. "Thank you for the recommendations."

Jude just nodded. She couldn't speak. Kat gave her one last look. Then she turned away. The bell over the door gave its familiar cheery ring as she opened it, then let it swing shut behind her.

And just like that, Jude let another incredible woman walk out of her life.

CHAPTER 2

KAT

Kat only made it two blocks from the bookstore before she had to stop and sit down—in part because her tote bag was unbearably heavy (she hadn't thought through the carrying-them-home part when she'd purchased the books), but mostly because she had a suspicion that her face had turned a mortifying shade of red, and that if she didn't stop and take a few deep breaths, she was going to be walking around the West Village looking like a tomato.

She sat on a bench in a little triangle-shaped park and focused on the trickling sounds of the fountain in the park's center. She watched pigeons strut around the water's edge, bickering over pizza crusts and fluffing themselves up to look bigger. But it wasn't enough to distract her from her humiliation. She had practically thrown herself at Jude, and Jude had rushed her out like she couldn't wait to get rid of her.

Kat had noticed Jude the second she walked into the bookstore. And not just because she was crying, either. Jude was seriously cute, tall and stocky with soft blond hair in a short boyish cut. Exactly the kind of butch that Kat liked to pine over during late-night Instagram spirals. When Jude's gray-green eyes had met Kat's, she'd had to stop herself from letting her mouth hang open. But it was Jude's *grin* that had made her feel completely lightheaded. It had tugged up one side of her mouth more than the other. Like a smirk, but nicer. As if you were in on the joke.

She had been so friendly, too. As she'd enthusiastically piled books into Kat's hands, Kat had felt a magnetic tug toward Jude, urging her to get closer. The pull had been so strong that she'd forgotten to worry that she had only ever kissed one girl before and what if she was terrible at it and what if Jude asked her out and then Kat totally embarrassed herself because she didn't know anything about lesbian dating and what if she—

Nope. Nuh-uh. She needed to reel these thoughts in. She needed to save her baby-queer spirals for the middle of the night at home, where no one could look over her shoulder while she took BuzzFeed quizzes with titles like "Are You a Top or a Bottom?" followed immediately by googling "What is top or bottom for lesbians?" The population of the West Village did *not* need to see that.

Kat took a deep breath and tried to stop obsessing over the many ways that she could potentially embarrass herself if she ever actually got to the point of going on a date with a woman. Which was looking increasingly unlikely, based on the encounter she'd just had.

Kat groaned and hunched over on the bench. The thing was, Kat could have sworn that Jude had been feeling the same way. But then something had changed. What had she done to make Jude suddenly lose interest like that?

Kat stood up and hoisted the tote bag over her shoulder. She was being ridiculous. She should just go back to the bookstore and ask Jude if she wanted to get a drink sometime. It was no big deal.

Kat made it half a block before she stopped again. She leaned against a lamppost, worrying the straps of the tote bag with her fingers.

It wasn't fear stopping her, necessarily. Asking someone out didn't scare Kat. If Jude had been a guy, then Kat would have undone another button on her shirt, marched in, leaned seductively over the counter, and instructed him to take her out for dinner tonight. She would have felt in control, confident, seductive.

But Jude wasn't a guy. And for some reason, that made everything seem different.

Kat had never asked a girl out before. The moves Kat used on guys might not work on women. What if the rules were different? What if she totally humiliated herself by asking Jude out in a straight girl way that turned Jude off? Or, worse, what if Jude felt creeped on? Kat hated when guys kept making their interest known after Kat had tried to politely turn them down. And this was Jude's workplace, where she *had* to be polite to Kat.

Oh my God. Kat was a sexual predator.

Her face burned even brighter red and she covered it with her hands, hoping the coldness of her fingertips would draw out some of the color. How did you approach a woman without making her uncomfortable? With guys, it was easy—even if the guy wasn't interested, he would probably feel flattered by being approached. Not unsafe. Kat didn't want to make any woman feel unsafe. She knew how unpleasant that could be.

Kat groaned into her hands. Why was being queer so complicated?

She spun around and started walking away from the bookstore, back toward home.

It was the middle of a weekday, but Bleecker Street was crowded. People rushed by her, hurrying into bodegas, peering through the windows of bakeries, and emerging from an old-fashioned Italian deli with foil-wrapped sandwiches the size of skateboards in their arms. Kat slowed to stare at a huge store dedicated entirely to cheese, then a smaller store that seemed to only sell soap shaped like cupcakes. She passed three different pizza places, all claiming to be the best in the city, as proclaimed by various pizza authorities, and a row of vendors selling jewelry from folding tables on the sidewalk. The amount of people walking around was overwhelming. They jostled her, pushing past without looking at her, shoving at all sides. It was stressful and overstimulating, but there was something nice about being part of the crowd. She could be out in the world, among people, but still in her own bubble of anonymity.

But the chaos wasn't enough to distract Kat from thinking about Jude.

The farther she walked, the more she reconvinced herself. Jude had *definitely* been flirting. The eye contact. The lingering handshake. That little smirk when Kat had asked for recommendations. Kat was good at reading people, and there was no way that had all been in her head.

She had to go back.

She had just changed directions for a third time and started striding back toward the bookstore when someone called her name. Not Kat but her full name: Katrina Kelly.

Shit, Kat thought, even as her body reacted instinctively, her spine straightening and her mouth curving into a smile. She thought about pretending not to have heard, but she'd already slowed. She couldn't run away now without being obvious about it.

So much for her bubble of anonymity.

She turned around. Two girls were hurrying up to her, wide-eyed and blushing. They were both wearing patterned jumpsuits.

"Oh my God, are you Lily from *P.R.O.M.*?" the blond girl in the lead asked. Her fingers tightened around her cup of iced coffee until the plastic buckled. "That was, like, my favorite TV show as a kid!"

"Yup!" Kat said brightly, trying not to wince at how loud the girl's voice was. "That's me! Do you want a picture?" Over the years, Kat had learned that it was always quicker to offer fans what they wanted than to wait for them to pull themselves together enough to awkwardly stumble through the ask.

"Oh my God, I *told* you," the blond girl said to her friend. "We're visiting from Boston and I was like, 'Oh my God, wouldn't it be so cool if we saw someone famous?' and she was like, 'We're not going to see anyone famous, this isn't L.A.,' and then I was like, 'I think that's Lily from P.R.O.M.,' and she was like, 'Who?' But I was right!"

Kat laughed politely, although she wasn't sure if the story was supposed to be funny. She noticed a few people glancing curiously at her as they walked past. She needed to get out there before more people recognized her.

"Here, let's take a selfie!" Kat stepped in between the two girls and put a hand on each of their backs, trying to hurry them along. She smiled as the blond girl held up her phone and snapped a couple of shots. When she finished, Kat pulled away, relieved. Now she just had to extract herself.

"I *have* to ask," the girl said, clutching Kat's wrist. Her hand was unpleasantly clammy from the iced coffee. "Are you dating Frasier Pierce? I heard a rumor that you were back together and, oh my God, I would be so happy I would die! Your romance was, like, the whole reason I watched the show."

Kat grimaced before she could help herself. Frasier was a pile of shit in human form, and she couldn't believe her self-esteem had ever been dire enough for her to actually date him. She hadn't seen him in years, either, so she had no idea where this dating rumor had come from. Frasier himself, probably.

Kat let out a bubbly laugh in hopes it would distract from her earlier pained expression. "Now, you know I can't kiss and tell!" Her voice had taken on a girly inflection so fake she wondered that the blonde didn't call her out on it. "But Frasier and I have remained *really* good friends since the show ended. I have to run, but it was *so* nice to meet you both! Thank you for being fans!"

She waved cheerfully to the girls and stepped decisively away from them into the street, risking getting taken out by an e-bike to make her escape. She started walking off as fast as she could.

That hadn't been her best fan encounter. Usually, Kat was smooth and gracious when people recognized her, able to keep them moving while still making them feel valued. Her manager occasionally trolled through social media looking for fans describing the times they'd met her, just to make sure that Kat was coming off as "nice and approachable" enough. But Kat had been caught off guard this time, and she'd let her eagerness to move on show through.

She should have been more prepared. Especially when walking around in public like this. She should have been wearing sunglasses, at the very least, but she'd forgotten to put them back on when she came out of the bookstore. She'd forgotten about everything except for Jude.

Kat had booked her first movie at the age of eleven, a minor role with one spoken line. She had continued to book increasingly larger parts until her breakout role in *Spy Pigs*, a shockingly successful children's film about a farm girl who realized her pigs were undercover spies. After that, she had starred in five different blockbuster movies and five seasons of *P.R.O.M.*, a monster-of-the-week dramedy about members of a dance committee who were also superheroes. Now she had eight million Instagram followers, excellent name recognition, and she couldn't go anywhere without people stopping her to take photos.

She was also completely uncastable.

Once she turned twenty-one and the network decided not to renew *P.R.O.M.*, Kat's career had ended. Three years later she was still famous, still high-profile enough to get tables at restaurants and invites to top parties, but she was a child star who had aged out of children's shows. Everyone from fans to casting directors looked at her and only saw Lily Carlson, the plucky superhero lead from the TV show.

Except for Jude. Kat was certain that Jude hadn't recognized her. That for once someone was flirting with her because they liked Kat and not Lily Carlson.

But apparently, Kat without Lily hadn't been enough.

Kat pulled her sunglasses out of her purse and put them on. The tote bag on her shoulder seemed to grow even heavier as she realized that there was no way she could go back to the bookstore. She'd been delusional to even consider it. Her career was already in shambles, and she'd never fix it if a story leaked to the press about Kat begging a bookstore employee for a date and getting turned down.

It had been nice to pretend for a little while. But that was all she'd been doing: pretending. Even if Jude *had* asked for her number, it never would have worked out. Once she found out who Kat was, she would have either gotten caught up in wanting a piece of Kat's fame or—if she was smart—run the hell away and found someone normal to date.

It was for the best that Jude hadn't asked her out, because at least this way Kat could pretend that if something had happened between them, it would have been magic. She could lie awake at night and dream about how soft Jude's blond hair might have felt beneath her fingers or what it would have felt like to have Jude push her up against those bookstore shelves and kiss her hard.

Dreams were almost always better than reality, in Kat's experience.

She started walking back toward her newly rented apartment in Chelsea. Suddenly, the energy of the city felt suffocating. There were too many noises and too many people. She'd only been here a week, but she missed the peaceful seclusion of L.A.

It didn't help that her stomach was starting to tighten into a hard, twisted knot as she realized just how foolish she'd been earlier. She'd asked Jude for queer book recommendations. She wasn't supposed to confirm her sexuality in public like that.

Worse, she'd asked for a literal guide to being queer. Sure, she'd given an abbreviated version of her name and paid in cash, but eventually Jude would realize who she was. Kat could see the tabloid article now: "Katrina Kelly Is Queer Poser; Begs Bookstore Employee for Advice."

Well, maybe they'd come up with a catchier headline. But the effect would be the same. Disastrous. What had she been thinking?

She *hadn't* been thinking. She'd stopped thinking as soon as she saw Jude reading the Eileen Styles book. Kat *loved* her books, and she'd never had anyone to talk to about them before. Plus, it had felt so nice to talk to another queer person. Jude had seemed so nonjudgmental and so excited to show off the bookstore's queer-books display. It had made Kat feel strangely safe, and she hadn't been able to resist asking one of the many, many questions that she'd been worrying about for the past two months, in between binging L Word episodes with her headphones on and using incognito windows to search things like "How do you know if you're bi or pan or gay?"

Kat felt a flush cover her face and spread down to her neck as she remembered asking Jude if she could call herself queer. Not only that, but she'd very obviously made up a fake friend to do it. She might as well have rented a billboard that said, "I'm insecure and don't know the first thing about being LGBTQ+."

That had been right before Jude had stopped smoldering at Kat with those beautiful eyes and turned into a cold customer-service robot.

Kat clenched her hands into fists. *Now* she knew what had made Jude change her mind. Kat had been wasting her time wondering if she wasn't pretty enough or if she'd said something wrong when the answer was obvious. She wasn't queer enough. Jude had decided that some inexperienced baby gay wasn't worth her time, and she'd hustled Kat out of the store as fast as possible.

Well, fuck her. Kat didn't need Jude. Especially not right now, when she needed to be completely focused on resuscitating what was left of her career.

Hopefully Jude would never realize who Kat was. And if Jude did decide to sell the story to a magazine, Kat would have her manager deny the whole thing.

Until something happened, there was no point in worrying about this anymore. Jude was just some random jerk, and Kat had already wasted too much time on her. She was going to forget about this whole encounter and move on.

Which would be easy, because she would never see Jude again.

CHAPTER 3

JUDE

"And then you just *let her leave*?"

Jude's already hot face grew even hotter. She was starting to regret telling this story. But after two days of mentally beating herself up for not getting Kat's number, she hadn't been able to keep her mistake to herself any longer.

"What was I supposed to do? Kiss a customer in the middle of the store?"

All three of her fellow booksellers let out a loud, simultaneous groan. Jude was suddenly glad that she had the checkout counter between her and her friends. It kept her out of shoulder-shaking range.

"No, you were supposed to ask her out!" Rhys Miller said from where he was leaning against the Biography shelf. "You two were clearly flirting."

"Well, then, why didn't she ask for *my* number?" Jude countered.

L. J. Jeong, the bookstore's event coordinator, who was sitting on the little step stool used to reach the upper shelves, shook their head, apparently too disgusted to even respond.

"Maybe because you didn't give her any signals that you were interested, because you're too much of a chicken," Talia Cohen said. She was perched on the edge of the Notable Nonfiction table, kicking her rainbow Chucks.

"I am not a chicken!" Jude protested, and everyone scoffed again.

"Dude, I love you, but you're such a chicken," Rhys said, crossing his arms. He was wearing a black short-sleeved button-down shirt, and Jude couldn't help noticing that his biceps looked much bigger than the last time she'd seen them. Testosterone was really working for him. "When's the last time you went on a date?"

Jude ignored him and started organizing the stack of receipts. Rhys knew when. He just wanted to hear her say it.

L.J. and Talia exchanged looks.

"Not since Becca?" Talia said. She tugged at the worn-out collar of her *Phantom of the Opera* T-shirt. "Really?"

"Damn. That was like two years ago." L.J. didn't bother to hide the disbelief in their voice.

Jude glared. "Yeah, well, it was kind of a tough one."

L.J. held up their hands defensively. "I know."

"We *all* know," Talia said. "But you have to move on, Jude. You can't be afraid forever."

"I'm not afraid," Jude snapped. She turned and stomped to the back of the store, where they had stacked the boxes that needed unpacking. She could feel her friends exchanging looks behind her back as she cut into the first box. She yanked out a stack of books and started piling them on the New Releases table. When the box was empty, Jude sighed and turned around.

"I was going to ask for her number," she said, avoiding her friends' eyes. "But I got nervous, and I choked." She ran her hands through her hair and groaned. "But this girl was perfect, guys. I fucked up."

"Yup," L.J. said in their typically blunt manner. "You really did."

Rhys shoved L.J.'s shoulder, almost knocking them off the step stool. "Maybe you can find her," he said. "It's a little bit creepy, but you could look at the name on her credit card."

Jude shook her head. She'd already thought of that. "She paid in cash."

Rhys sucked his lips in between his teeth, thinking.

"You should post a missed connection!" Talia said, fluttering her hands with excitement. "On Lex and Craigslist. I do that all the time."

"All the time?" L.J. said, with slight scorn. "How often is 'all the time'?"

Talia shrugged. "Like once a week or so. Whenever I see someone hot on the subway or at the bar."

L.J. rolled their eyes. "Why don't you just talk to them?"

"You mean just walk up to a total stranger in public and say, 'Hi, you're hot,' with no preamble?" Talia asked.

"I mean, there's not no preamble," L.J. said. "First you look at them a little bit. Make eye contact. And then when they look back at you and blush and give you subtle cues, *then* you go over and say something."

"Okay, but that's a *you* thing," Talia countered. "No one is turning into a blushing mess just because I *looked* at them a little bit on the subway. We can't all be the Casanova of Crown Heights."

It was L.J.'s turn to blush. "Will you let that go?"

"Hey, if you didn't want a group of girls to make a zine dedicated to your sex appeal, you shouldn't have slept with so many studio art majors."

L.J. scoffed. "Okay, Tinderella, when's the last time you walked into a gay bar without seeing five people you've been on dates with?"

"Okay, okay. Break it up." Rhys stepped in between Talia and L.J. and held out his hands. Without Rhys refereeing, the two of them would spend roughly 80 percent of their time bickering.

"The focus is on Jude's terrible dating life, not yours. Although, Talia, how often do you actually get a response when you post a missed connection?"

Talia's face fell. "Well, it *could* happen."

Jude groaned. "I'll never find her," she said. "This girl was probably my soulmate, and now I'm going to die alone because I was too scared to ask for her number."

"Okay, that's a *little* bit dramatic, buddy," Rhys said, clapping a hand on Jude's back. "There will be other girls. You just need to take more chances. Get outside of your comfort zone a little."

"Not right now, Rhys. Please." Rhys had given Jude a variation of the comfort-zone speech every few months since her breakup with Becca two years ago, urging her to try new things and meet new people. And sure, Jude liked her routines. But it wasn't like she was a *hermit* or anything.

"Fine, fine." Rhys went back to leaning against the shelf. "But at least—"

The door to the back room opened, and he fell silent as Stephen Delk, owner of the local franchise Book City and the current owner of The Next Chapter, stepped out, pulling on his coat. Stephen raised his eyebrows.

"It's never a good sign when you walk into a room and people stop talking," he said in the smooth tone that had once made *The New Yorker* call him "charming and impertinent."

Jude managed a weak smile. "Just chatting about the events calendar for next month," she said. "We're debating adding a teen book club."

"You guys and your book clubs." Stephen straightened his collar and strode to the door. "But as long as they're buying the books, I suppose it doesn't matter. Not like those volunteer nights. Which have stopped. Right?"

"Right." Jude dug her fingernails into her palms. For years, The Next Chapter had partnered with a prison advocacy group to host letter-writing campaigns and protest-sign-making parties.

But as they didn't actually sell books during those after-hours events, Stephen had put a stop to them. He claimed it was for insurance and liability reasons, but Jude was pretty sure he just didn't want his employees using *his* bookstore like it was their own.

Stephen paused with his hand on the door handle, his gaze sharpening on the display table closest to the exit. "Why isn't the new Nick Rooney book on the New Releases table?"

"Is it not?" Jude asked in a hopefully innocent tone. Nick Rooney wrote extremely conservative and, unfortunately, extremely popular books on social theory.

"We've been over this, Jude. It's not up to us to decide what people read. We offer them both sides." He glared at Jude, who glared back for a few seconds before remembering her need to stay employed and lowering her gaze. "Besides, conservatives sell. I want those books front and center by end of day. Got it?"

"Got it." The words felt hard and bitter in her throat.

"Good." Stephen yanked open the door and stalked out.

"God, that guy is the worst," Rhys muttered once the door closed behind him.

"A total dumbass, too," L.J. said. "He *knows* our brand is a queer and feminist bookstore. That's where our three hundred thousand Instagram followers come from. Selling 'both sides' might work at Book City, but the reason we work here is because we're specialized."

Jude grunted in agreement as she went to the back room and unearthed the box of Nick Rooney books she'd hidden behind the fridge. She had spent years building that Instagram following through tongue-in-cheek book recommendations and literary memes. It was a huge part of why the bookstore was still open. But did Stephen recognize that? Of course not.

"We're way over three hundred thousand now, actually," Jude said, shouldering back through the swinging door with the box. "We got a wave of new followers after that meme you came up with, Talia."

She dropped the box and pulled out her phone to show Talia their new follower count but stopped when she saw that the account had more than a hundred notifications.

"Hey, check this out," Jude said. "Someone must have tagged us in something, because the Instagram is blowing up."

She opened the post, waiting as it loaded slowly due to the store's bad Wi-Fi. The photo was just a tote bag from the store next to a stack of books. Some bookstagrammer, maybe. Jude checked the username.

"Someone named Katrina Kelly," she said, clicking on the profile and watching the little loading circle spin.

"Did you say *Katrina Kelly* just tagged us in a post?" Talia jumped off the table and grabbed Jude's phone.

"Who?" Jude said.

"Are you kidding? Didn't you watch TV growing up? The girl from *Spy Pigs*? Lily from *P.R.O.M.*?"

Jude glanced at Rhys, who shrugged, but L.J. was nodding, too. "I had such a crush on her in that show," they said. "She was the one with the catchphrase. What was it?"

"'Just because we're saving the world doesn't mean we can't look our best!'" Talia recited.

Jude rolled her eyes. "Can't believe I missed that one."

"Everyone is saying that Katrina is secretly queer," Talia said, still scrolling through Jude's phone.

"Who's 'everyone'?" L.J. asked.

Talia waved a dismissive hand. "You know. The internet."

"Ah, yes," L.J. said. "Your real friends."

Talia flipped L.J. off, then handed Jude her phone back. "Anyway, she has eight million followers, so this is great for our account."

"Oh, that's awe—" Jude started to say. Then she stopped, cutting off her words with a strangled whimpering sound.

"What's wrong?" Rhys pushed off the bookshelf with his shoulder blades, looking concerned. But Jude just stared at the photo that had caught her eye: a glamour shot of Katrina Kelly standing on a cobblestone street in SoHo, wearing a leather jacket and looking thoughtfully into the distance.

"Jude?" Rhys prompted.

Jude looked up. She couldn't remember any words. Certainly not any words that would convince him that what she had to say wasn't delusional. She held the phone out to Rhys, gesturing at it frantically as if that might help him understand what was going on. Rhys raised his eyebrows. Finally, Jude managed to swallow and croak out of her suddenly dry throat, "That's *her.*"

"That's who?" Talia said, but Rhys's eyes widened.

"*Katrina Kelly* is the girl you were too scared to ask out?" he said.

Jude nodded wordlessly.

L.J. scoffed. "No way," they said, coming over to look at the photo, too.

"Are you sure?" Talia said, sounding doubtful.

"I'm sure," Jude said.

Rhys broke the silence with a long whistle. "Well," he said. "She's hot."

"And you're sure she was flirting with you?" L.J. said.

"Yes." Jude took her phone back and scrolled through the dozens of perfect pictures on Kat's profile—in New York, in L.A., on a tropical-looking beach somewhere, on a boat.

"Well, that would explain why she didn't ask for your number," Rhys said. "Someone famous like that probably can't go around asking normal people out."

"You *have* to DM her," Talia said.

"Are you nuts?" Jude said. "You just said she's super famous. I don't have a shot in hell with her."

"Well then, why not?" Talia demanded, putting a hand on her hip. "If you don't have a shot, what do you have to lose by asking?"

Jude could feel a shift in her heartbeat at those words, her heart not necessarily pumping faster but pumping harder, clenching in her chest like a fist. What did she have to lose? Plenty.

"I bet she doesn't even check her DMs," Jude protested. "She probably has some assistant running her social media for her."

"You said that she seemed perfect for you," Rhys said. "You really don't want to even try?"

Jude turned away, straightening the books on the Black Voices display. Finally, she said, "What would I even write?"

"Tell her that you think she's super cute and you want to make out," Talia suggested.

"Tell her that you're a dipshit who was too scared to ask for her number," L.J. added, sinking back onto the step stool.

"Explain that you got nervous when she was in the bookstore, but you really enjoyed meeting her and felt like you had a connection," Rhys suggested. "And no worries if she's not interested, but you would really love to see her sometime."

Jude took her phone back out and reopened Kat's page. She hesitated for a moment, then clicked "Follow" and opened a new message. She started typing. *Hi, this is a little weird but*

And then she stopped. Who was she kidding? Kat would never reply. And even if she did, even if by some long shot she agreed to go out with Jude, there was no way it would work out. Kat was famous and glamorous and ambitious. She had a life bigger than Jude could even imagine. How could Jude ever be enough for someone like that?

Letter by letter, Jude deleted the message. Then she closed the app and turned off her phone. There was no point in even trying. Jude would never see Kat again.

CHAPTER 4

KAT

Katrina Kelly was going through a rebranding.

Kat hated that word. *Rebranding* sounded like something that should happen to a health food company that had accidentally given a lot of people zinc poisoning, or a politician who'd been caught sexually harassing his interns. It had a distinct note of wrongdoing to it—as if Kat must have done something particularly shameful to land herself in this position, when in reality all she had done was grow up.

She didn't look sixteen anymore. That was the crime she'd committed against the entertainment industry. And now she was serving out her sentence in the most remote conference room at the Creative Talent Agency's New York office.

"Just through here." The slick-haired assistant who had walked her down several hallways, each of which Kat swore had gotten incrementally darker, hooked a thumb into one of his red suspenders as he gestured her around yet *another* corner. Katrina was fairly certain the CTA office hadn't been this large the last time she was here. But then again, the last time she'd visited she'd been finishing off the press tour for *Mission Im-Paw-ssible* (the sequel to *Spy Pigs*—a box office hit, but widely dismissed as lacking the charm of the original), and they'd put her in one of the big conference rooms on the main floor.

Suspenders led Katrina through a few more confusing turns. If he abandoned her here, she would never find her way out again. She wasn't sure this even still *was* the CTA office. Possibly they had rented out another building for the sole purpose of snubbing her.

"Here we go." Suspenders gestured at a dark room. Katrina peered inside. There were no windows. Through the gloom, she could just barely make out a small round table, only big enough for three chairs. She sighed.

The assistant shot her a glance that might have been intended as sympathetic but mostly came off as smug. He snapped on the lights.

"Can I get you anything? Coffee? Tea? Juice?"

"Water would be great," Katrina said, trying to maintain some semblance of dignity.

"Of course."

He disappeared back through the labyrinth of hallways, and Kat looked around the room. There was a tray of snacks against one wall, but otherwise it was empty. She'd forgotten to eat breakfast, she realized. She should probably open one of the granola bars, but the thought of trying to force anything into her stomach made her nauseous.

It was just nerves, she told herself. Once she had a plan to fix her career, she'd get back on a regular eating schedule. It wasn't a big deal.

She took out her phone to occupy herself while she waited. Automatically, she flipped open Instagram to check how her post of the tote bag from the bookstore had done. It had been twenty-four hours, and she had a hundred thousand likes. Shit. She should have posed with the bag instead—pictures with her face in them always did better.

Until three years ago, Kat hadn't cared about her social media.

She'd been so famous that she didn't need to worry about keeping her fans invested and engaged—her regular appearance in movie theaters did that for her. She'd always had Instagram, but an assistant had run it for her, keeping her page stocked with glamour shots and behind-the-scenes photos.

Now social media was the one tangible thing she could offer to casting directors—the ability to get their movie in front of eight million people on a regular basis. She couldn't afford an assistant anymore, but she hired a photographer once a month to take shots of her in different locations, so she had glamorous photos to post to her grid two or three times a week. She did a story every day, letting fans see her skin care routine, her daily workout, what she ate for breakfast. Giving fans a glimpse of the "real" her—but not so real that it ruined the magic. She showed them a carefully curated, upbeat, real-talking-without-saying-anything-depressing version of her authentic self, as mandated by the social media expert she'd hired to audit her online presence last year. She was supposed to be open about the difficulties of fame without seeming to take it for granted. To be warm and friendly without seeming desperate. To be sad, sometimes, without seeming weak. To be happy without gloating. To go on fancy vacations and eat in trendy restaurants without flaunting. To perfectly strike the balance between being relatable and being inspirational.

A lot of the comments on her latest post were focused on the books she'd purchased—*The Color Purple*, *To the Lighthouse*, and *Bad Feminist*. Some of them argued that these books were proof that Katrina Kelly was queer, while others argued that these books were proof that Katrina Kelly just liked to read. Which was, of course, the whole point of buying those exact books. To get people talking.

Kat stopped herself before she scrolled too far—she didn't need that hit to her self-esteem today. Instead, she opened her

DMs. As usual, she had more messages than she could possibly respond to. She'd stopped looking at requests from people she didn't follow back, as she'd been scarred by disturbing messages one too many times. Of her primary messages, half were actors with even worse careers than her, trying to build a connection by responding to her stories with personal anecdotes, which she mostly ignored and occasionally hearted. But she did try to keep up with messages from higher-up industry people, bigger brands, and the people she spent time with in L.A., ostensibly her friends, so she scrolled through the list, her eye snagging on one particular message. It was from The Next Chapter. When Kat had tagged them in the post, she'd opened a message thread between them, and the bookstore had responded.

Hey, this is Jude. I really enjoyed meeting you in the store the other day. I hope you're liking the Eileen Styles book. If you're interested, I would love to take you for a drink to talk about it sometime.

Kat stared at the message. Jude wanted to see her again. Kat hadn't been making up their flirtation at the store.

Or had she? Was Jude only interested now because she knew Kat was famous?

Kat hated not knowing whether someone was interested in her or her fame. Ninety percent of the time, the answer was easy: most people were interested in Katrina Kelly the movie star, not Kat the person. But she and Jude had had such instant, easy chemistry . . . Was it delusional to think that Jude might actually just want to get to know Kat for Kat?

Thankfully, the door opened at that moment and Kat's manager came in before she had time to descend into a spiral.

Jocelyn Davies was white, with sleek bobbed hair and an aura of annoyed efficiency that made her seem taller than she actually was—although the four-inch heels helped, too. She spoke very fast and always seemed to be in a rush, but she was the person who'd guided Kat's career to the heights it had (so briefly) reached. She had even temporarily moved to New York to help Kat with the next phase of her career.

"*There* you are," Jocelyn said, hurrying over to kiss Kat on both cheeks. "It took me forever to find you. I've never even *been* to this corner of the office." She frowned, as if Kat had specifically requested to be placed in the most hidden conference room, but then her frown abruptly turned into a beam. "Good news! I've found our play."

Kat sat up straighter. This was exactly what she needed to drive Jude out of her head—a plan. "What is it?"

Jocelyn sat down and leaned eagerly across the table. "Richard Gottlieb. Do you know Richard Gottlieb?" She snapped her fingers three times, urging Kat to be quick.

"I don't think so."

"Of course you don't! He's not a Hollywood guy. He's a theater guy. One of those literary, pretentious types. Very gay. Wears a lot of scarves. He's won all sorts of awards—nothing you'd have heard of, minor theater awards, you know. And guess what?"

Kat grinned. "He has a show?"

"He has a show." Jocelyn grinned back. "It's called *Philosophies of Desire*. Auditions in six weeks. Off-Broadway for now, but everyone's saying this one will go all the way. I see Tonys in our future, my dear."

"It's not a musical, is it?" Kat asked, her stomach sinking. She'd recorded a few singles during her *P.R.O.M.* days, at the network's request, but they'd had to use so much auto-tune that she had come out sounding vaguely demonic. Apparently, they'd been resurfacing in a lot of horror TikToks lately.

Thankfully, Richard Gottlieb wasn't into musicals, Jocelyn explained. He was an up-and-coming writer/director. His new play was about a morally gray young woman who seduces a respectable middle-aged male professor. It was literary and serious and a little bit scandalous—the perfect role for a child star looking to launch a new career with a sophisticated adult image. It would be Kat's *Equus*.

Kat's breathing came a little easier as Jocelyn spoke. Her career might be in shambles, but Jocelyn Davies had found a way to fix it. Ideally, she'd be acting in Oscar-bait blockbusters within two years.

Jocelyn laid out the strategy. Kat's name recognition would help her land an audition, but they couldn't rely on that alone to lock down the part. Kat would spend the six weeks until casting infiltrating Richard Gottlieb's social circle. She would go to opening nights, galas, private parties—any event he was attending that Jocelyn could pull strings to get Kat into. In the meantime, Kat would read over his body of work, study all his favorite plays, research his influences, memorize the names of prominent Broadway stars, and study French impressionism—apparently Richard was a big fan of French impressionism. She would win the director over on a personal level while showing him that she had influence in the theater world and the fan appeal to draw a crowd.

Pushing your way into a role using every trick in the book wasn't exactly what people dreamed of when they imagined fame. It was humiliating, really, but Kat didn't care. Because the alternative was being a washed-up, out-of-work former child star with no money and no career. Which was far *more* humiliating.

Katrina Kelly was making a comeback. No matter what it took.

"Am I brilliant or what?" Jocelyn said once she'd finished laying out the attack plan.

"You're brilliant," Kat said. Jocelyn had been her manager since she was ten, and she'd never been wrong yet.

Jocelyn leaned back in her chair and added, almost as an afterthought, "Obviously, we'll need to move up the timeline on your sexuality reveal."

"What? Why?"

"Gottlieb's not going to cast you if he thinks you'll negatively affect the highbrow reputation of his play. Right now, your brand is all wrong for his. We need to force him to take you seriously. Show him there's more to you than just your ability to run into a cake."

Kat sighed. You run into a giant cake in a movie *one time* . . . Jocelyn was right, though. Half the people who asked her for photos on the street just knew her as "that cake girl." Which was exactly why she needed to change her image.

Two months ago, when Kat had told Jocelyn that she wasn't straight, she had done it as more of an FYI. The same way she would have told her manager if she'd been arrested for drunk driving—giving her all the information, just in case damage control was called for. She had expected Jocelyn to feel the same way Kat did: that this was information better kept hidden from the public eye.

Instead, Jocelyn had recommended the opposite. Being queer was trendy now. Coming out would make people look at Kat differently, see something besides the child star and talk about something besides *P.R.O.M.* It would endear her to a brand-new, devoted audience. Kat had nearly cried as Jocelyn told her that she deserved the chance to be her true self.

Three hours later, Jocelyn had devised the Katrina Kelly Queer Branding Shift.

That was why Kat had gone to The Next Chapter—the bookstore had a good social media presence with a strong queer brand. Her visit and subsequent Instagram post were part of phase one. She had also been photographed reading *The Price of Salt*. She'd gone to an Indigo Girls concert. She had mentioned in an interview that *Thelma and Louise* was her favorite movie. Nothing concrete, nothing official. Just tiny little hints, which fans could piece together if they so desired.

And they did. Already, there were subreddits and TikTok deep dives dedicated to debating whether Katrina Kelly was gay and trying to connect her to various female celebrities. It was the most public interest Kat had gotten in years.

But she was supposed to have months before she officially came out as queer. Months to get used to her new identity and figure out what the hell she was doing. She hadn't even told her parents yet. Not that she told them anything these days, since that would require actually talking to them. But still.

"So . . ." Kat said, trying not to betray the panic she was currently feeling. "I just post on Instagram that I'm gay? Or bi, or whatever?"

"Of course not." Jocelyn's phone dinged and she picked it up to read whatever message she'd gotten. "Concrete labels are out. What you need is a girlfriend."

Kat felt like she might choke. Damn that assistant for not bringing her water. "A girlfriend?"

"Some queer celebrity. Kristen Stewart or Cara Delevingne, except I don't think either of them is single. But someone like them. Someone confirmed queer who you can be seen with."

"I can't just jump right into dating Cara Delevingne." Kat's panic was definitely audible now.

"You won't." Jocelyn frowned irritably at her. "I just told you she's not single." She squinted at Kat. "Wait, what about that girl from your show? Madelyn West?"

Kat's teeth found the inside of her cheek and dug in. "Not her."

Jocelyn peered up over her glasses, studying Kat. "Are you still mad about that whole thing?"

Kat shrugged and didn't respond. Because yes. She was very much still mad about that whole thing.

Jocelyn clucked her tongue. "Okay, but Madelyn is in that queer show now. *The Qties*. She has a dedicated gay following. She could be just what you need to boost your image."

Kat bit down a little harder. The fact that her former best friend had managed to transition into having an adult acting career was just another reason why Kat resented her. Particularly since Madelyn was a huge part of the reason Kat no longer had a career.

"I'll have my assistant make a list of actresses who are single and gay. Maybe there's someone else in *The Qties* you could date."

Kat groaned.

"This is important," Jocelyn said. "The queer rumors are catching on. If you don't start confirming your sexuality soon, people are going to think you're gay baiting them and start to turn on you."

"This section of the rebrand is literally labeled Gay Bait Phase in your planner," Kat said.

Jocelyn waved this detail away. "Remember when wearing skirts over jeans on the red carpet was a trend and I put my foot down? Was I right?"

Kat winced. "You were right."

"I know I was. And I'm right this time, too. It's time for you to deliver the goods. Let you be seen around town with some hot piece of ass with a boy's haircut."

Kat flushed. First of all, *the goods*? Second, she knew Jocelyn had her best interests in mind, but she wasn't sure if she was ready for all of this. Kat had seen the *Qties* cast at events, and they all seemed so . . . confidently gay. Moving in a group, laughing like they were best friends. Wearing suits and sequins and floral vests and fedoras. What if Kat committed some lesbian dating taboo and came off as a straight girl just fishing for attention? What if she hooked up with someone on the show and humiliated herself in bed and then the entire *Qties* cast found out and from there the message spread to every sapphic-aligned celebrity in North America? Kat would be the laughingstock of the celesbians.

No. She definitely couldn't date a *Qties* star.

"What if . . ." Kat paused to swallow nervously. She almost

never questioned Jocelyn's plans. "What if I dated someone who wasn't famous?"

Jocelyn narrowed her eyes and didn't respond. Kat rushed to explain herself further.

"I mean, there are only so many queer celebrities who are famous enough, right? I don't want to work my way through the pool too quickly. And right now, no one even knows I'm queer, so why would the Kristen Stewarts bother with me? Plus, I don't even know what the queer cliques are, so what if I date the wrong celebrity and then Miley Cyrus hates me forever or something? Whereas if I date someone normal, I kind of announce to the world that I'm queer and I can see if any celebrities step forward. And I could also get some . . . some practice. So it doesn't seem like I don't know what I'm doing with. You know. With . . ." Katrina's mind suddenly went blank. "Girl-dating."

Jocelyn drummed her fingers against the table, which Kat knew meant she was at least considering the idea. Finally, she said, "You might have a point."

Kat wanted to sigh in relief, but she held it in. She wouldn't have to embarrass herself by trying to slide into Reneé Rapp's DMs. At least, not yet.

"But we'd have to find the right normal person." Jocelyn said. "Someone who can give you a little credibility, but won't cause any issues when you upgrade in a month or two to someone with status." Jocelyn rapped her fingers against the table once more, loudly and decisively. "Okay! I like it. New plan: find some normal, attractive lesbian for you to date."

Kat must have looked too happy, because Jocelyn gave her a knowing look. "You already have someone in mind, don't you?"

Kat took a deep breath.

"Actually," she said. "I do."

CHAPTER 5

JUDE

Jude's will to make it through the day gave out around the same time as the bottom of a box filled with copies of a viral book called *Liberal Snowflakes: How Left-Leaning Colleges Make America's Youth Weak*. It had been on the nonfiction bestseller list for weeks, but Jude had managed to avoid ordering it until their last staff meeting, when Stephen had insisted that not only were they putting it on shelves, they were also having the author in to give a talk in three weeks.

Jude had spent a full half hour trying to convince him that compromising the store's brand would mean losing customers. But Stephen's view was that a bookstore should be dedicated to free speech, which meant showcasing both sides. Then he reminded her that the store belonged to *him* now, not her family, and maybe it was time he started taking a more active role in running the business.

Fifteen minutes later, he'd sent an email looping L.J. in with the *Liberal Snowflakes* author's publicist to schedule an event.

Still, Jude didn't intend to make the books easy to find. She had been in the process of lugging the copies to the shadowy back of the satire section, ignoring both the Notable Nonfiction and the New Releases displays entirely, when the bottom of the box had given out and several liberal snowflakes had landed on her toes. Instead of picking up the books and continuing on, or even cursing and throwing a few of them, Jude had just stared at the fallen copies before sinking down and lying on the ground next to them, staring up at the framed photo of her and her mom hanging on the store's back wall.

Jude's mom, Susanna, had opened The Next Chapter eighteen years ago, fulfilling her lifelong dream of owning a bookstore. When she first signed the lease, she and Jude had come to the store every single night on their way home from afterschool care. Susanna would unlock the door and lead Jude a few steps into the building, then flick on the lights with a dramatic gesture. "Look," she would say, with a reverent whisper. "This is what a dream in progress looks like."

Most nights, the store looked exactly the same as it had the night before. Concrete dust and plastic sheeting and bare, cold walls. Jude would complain sometimes about having to stop by the store to stare at the same old room every day, but her mom would shake her head. "Building dreams isn't glamorous, Jude. It takes a lot of hard work. Sometimes you can't even tell you're making progress until you're already there."

Jude would roll her eyes and groan, but she didn't put up too much of a fight about visiting. Because some nights, everything would suddenly be different. She came in one day to find a beautiful, sparkling wooden floor laid where before there had only been treacherous two-by-fours. One evening, as if by magic, shelves appeared along the walls—tall, dark wood bookshelves running all along the room. A dream, suddenly come to life.

The Next Chapter opened when Jude was seven. She spent most of her childhood running through the store, helping with little tasks and getting in the way, until she turned fifteen and her mom had shown her how to use the register and announced that she officially had a part-time job. She'd worked there until she'd moved to Chicago to go to college. When she left, she figured the store would always be part of her life, as familiar to her as the apartment she'd grown up in—a home she could return to whenever she came back to New York.

But then her mom had gotten breast cancer. When she went in for her third round of treatments, she'd sold the bookstore to Stephen Delk, who already owned four bookstores in the city, under one condition—that she be allowed to buy the store back at market value if she ever wanted. When she'd died shortly after Jude's college graduation, Stephen had agreed to extend the same offer to Jude, as long as she stayed on and ran the bookstore, since she was the only other person with a working knowledge of the inventory system.

And here she was, three years later and no closer to having the amount of money she would need to buy the store back. And now Stephen was planning to "take a more active role" in daily management.

Jude closed her eyes, then opened them again when she heard footsteps coming up behind her.

"I should really write you up for slacking on the job," Rhys said. Jude saw his cane come to a stop at the edge of her peripheral vision. He must have been having a bad pain day.

Rhys was only twenty-five, but he had hypermobile Ehlers-Danlos Syndrome, which meant his joints were unstable. They dislocated often and caused him pain, particularly in his knees and back. He didn't talk about it very much, but Jude knew that he was always in some pain, even on good days.

"Well, if you do, *I'll* write *you* up for insubordination," Jude said.

"Hmm. Mutually assured destruction. Touché." Rhys leaned against the Travel section, where he could keep an eye on the front door and also look down at Jude. "Do you want to talk about it?"

"Talk about how Stephen is determined to ruin the brand

we've spent years building and turn this place into an impersonal chain store? No thanks."

Rhys nodded slowly. "What about talking about how you've been extra moody since you didn't ask that girl out?"

Jude glared at him, then sat up and started gathering the scattered copies of *Liberal Snowflakes* into a pile. She noted with satisfaction that several of the dust jackets were bent at the edges. It wasn't *her* fault that these conservative publishers hadn't invested in sturdy enough boxes.

"Got it," Rhys said. "But maybe you should download—"

Jude hoisted a book into the air threateningly. "If you say a dating app, you are getting a hardcover to the head."

Rhys sighed. "Go take a break," he said. "These liberal snowflakes will still think they're special when you come back."

Jude left the pile of books on the ground, eager for an exit from the conversation, and went into the back, a large concrete space that was half book storage and half staff room. Talia and L.J. were already in there, sitting around the worn wooden table and trying to throw grapes into each other's mouths. As Jude came in, L.J. caught one and Talia cheered.

"Heya," L.J. said through their mouthful of grape.

Jude nodded at them and slumped down in front of the computer, pretending to check their inventory so she didn't have to talk to them.

Rhys was right. She'd been in a worse mood than usual since meeting Kat. Jude hadn't dated anyone since her ex, Becca, had completely shattered her heart more than two years ago. She hadn't even been interested in anyone. But then Kat had walked into her life, and for a second Jude had thought . . . *What if?*

But hope was dangerous. It made life feel even emptier when it inevitably went away.

She heard Rhys say something to a customer, and then his footsteps coming toward the storeroom. She straightened up and tried to make herself look less existential-crisis-y.

Rhys shut the door behind him and leaned against it, his eyes wide. All three of them turned to face him.

"So, I have a confession to make," he said, in a faux-casual voice.

"You're in love with me?" Talia guessed.

"You're in love with Stephen?" L.J. suggested.

"You're in love with Stephen and he's pregnant with an evil capitalist baby?" Talia added excitedly.

"Oh, oh!" L.J. said. "You're in love with Stephen and he's pregnant with your evil baby *and*—"

"Oh my God, you are *not* as funny as you think you are," Rhys said, cutting them off. "No. I, um . . ." He looked at Jude, his cheeks turning oddly pink. "Do you remember Katrina Kelly?"

Jude raised her eyebrows.

"Right. Yeah. Of course you do." He ran a hand through his hair, then said in a rush, "I messaged her from the bookstore account pretending to be you and asked her out."

"You WHAT?" all three of them shouted at once.

"I know!" Rhys said. "But you said you guys had this really great connection and I figured there was only a slim chance that she would respond but you'd regret it forever if you didn't try and I—"

"Dude." L.J. shook their head. "Total invasion of privacy."

Rhys winced. "I know, I know. It was really bad. And I'm sorry. But not *that* sorry because"—he glanced at the closed door behind him and then lowered his voice—"she's in the store right now and she just asked for you."

Talia shrieked. Jude choked. Actually, literally choked on a mouthful of spit and started hacking and coughing.

"Okay, that's fine," Rhys said, clapping her on the back. "Get that out in here. And then when you go out, you can just be calm and relaxed and take deep breaths, right?"

"Um," Jude said.

"Stand up so we can see how you look," Rhys said.

Jude stood. Her three friends stared at her, unsatisfied expressions on their faces.

"Let me fix your hair," Talia said, coming over.

"What's wrong with my hair?"

"Just—come here."

"Ew, don't use spit! That's disgusting."

"It's not my fault you've never seen a comb," Talia hissed.

"Try tucking in your shirt," L.J. suggested.

Jude complied. They all frowned at her.

"Okay, never mind," L.J. said. "Untuck it. But use an iron once in a while. Jesus."

"This is *not* helping my confidence levels," Jude complained.

"Okay. Deep breaths." Rhys stared into her eyes like a boxing coach. "You are hot. You are funny. You are smart. You can do this."

Jude nodded. "Okay. Cool. I'm gonna walk out there. So calm."

"Attaboy." Rhys smacked her ass and then gave her a little shove toward the door. "And for God's sake, don't forget to ask her out this time."

Jude nodded again. Her throat was so dry she could feel each breath rasping over the surface. She rolled her shoulders back and opened the door.

Kat was at the register, looking at her phone. Jude stood there for a moment, ogling. She hadn't fully believed that Kat was actually here until this moment.

Maybe she just wanted to return the books she'd bought. Maybe she'd hated all of Jude's suggestions and she wanted to lodge an official complaint.

"Um," Jude said, "hi?" She immediately cringed. *Um, hi?* was not the confident pickup line she would have chosen under more rational-thinking circumstances. She had a sudden vision of all three of her friends pressed against the storeroom door, smacking themselves in the forehead.

Kat looked up. Their eyes met, and she stared at Jude for a

few seconds, her eyes wide. Distantly, Jude was aware that she couldn't breathe. But needs like breathing suddenly seemed trivial.

"Um, hi," Kat repeated with a slight smile. She was wearing a pair of tight leather pants and a black jacket with a gold cowboy-style fringe. It would have looked ridiculous on a normal person, but on her it looked absolutely heavenly.

"It's nice to see you again." Jude walked a little closer. She felt suddenly like she had too many hands and not enough places to put them. Crossing her arms seemed unfriendly, but holding them at her sides seemed unbelievably awkward and strange. Good lord, what did she normally do with her hands?

"You too." Kat looked away, her cheeks slightly pink. "I got your message."

"Oh, right! My message." Jude was going to kill Rhys. How was she supposed to reply if she didn't even know what she'd allegedly said?

Kat stared at her expectantly for several long seconds. Then, she said, "Well, do you want to get that drink?"

"Oh! Yes." Jude was still dealing with the excess-of-hands problem, except that now they were also very sweaty. She tried to rub them subtly on the front of her jeans. "Um, do you mean right now?"

"Yeah." Katrina's shoulder twitched, almost like a shrug. "You free?"

"Um, the store doesn't close for another—"

The storeroom door cracked open. "She can go!" Talia called through the crack.

"Oh." Jude's face started to burn. "Well. I guess that's that, then. Um. Shall we?"

CHAPTER 6

KAT

"So, what brings you to New York?" Jude asked once the waiter had placed their drinks on the table. They were in a bar that Jocelyn's assistant had found for Kat, on the top floor of a tall building only a few blocks away from the bookstore, near the Hudson River, with dim red lighting and sleek black furniture. Half of the walls were windows and half of the walls were mirrors, which created the dizzying effect of not knowing which was which.

"Well, I've mostly been in L.A. for the last twelve years," Kat said. "I wanted to try living somewhere that doesn't center Hollywood." Technically true, even if she was making it sound more like her choice than it actually was.

"And what do you think so far?"

"I love it," Kat admitted. "I've been to New York for press events and opening nights, but I've never had the time to actually walk around by myself before. There's always something interesting to see."

Jude beamed, and Kat felt herself relax a little. "My mom used to say that if you couldn't find something exciting in Manhattan, you were the problem. Even if you've walked the same block a thousand times, you'll always find something new."

God, Jude was cute. Especially when she smiled that lopsided, easy grin. Kat had half expected that when she saw Jude again, there wouldn't be the same kick-to-the-stomach type of attraction. But when Kat had looked up to see Jude walking toward her from the back of the store, she'd felt mesmerized by the softness of her hair and the messy way it defied gravity by sticking up in all directions. She loved the carelessly perfect way Jude's rumpled blue button-down shirt showed off her torso—loose enough to be masculine but tailored enough to convey lean strength through the fabric.

Kat realized she was staring and hurried to add something to the conversation. "How long have you lived in the city?"

"My whole life, practically. I was born in Jersey, but my mom moved us to the West Village when I was five."

"Does she still live around here?"

The half smile melted downward. "Uh, no. She actually died three years ago."

"I'm so sorry."

"Thanks," Jude said. "What about you? Are you close with your family?"

"Me? No. I pretty much stopped talking to my parents after I found out they'd stolen most of my life savings."

Shit. Kat shouldn't have said that. She'd been thrown off-balance by how comfortable she felt with Jude, and she'd forgotten who she was for a second. Katrina Kelly couldn't share anything that she didn't want to find herself reading in *Entertainment Daily* in three weeks.

Jude's eyebrows lowered over those beautiful eyes. "I'm so sorry."

"It's not a big deal." Kat tried to keep her voice breezy, channeling Interview Katrina. "I'm very lucky that I even had money in the first place. Not everyone gets the chance to live their dreams at a young age."

"I'm sure it was really tough sometimes, though," Jude said. "Even if you wanted it."

Kat sipped her drink and didn't respond. It was possible Jude didn't mean anything by that comment. But too often, she found that the men she'd gone on dates with wanted a sob story. They wanted her to open up and tell them about the tragic figure behind the child actor. They wanted to get to know the "real" Katrina.

Or at least, they said they did. What they actually wanted was another fantasy. A fantasy behind a fantasy. A princess they could rescue. But then, when Kat turned out to be more than just a tragic archetype? When she turned out to be a real person with morning breath and messy hair and grumpy days?

Well, then Kat would be reading about her secrets in *Tiger Beat* or *J-14* while blocking another phone number. Just like with Madelyn.

As if sensing Kat's reluctance, Jude changed the topic. "Have you read the Eileen Styles book yet?"

"Oh my God, I *loved* it," Kat gushed. "*Curled Around Your Finger* might be her best one yet."

"I can't believe they didn't win!" Jude said. "I totally thought they were going to pull off the best underdog comeback in history."

"Okay but don't you think that would have been too much?" Kat said. "I mean, they already won by ensuring the women's curling league would continue to operate. They can't *also* win the tournament."

"Maybe I'm an idealist," Jude said. "But I wanted a completely happy ending."

"But that scene at the end? When Ella races across the ice to say she doesn't want Sam to quit her team after all? And it seems like she slips but then she lands on one knee and proposes? That was *so* good."

"True. And it wouldn't have hit the same way if they hadn't lost the finals earlier." Jude's half-hitch grin had reappeared. "You're right. I concede the point."

"Also, that sex scene in the locker room after semifinals? Unbelievably hot." Kat said it without thinking, then felt her face flush. She hadn't meant to steer the conversation to sex.

Jude leaned in slightly. "I read it four times," she admitted in a low voice. "I had no idea you could spank someone with a curling rock."

"I'm not sure you actually *can*." Kat snorted. "I looked it up and they're forty-two pounds. So, unless you've been lifting a *lot* . . ."

"Well, Eileen has never let physics get in the way of a good sex scene." Jude's usual half smile melted into a full one, and her eyes danced at Kat across the table.

Kat glanced down, then back up into the gravitational pull of Jude's gaze. It made her chest ache to hold eye contact, but in the most delicious way. She wanted to lean into that ache, to stare at Jude until she could no longer breathe. It had been a long time since she'd flirted like this—with a feeling like you were passing a ball of energy back and forth, making it grow with every little glance and touch. Like you were having an entire conversation without speaking.

"So, what made you decide to message me?" Kat said, in a low, flirty tone.

To her surprise, Jude leaned back, breaking the magnetic field between them.

"Oh." Jude rubbed a hand through her hair, rumpling it even further. "Well. Actually, I, um, didn't send the message. My friend Rhys did. I told him that I met you in the store and he, uh, reached out without telling me."

A cold snap iced Kat's insides. She picked up her drink to give herself something to do, but she suddenly didn't feel like drinking it anymore.

"I mean," Jude tugged at her collar, pulling it away from her throat like it was too tight. "I didn't— Like, he messaged you because . . ." She stopped, twisting her wrist in a nervous circle.

Kat put her drink back down. She knew why Jude's friend had messaged her. Because he wanted a good story about someone famous. He'd probably sent the DM as a joke, never imagining that Kat would be insecure enough to respond.

Had Jude even wanted to go on this date?

She'd thought the message meant that Jude had been thinking about their meeting as much as Kat had. That maybe Jude had been replaying their conversation in her head, too, wishing for the chance to do things differently. But Kat had been projecting, the same way she'd been projecting in the bookstore.

And here Kat was, spilling details about her relationship with her parents and making comments about queer sex scenes. If Jude had told her friends about their first meeting in the bookstore, she would certainly tell them about this date, too. Then they would tell other people, and someone would post online, and the whole world would suddenly be tweeting about how Katrina Kelly loved to get spanked with sporting equipment. Which was *not* the plan. She was supposed to be seen dating a woman, not embarrass herself by oversharing personal details with someone who wasn't even into her.

She needed to get out of here.

"Right." Kat raised her hand, flagging one of the waiters down, and passed him her credit card. Jude opened her mouth to protest, but the waiter walked away before she could.

"I'm really sorry," Jude said, but she was still fidgeting with her hands, which made it hard to believe she was sincere. "I didn't mean—"

"I have to go. I have dinner plans," Kat said. Jude's eyes slid to her watch. "Early dinner plans."

Jude's mouth opened, then closed. Finally, she said, "Okay."

They sat in awkward, fidgety silence until the waiter brought the check back. Kat signed it. Then she stood up and strode out of the bar so fast, Jude didn't even have time to say goodbye.

CHAPTER 7

JUDE

When Jude knocked on the locked door of the bookstore, Rhys looked up from the cash register with annoyance, raising his arm to gesture to the large CLOSED sign. When he saw Jude, his face melted into a smile instead, but it disappeared within seconds as he took in Jude's expression. He checked his watch, probably noting that less than an hour had passed since he'd last seen her, and then he grabbed his cane from where it was leaning against the counter and hurried over to let her in.

"I never liked her movies anyway," Rhys said as a greeting, locking the door behind her again. "I mean, *Spy Pigs*? If pigs have a centralized intelligence agency, then why haven't they taken down the meat industry yet? Seriously. Plot holes everywhere. It's embarrassing."

Jude gave Rhys her best attempt at a smile.

"Come on," he said. "I think this calls for a globe bar night."

He ushered her into the back room, where Talia and L.J. had just finished clocking out and pulling on their jackets. When they saw Jude, they slid the jackets right back off.

"Globe bar?" L.J. asked. When Rhys nodded, they strode over

to the large, stately globe in the corner of the room and opened it to reveal the bottles of alcohol hidden inside.

"Everyone's talking about globe bar!" Talia said, as she pulled ice cubes from the mini fridge/freezer combo and added them to mugs from the coffee station. "It's New York's hottest club!"

L.J. poured whiskey into each of the mugs and pressed one into Jude's hands. She sat down in the rolling computer chair.

"Do you want to talk about it?"

Jude took a sip of half-cold, half-lukewarm whiskey. "It went well at first," she said. "Which is actually the worst part. I mean, if the whole thing had been bad, whatever, right? But she's really special, this girl. And I blew it."

She told them about how well things had been going—the flirty energy between them, how they'd gushed about the book together. The way Kat's face had instantly shuttered when Jude told her she hadn't sent the DM, and how Jude had started to panic until words melted in her mouth, leaving her unable to explain how much she'd wanted to see Kat again.

"Dude!" L.J. said. "Why didn't you tell her you sent the message?"

"I couldn't lie to her! What if we started dating and our whole relationship was built on this DM that she thought I sent?"

"I dunno," Talia said. "This seems like a case where a little while lie would be okay. Because you do really like her."

"I *did* really like her," Jude said glumly. "I'm definitely never going to see her again."

"I'm really sorry, man," Rhys said. "I thought I was doing a good thing by sending that DM, but I really messed things up for you, didn't I?"

"No," Jude said. "You were right. I never would have messaged her on my own. It's my fault for being too scared to reach out to her in the first place." She took a gulp of the whiskey, then grimaced. "I'm never going to find love, because I'm too much of a fucking coward to actually go after anyone, because I'm so scared of getting hurt."

There was a long silence. Ice cubes clinked against mugs as everyone drank.

"Well, I'm right there with you," Rhys said.

Jude rolled her eyes. "You're not a coward."

"No, but I am fucked dating-wise. I'm so demi I take, like, two years to develop feelings for anyone. At which point, they've decided I'm not interested in them and categorized me as just a friend. Plus, it's kinda hard to go on dating apps and say, *Hey, anyone interested in meeting up for drinks and then engaging in a drawn out, multiyear slow burn?*"

Jude gave him a small smile.

"Well, I have the opposite problem," Talia said. "Every time I go on a date, I get completely obsessed with the person and drive them away. I fall too hard, text them constantly, freak out when they don't reply, and then tell them I love them on the third date. It's like a recipe for getting ghosted."

"Have you tried just *not* doing those things?" L.J. suggested.

"I can't help it!" Talia said. "I can tell I'm acting crazy but I just can't make myself stop. So I'm kinda fucked romance-wise, too."

They all looked at L.J.

"What?" they said. "I'm perfect."

Talia hit their knee.

"I mean, I date people a lot," L.J. said. "I'm doing fine."

Talia hit them again.

"*Fine.*" L.J. let out a long, aggrieved sigh. "I guess, if I was being forced to talk about it under threat of physical violence from my friends, I would say that I have a hard time connecting with anyone emotionally. And ever since I realized I was trans, I've also realized that I've been kind of numb my whole life. Like, to keep the trans thing shoved down, I had to shove everything down. And since I came out, I've started actually feeling my feelings. And it's terrifying as shit."

"There you go," Talia said, clapping them on their back. "Proud of you."

L.J.'s cheeks turned ruddy. They kept their eyes firmly focused on their whiskey mug as they said, "It's actually kind of thanks to you, Rhys."

"Me?" It was Rhys's turn to blush.

"I mean, watching you transition over the past few years," L.J. said, still speaking to their mug. "You've been so open with talking about it. And seeing how happy you are now, and how unafraid you are to talk about the parts that are hard. It, um, it makes me want to be like that, too. So I've been, like, going to therapy and working on my feelings and shit. So, like, thanks for that."

They glanced over at Rhys, and the two of them held eye contact for a few seconds, both completely bright red now.

"Thanks," Rhys said in a slightly shaky voice. "That means a lot. And I think what you're doing is really brave."

They both looked away, now very determinedly not making eye contact at all.

Oh fuck. Jude clutched her mug, her heart sinking.

Rhys had been Jude's best friend since he had taken a part-time job at the bookstore when they were both sixteen. They had gravitated toward each other the way queer teenagers do, forging an immediate bond that got even stronger when Rhys came back to the bookstore after college, intending to work there for a few years before getting his master's in library science. Talia had started working at the bookstore four years ago—it was the perfect job while she tried to make it as a playwright. And L.J. had joined two years ago, working there part-time as they finished their degree at FIT before switching to full time after graduation while they got their cosplay costuming business off the ground.

For all three of them, the bookstore was a temporary stop on their way to something else. But for now, as the only full-time employees on the bookstore's payroll, they saw one another nearly every day. Together with Jude, they were the Core Four.

But what would happen to the Core Four if Rhys and L.J. started dating? They'd cut the core in half. Rhys wouldn't need to list Jude as his emergency contact anymore. L.J. would be his go-to invite for slam poetry readings and New York Liberty games. They would become a couple and want to make couple friends and do couple things. And Jude would be left behind. The way she always was.

Jude's phone dinged in her pocket and she took it out, eager to look at something that wasn't Rhys's and L.J.'s blushing faces. The bookstore account had gotten a DM.

A DM from Kat.

"Oh shit. She messaged me," Jude said. "Probably to tell me never to contact her again." Jude had assumed Kat would ghost her, but apparently she was the straightforward-communication type.

"What does it say?" Rhys asked. Jude hovered her thumb over the message, trying to ignore her dread. It was just a rejection. Nothing she didn't know already. This message wouldn't shatter her. She would recover.

Wouldn't she?

"Hey, I know this is short notice, but I have to go to this charity gala thing tomorrow night. Do you want to come?" Jude read out loud.

The group stared at her in stunned silence.

"Damn," L.J. finally said. "I guess she wasn't as upset as you thought."

"No, she was definitely upset. She was so mad she left without finishing her drink."

"Well, she's giving you another shot," Rhys said. "Tomorrow you can apologize and make it clear that you're really into her."

Jude read the message again. "A charity gala, though? I can't go to a charity gala."

"Why not? Are you anticharity?"

"I've never been to a gala in my life. I'll completely humiliate myself trying to . . ." Jude paused as she tried to imagine what people did at galas. "Eat oysters with a tiny fork?"

L.J. raised an eyebrow, looking unimpressed. "You've been using a fork for years, dude, I think you can figure it out."

Jude shook her head. This didn't make any sense. Why had Kat been upset enough to walk out on her, but then invited her to a party an hour later? What had changed?

But . . . did it matter? Rhys was right. Jude had another shot. Didn't she have to take it?

She turned to Rhys. "I don't have anything to wear."

"Attaboy!" He grinned at her. "I have an old suit from my uncle. L.J., could you tailor it to fit Jude?"

L.J. scoffed. "I just finished a drag king Naruto costume with *three thousand* sequins. I think I can handle a little tailoring."

"Excellent." Rhys rubbed his hands together. "I think this calls for an eighties-style getting-ready montage."

CHAPTER 8

KAT

This date was going to be terrible. Kat was going to make sure of it.

When she'd walked out of the bar the night before, Kat had been determined to never see Jude again. But halfway through her walk home, she had realized her mistake. She'd promised Jocelyn that she'd bring a date to the gala tomorrow. And once you promised something to Jocelyn, you did not let her down.

Kat had wandered around Chelsea for a while, trying to think of another option. *Any* other option. But short of getting on Tinder and inviting a complete stranger to go with her, she had nothing. And she really didn't want to mess up Jocelyn's whole sexuality-reveal timeline.

So she'd messaged Jude. But this time, Kat wouldn't embarrass herself.

In the car on the way over, she went over the rules in her head: No flirting. No witty banter. No gushing about gay books. And absolutely no sharing of personal details. Kat would be professional and aloof. They would show up together, start a few rumors, get their photo taken, then leave and never see each other again.

When she got out of the car in front of the upscale midtown hotel where the Stars for Sound charity gala was being held, Jude was waiting on the sidewalk, wearing a navy suit with a crisp white button-down and a gray tie with a matching pocket square. She had combed her hair and the clean line of her part somehow emphasized her strong jawline even more than usual. Her lips pulled up into that small sideways smile as Kat walked over.

This date is fake, she told herself desperately. *This person isn't actually into you. She's just hot!*

But she was *very* hot.

"Hi." Jude ducked her head slightly as she smiled, like a shy little kid.

Professional and aloof, Kat reminded herself.

"Hi," she said, without stopping, striding for the hotel doors. Jude hurried after her.

"How are you?" Jude said.

"Fine. You?"

"Um." Jude held the gilded door open for her. "Also fine, I guess."

"Great." Kat walked a little faster, heading toward the flower arch decorating the entrance to the ballroom across the lobby. The quicker they got this over with, the better.

But when she reached the door, Kat paused. When she walked into that ballroom with Jude, she would be confirming all the rumors. She would essentially be coming out as gay. Or bi. Or pan. Or whatever she was. Wasn't it ridiculous to come out before she even knew what she was coming out as? Was she making a huge mistake?

It didn't matter. Her career needed this. And without an acting career, who was Katrina Kelly?

Absolutely nobody.

Kat reached out and took Jude's hand. Jude looked surprised, but she didn't pull away. Then Kat pushed open the door to the ballroom and led Jude inside.

As she'd predicted, the entire room turned to look. At events like this, everyone had one eye on the door, watching to see if anyone interesting would come in. A hundred gazes lingered on their joined hands, and Kat's stomach burned like she'd just taken a shot of whiskey, but she kept moving, leading Jude toward the bar. When they got there, Kat leaned up and whispered in Jude's ear, "What do you want to drink?"

Jude looked a little confused, but she leaned down and whispered her drink order back, the way Kat had suspected she would. To anyone watching, it would look like they were exchanging intimate private words.

"Damn. This place is fancy," Jude said once they'd accepted their glasses of wine and moved to the side. "Do you go to a lot of events like this?"

"Yes."

Jude waited, but Kat didn't elaborate. The less she said to Jude tonight, the better. Instead, she surveyed the crowd until she spotted a producer, one of the six people Jocelyn had told her to network with tonight. She headed toward him, leaving Jude to trail awkwardly behind her.

"Evan!" she cooed, adding a tone of surprised delight to her voice. "So good to see you!"

They exchanged kisses on the cheek, and Evan had just started updating her on his two daughters when Kat glanced toward the door at the exact moment Madelyn entered the ballroom.

Kat tried to stay engaged in her conversation, but it was impossible. Her eyes kept returning to the front of the room. Madelyn had shaved one side of her long blond hair into an undercut, and she was wearing tight white pants and a strappy black shirt that showed off her stomach, along with heavy black eyeliner and high-heeled boots.

Kat bounced her eyes back to Evan. This shouldn't matter. No, it *didn't* matter. Kat had seen Madelyn at dozens of parties since *P.R.O.M.* had stopped filming. She'd known that Madelyn lived in New York between filming seasons of *The Qties*. Seeing her tonight was perfectly natural, and it shouldn't throw Kat off her game at all.

Still, it seemed like a bad omen that during her very first public appearance as a queer person, she was being confronted with the first girl she'd ever kissed.

No. Kat couldn't think of her like that. She shouldn't remember the kiss. She should remember that Madelyn had ruined Kat's entire career.

The next time Kat glanced over at Madelyn, they locked eyes. And then Madelyn started walking over.

Kat hurriedly refocused on the conversation, nodding along fervently at whatever Evan had just said. Still, she could feel Madelyn's presence behind her a second before a hand tapped her shoulder.

"Kat! Hi!"

"M*aaa*delyn!" Kat's voice took on an odd singsong croon as she turned around. "How *are* you?"

"I'm great. Just finished up filming season three." Madelyn smiled, and Kat bit down on the inside of her cheek. She knew exactly what Madelyn was doing—flaunting the fact that she had managed to grow her career while Kat's had sputtered to a flaming halt. "Are you living in New York now?"

"Just moved here." Kat gave her the fakest smile she could.

"We should get together, then." She let her eyes linger on Jude. "It seems like there are a lot of . . . changes for you to catch me up on."

"Definitely. Text me! We'll get lunch!"

"Seriously," Madelyn said, her voice dropping into earnestness. "I'd really like to see you. I think it's time we put what happened behind us, don't you?"

For a second, Kat forgot to keep her performative smile on.

Whatever expression was on her face, it made Madelyn take a step back.

"Okay." Madelyn lingered for a second. "Well. Maybe I'll see you soon."

With difficulty, Kat forced her face back into pleasant neutrality. "Ta-ta!" She fluttered her fingers in a dismissive wave, and Madelyn walked off.

"Excuse us one minute," Kat said to Evan. She took Jude by the elbow. "Come on. Let's get our picture taken."

"Oh. Sure." Jude followed her over to the step-and-repeat. "Um, are you okay?"

"Of course I'm okay. Why wouldn't I be?"

"You've barely said anything to me," Jude said. "And you seem a little upset."

"Of course I'm not upset," Kat said. "I'm just working."

She stepped in front of the banner and wrapped her arm around Jude's waist. Jude hesitated for a second. Then she put her arm around Kat's shoulder, pressing their sides together. Kat could feel the warmth of Jude's body against hers. It made her want to lean in and discover the shape of that body, to press her nose to the crease of Jude's neck and inhale the warm cedar-and-cinnamon scent of her cologne.

She nearly forgot to smile as the photographer lifted the camera. As soon as the shutter clicked, Kat stepped away, putting a safe distance between her and Jude.

Just then, Tony-nominated Broadway actor Jonathan Costello swooped out of the crowd with his arms raised.

"There you are, Katrina! Oh, I've missed you so much! It's been far too long!"

He wrapped Kat up in a hug, and she resisted the urge to roll her eyes. She had met Jonathan once, two days before, at the CTA offices. But pretending to be Kat's biggest fan was part of the deal Jocelyn had struck with his agent. Jonathan was a

Broadway star hoping to get into film. Kat was a movie star hoping to get into theater. There was a lot they could offer each other.

Based on the performance he was giving now, Kat didn't quite believe that Jonathan would make it in Hollywood. But that didn't matter as long as he introduced her to Richard Gottlieb, the writer and director of *Philosophies of Desire*. Kat needed to meet him tonight and make a good impression. Her entire career depended on it.

"I have some people you *must* meet," Jonathan said. His accent had become slightly British, in what Kat assumed was a failed attempt to act natural.

Kat rolled her shoulders back, trying to shake off the encounter with Madelyn. Go time.

She took Jude's hand and let Jonathan lead them over toward Richard Gottlieb. She recognized him from the headshot Jocelyn had given her. He was tall and white with dark curly hair and a short, fussy goatee, wearing a black suit with a black shirt. He was standing next to his husband, Ashton, a muscular blond whose headshot Kat had also been given.

"Richard! Hi!" Jonathan called, bouncing over. "It's *so* good to see you."

Richard turned, looking Jonathan over with a blank expression. "Hi." His tone was not warm. Jonathan raised his arms for a hug, but Richard stepped backward. "I'm sorry, do I know you?"

Kat felt her stomach tense. Jonathan's cheeks started to flush. "I auditioned for your show. *Expositions*."

"Ah." Richard flicked his eyes up and down Jonathan's body. "Did you make it to callbacks?"

"Uh." The red spots on Jonathan's cheeks flushed a deeper color, and he flashed a small, guilty look at Kat. "No, I didn't."

"Well." Richard took a sip from his wineglass. "That would explain it, then."

Kat was going to *murder* Jonathan. He'd promised Jocelyn that he was "on intimate terms" with Richard. What good was an introduction if Richard didn't actually know the person introducing her?

She kept her smile up, but her grip tightened on Jude's hand.

"Well," Jonathan said, making a brave effort to continue. "Um. So nice to see you again. And this is Katrina Kelly!" He made a Vanna White gesture in her direction, but there was a distinct note of desperation to it. "She just moved to town from L.A."

Kat dropped Jude's hand so she could shake Richard's. "It's very nice to meet you," she said. "I'm a big fan. I loved *Seasons of Change*."

Richard lifted one dubious eyebrow. "It's not often a Hollywood person comes all the way to St. Ann's Warehouse to see a play."

"Well, I'm a big fan of experimental theater." Hopefully she sounded convincing.

"Really?" Richard said. "What did you think of the staging?"

Shit.

Kat had not flown from L.A. to see *Seasons of Change* two years ago. In fact, during its rather short run, she'd been filming a Netflix original show about a vampire who wanted to be a pop star (canceled after one season). She'd read the play so she'd be prepared to flatter Richard about it, but the script hadn't included any notes about how the production was staged.

"I loved it," Kat said. "So original!"

"Hmm. 'Original,'" Richard repeated. "I suppose you could say that." He exchanged a glance with his husband, barely bothering to conceal his smirk. *Fuck, fuck, fuck.* What was the line Jocelyn had given her again? Something about how the play's overexplaining narrator represented . . . commercialism? Surely that couldn't be right.

She could feel sweat on the back of her neck. She opened her mouth, but before she could speak, Jude jumped in.

"Oh, I remember you raving about that play!" Jude said. She turned to Richard. "Kat was talking about it just the other day. She kept going on about how the complete lack of props or set effectively represented the emptiness of capitalism." She turned back to Kat, snapping her fingers thoughtfully. "What was it you said? That the disorientation the audience feels at the lack of context mirrors the way we're all disoriented and cut off from our true natures in postindustrial society?" She laughed cheerfully. "Honestly, hon, I don't understand half the things you say sometimes."

Kat laughed, too, hoping it sounded less manic than it felt.

Richard had stopped smirking. Instead, he nodded earnestly at Kat. "That's exactly what I was going for! Disorientation as a way of immersion. Honestly, my plays have gotten so much more expansive since I gave up on the idea of 'owing' a comprehensible experience to the audience."

"Oh, yes." Kat nodded back at him. "I completely agree." She was still sweating. Her throat felt like it was closing up. She needed to say something impressive.

"I'm Jude Thacker." Jude held out her hand, and Richard shook it. "We actually sell some of your plays at the bookstore where I work."

"Not bestsellers, I assume?" Richard said.

"Not quite," Jude said, chuckling. "The average bookstore customer isn't quite ready for you, I don't think." She glanced at Kat, who still couldn't think of anything to add to the conversation. She could feel her pulse racing in the sides of her neck. What was wrong with her?

"But that's actually how we met," Jude said, the lie coming out smoothly. "Kat came into the bookstore and bought one of your plays. Which one was it, again?"

She turned to Kat, whose mind spun for a second before she said, "It was *(de)forestation: a metaphor.*" The notes Jocelyn had made her memorize started to come back to her. "I loved the way it kept shifting around in time."

"I'm glad to hear that," Richard said. "A lot of critics found it unnecessary."

"Not at all," Kat said. "How else would it be clear that power has been a corrupting force in every time period?"

"Precisely!" Richard snapped his fingers. "What brings you to New York?"

"All the good theater is here," Kat said. "L.A. theater is far too commercial."

"Well, if you're such an experimental theater fan, the two of you must come to the little soiree Ashton and I are throwing tomorrow. I'll introduce you to Francoise Auclair." He winked.

Kat's stomach gave a happy swoop. She had no idea who Francoise Auclair was, but an invitation to Richard Gottlieb's house? Already? "I would *love* that."

"Email my assistant. She'll send over the details."

"I will. Definitely." Kat glanced around, trying to think of a graceful way to end the conversation. Her eyes connected with Jude's.

"Kat!" Jude said suddenly, cocking her head as the band started up a new tune. "It's your favorite song!" She turned to Richard. "I'm so sorry, but do you mind if I steal her for a minute? I can't miss this opportunity to dance."

"*Excellent* choice in favorite song." Richard Gottlieb beamed at her. "Ashton and I will have to come join you once we finish our drinks."

"We would love that!"

Jude placed a hand on Kat's lower back and swept her away toward the dance floor. Kat allowed herself to be swept. Her head didn't feel fully connected to the rest of her body anymore.

"What song is this?" she said, when her tongue finally became unstuck. It was something classical, but she didn't know anything beyond that.

"No idea," Jude whispered. "It just seemed like you needed a breather. I'm really sorry if I overstepped. I probably shouldn't have made all that stuff up."

"Not at all. You totally saved me."

Jude glanced back over her shoulder at Richard. "Unfortunately, I do think we need to dance now."

"Okay." Kat glanced around at the gliding couples. "Do we—How does this work?"

"Can you waltz?" Jude asked.

"Can *you*?" Kat responded skeptically.

Jude grinned and held out a hand for her to take. "Why don't you find out?"

Kat placed her hand in Jude's and Jude tugged her inward, putting a hand on her waist. They were very close together. She had to tip her chin to look Jude in the eye, and the proximity made her feel a little breathless. She raised her hand to Jude's shoulder.

Kat had taken enough dancing lessons in her life to follow along as Jude guided her into a confident three-step. After a few stumbles, she found her feet, and Jude swept them along, gliding in rhythm with the other couples. Her hand pressed against Kat's waist, gently leading her into each new movement.

In many ways, dancing with Jude was similar to dancing with Johann, her costar from *Agent Princess,* who was the last person she'd ballroom danced with (for a scene where the titular princess-spy had to gather intelligence at a party celebrating the crowning of the king of Flenovia). But it had some key differences. For one, Kat didn't remember being aware of every finger of Johann's hand, or feeling a little *zip* of sensation up her side every time their pressure changed. She didn't remember the scent of his cologne feeling like a drug she was desperate to inhale, urging her to step closer and closer to her partner. She didn't remember this sparkling sensation across her skin when their eyes met and they gazed at each other as they moved effortlessly across the ballroom, giving her the breathless feeling that they were moving exactly in tandem.

"Where did you learn to do this?" Kat asked.

"My mom. She loved to dance."

"Thank you for saving me back there," Kat said. "I don't know what happened. I just froze."

"You were totally fine," Jude said. "If anything, you seemed like such a big fan you were awestruck into silence. He ate it up."

"Liar," Kat said. Then, "Have you actually seen that play?"

"Yeah. My friend Talia writes reviews for a theater blog, so she gets free tickets to shows." Jude snorted. "It was the most pretentious thing I've ever seen. Completely incomprehensible."

"Well, you seemed to understand it pretty well. Better than I did, anyway," Kat said. She bit her lip, then added, "Do you think I made a terrible impression?"

"Not at all," Jude said. "No offense, but why do you care so much?"

Kat sighed. "He's casting for a new play next month. I really want to be in that show."

"Is it good?"

"The play?" Kat shrugged. "I'm sure it's fine. But it would be huge for my career."

"Ah." Jude nodded thoughtfully. The band finished their song with a flourish, and the dancing couples around them stopped to clap. As they started up a new one, Jude leaned over and said, in a low voice, "Do you want to get out of here?"

Kat hesitated. She'd promised herself that she'd be cold and aloof. But Jude had just saved her ass. Surely it wouldn't be that bad to get one drink with her?

"I really do."

Jude grinned. "Great. I know a place nearby."

CHAPTER 9

JUDE

"Just for fun, when would you estimate was the last time this place was inspected by the health department?" Kat asked as they slid into a booth at Jude's favorite diner, looking dubiously at the dingy newspaper articles on the wall and the ripped red cushions on the chrome stools at the counter.

Jude put her hand on her heart. "I promise this place has had no recent rodent infestations."

"*Recent?*"

"Sure, a *few* people may have died in the past, but don't you believe in giving second chances?"

Katrina glared. Jude laughed. "This place is really good, I promise. My mom used to bring me here as a kid."

"Okay. I'll take my life in my hands, then, and order"—Kat flipped through the extremely long menu—"the lobster? Really?"

"Okay, definitely don't order that," Jude said. "I can vouch for the pancakes, but not for anything of the shellfish variety."

Kat was deep in the menu now. "Pasta with clam sauce? Moussaka? Beef bulgogi? There are, like, eighteen different cuisines in here."

"That's a New York diner for you. If it doesn't have a menu

that looks like it was composed by a poet in a fever dream, then it's not authentic."

The waiter came over, and they placed their orders. Once he left, Kat slumped down in the booth, her entire body going limp. "Oh my God, I'm so happy to be out of there."

Jude smiled at her. At the beginning of the night, Kat had seemed like a different person. She'd barely looked at Jude, and Jude had wondered why she'd even invited her. Now it felt like some filter had dropped away, and the real Kat was back.

"Don't you have to go to that kind of party all the time?" Jude asked. "Aren't you used to them?"

Kat sighed. "I should be," she said. "But it's different now. When I was a kid, all I had to do was take directions and not complain. But now, getting cast, staying relevant, it's all so political. And usually I can handle that, but today, I don't know . . . I just got overwhelmed." She hesitated for a second, then added, "This was my first time being seen in public with another woman, too. I think that threw me off a little."

"Oh," Jude said. Why hadn't Kat told her that in advance? That seemed like important information for her to have. "Is that why you invited me? You wanted to be seen with a woman?"

Kat blushed. "No, no, no," she said hurriedly. "I needed a date. And I had just met you and you seemed really nice, so I thought, why shouldn't I bring a woman? I'm ready for people to know I'm gay. Although, actually, I don't even know if I am gay." Jude raised her eyebrows and Kat hurried to amend. "I mean, I definitely like women. I just don't know if that's all I like."

Jude nodded. "That makes sense."

"Does it?" Kat looked down at the table. "I mean, shouldn't I just *know* that? If I have to think about it, isn't that some sort of sign?"

"I don't think so." Jude smiled at Kat gently, even though Kat was avoiding her eyes. "When people spend your whole life telling you that you love hamburgers and asking aren't you excited to have hamburgers and don't you think that hamburger looks delicious, it makes sense to like hamburgers. But then if you go somewhere like this with a forty-page menu and realize there are a lot of different foods out there, it makes sense that you'd start thinking, Hey, maybe I'm actually a steak person. Or a vegan chicken substitute person. And it would take time to try those foods and decide what kind of person you are. Maybe you like all the foods. Or maybe you try steak and it's so good that you think, man, I can't believe I've been settling for hamburgers all these years."

Kat snorted with laughter—actually snorted, wrinkling her nose up adorably. Jude grinned at her, feeling giddy. She couldn't believe she was actually sitting here, in her favorite diner, with Kat.

"So, men are hamburgers and women are steak, then?" Kat made the words sound flirtier than they had any right to be.

Jude held up her hands. "Don't hold me to this metaphor. But, okay, yes. Women are *much* higher quality than men."

Kat looked up at Jude through her eyelashes. "Guess I'll have to give steak a try, then."

Jude swallowed. She hoped her eyes weren't bugging out of her head like a cartoon character. She tried to channel every last possible scrap of smoothness that she had as she leaned forward slightly to say, in a low voice, "I think you should."

They held each other's eyes. It seemed like they were breathing in sync, like Jude could feel every breath that Kat took moving through her own lungs. Their bodies seemed to be humming at the same frequency, and Jude wished desperately that there wasn't a table between them.

A throat cleared, and they both snapped back in their seats as the waiter dropped two plates in front of them. Jude could see a faint blush on Kat's cheeks as she busied herself with the syrup.

"You know, that's the metaphor they use in church, too," Kat said.

"What is?"

"About why you should wait for marriage to have sex. 'Why have hamburger when you can have steak?'"

"Ew. I did not mean to channel that energy," Jude said, biting into her burger. "Did you grow up religious?"

"Yeah, fairly. I grew up in a suburb outside Albuquerque, and church was a big part of my parents' social scene. Although they definitely used it in part as free babysitting. They worked a lot, so they would drop me off for whatever kids' class the church was having, and someone's mom would take me home afterward." Kat popped a bite of pancake into her mouth and shrugged. "It wasn't so bad. I got a lot of coloring books full of gruesome bible scenes."

"Can I ask how you got into acting?"

"Through church, actually," Kat said, reaching over and helping herself to one of Jude's fries. "We used to do these pageants. The big one at Christmas, of course, but in Sunday school we would do little skits to act out bible scenes. And I loved it. I used to beg my mom to let me try out for a Disney show. But my mom wasn't about to drive me ten hours to L.A. So when I was nine, I went on the family computer, started googling, and found some local commercials that were casting instead."

"Damn," Jude said. "And to think I was just messing around on Neopets."

"Well, I did a lot of that, too," Kat said. "Hasee Bounce was my jam."

"So, your mom let you try out for commercials?"

"Yup. There was one being cast not too far from our house with auditions on a Saturday, so she finally gave in. Burt's Auto Dealership. I didn't even have lines. I just had to walk onto the lot and look wowed by all the shiny new cars. But they paid me two hundred dollars. And once she realized we could make money, my mom was suddenly a lot more willing to drive me to auditions."

Kat smiled like it was a joke, but Jude could see bitterness in the sides of her mouth, and how she stabbed her pancakes with particular force. Jude hesitated before her next question. She didn't want to pry, but she also wanted to understand what kind of life Kat had lived, how she'd become the person she was today.

"How did you get to L.A.?"

"My mom lost her job. She was a receptionist at a law firm, and they laid her off. Money was tight, and she had some free time on her hands, so she drove me over there. I went to nine auditions in three days and I got one." Kat shrugged. "The pay was good enough that my mom let me keep trying out. After a couple of small roles, I signed with my manager, Jocelyn, and then I got the big one."

As she talked about acting, Jude could feel Kat's walls starting to creep back up—her shoulders tensing, her voice becoming less expressive. Buttoning herself back up. So she changed the subject. "How are the pancakes?"

"Oh my goodness, they're incredible. Here." Kat pushed her plate across the table and Jude took a bite, smiling to herself.

Kat laughed, watching Jude chew. "You really love these pancakes, don't you? I'll admit it, your restaurant did not turn out to be as gross as I thought."

"First of all, it's a *diner,* not a restaurant," Jude said, swallowing. "Big difference. But the smiling is because I'm having a really nice time. I was worried that I'd hurt your feelings by telling you I didn't send that DM, so I was really glad when you asked me out again. Because I really wanted to see you, even if I wasn't the one who messaged you."

Kat looked down, the laughter fading out of her face. She slowly cut another bite of pancake. Jude wished she hadn't said anything. Had she made things weird? She ate some of her burger to cover her discomfort.

"Can I ask you something?" Kat said suddenly, putting her silverware down.

"Of course."

"When did you know you were queer?"

Jude paused to think. "Well, I was always really tomboy-like. Even when I was a little kid, people were always asking if I was a boy or a girl, and I always wanted to do whatever the boys were doing. I went through a phase in middle school where I wore skirts and tried to be more like the other girls, but that didn't last very long. And I'd kind of always had crushes on girls. So part of me always knew, but I didn't officially come out until the second half of high school."

"What was that like?"

"I mean, shitty. It's New York, so most people were liberal and supportive of gay people in theory, but in practice . . ." Jude shrugged. "It wasn't like I got beaten up in the hallways or anything. People just whispered about me. Laughed when I spoke in class or asked me why I wanted to look like an ugly man. That kind of thing. But when I was sixteen, I met my friend Rhys—the one who works in the store. We didn't go to the same school, but having a queer friend made me feel so much better. It made me realize that my experiences were normal, and I wasn't a freak. Having queer friends is really important, especially when you're first coming out."

Jude watched Kat drag the tines of her fork through the pools of drying syrup on her plate. Her brow was furrowed and her lips were pressed together, as if in concentration.

"Want to hear something weird?" Kat finally said. "I knew then, too. I was thirteen, and I had this crush on one of my costars—this girl a few years older. And I remember thinking, Wow, guess I'm into girls. And some part of my brain was just like, No thanks, that sounds really complicated, let's shove that one down for another decade or two." She let out a hollow laugh, as if that would convince Jude that she didn't really mean it when she added, "Isn't that messed up?"

"I don't think so," Jude said in a soft voice.

"You don't?"

It would be possible to get lost forever, Jude thought, in the gaze that Kat was giving her right now. In those big, vulnerable eyes looking so hopefully at Jude. When was the last time someone had looked at her like that, like Jude was a safe harbor in a storm? Like she was strong instead of fragile?

"I think it makes sense," Jude said. "I mean, you were a kid. You knew that dealing with all of that would be really complicated and that the adults around you wouldn't be supportive. So your brain decided to wait to process it until you were ready."

"But I wasted so much time," Kat said. "I missed out on having the chance to do all of this when I was the right age. And now I have to figure it out years after everyone else, and totally embarrass myself because I have no idea what I'm doing. Plus, it's not like I can just walk into a queer bar and see how it goes, because I'd be recognized."

"You're not late," Jude said. "Some people don't figure this out until their forties, fifties, sixties—eighties, even. You're so much earlier than so many people."

"It doesn't feel that way," Kat said. "It feels like I'm starting at a new school halfway through the semester, and now I'll never find friends to sit with at lunch."

Jude reached her hand across the table without thinking, palm up. "I'll sit with you at lunch."

Kat hesitated. Then she reached out and put her hand in Jude's.

Jude stopped breathing. Her whole body felt light, as if she were floating a few inches off her seat. Kat's soft hand fit in Jude's palm like it was made to be there. Her thumb rested on Jude's wrist, light enough to cause goosebumps. Jude felt a sudden urge to lift their hands and press the back of Kat's hand to her lips.

Before she could, Kat pulled away. "I should get home."

Jude wanted to stay at this diner all night, listening to Kat talk. She wanted to unwrap the layers of this beautiful human in front of her, find her way past the various fronts and faces Kat put on.

But she could take her time. Clearly, that was what Kat needed.

Kat stood to go, pausing for a moment, lingering by the table. "You'll come with me to Richard Gottlieb's party tomorrow, right?" she finally said. "He invited both of us."

Jude couldn't help the enormous grin that filled her face. "I wouldn't miss it."

CHAPTER 10

KAT

The day after the charity gala, Kat woke up and ran seven miles.

She wasn't supposed to run like that. Not overexercising was a key part of her eating disorder treatment plan. During her *P.R.O.M.* days, Kat had worked out every morning before filming and every night before bed, barely sleeping so she could spend more hours on the treadmill or elliptical, constantly telling herself that if she did just fifteen more minutes, then she would finally feel like she'd earned a rest.

It had been almost four years since she'd spent two months at the Serenity Center, the most discreet inpatient eating disorder treatment center in California, and, for the most part, Kat was okay. The urge never fully went away, though. Treatment had helped her turn down the volume, but there was no off switch. Her therapist back then had told her that was normal—the disorder would probably be a voice in her head for the rest of her life, and it would get louder at some times and quieter at others. Resisting the impulses to restrict calories and overexercise helped her keep that voice quiet, but sometimes the anxiety got so bad, she would do anything to drown it out. And then she would run and run and run until she couldn't think anymore.

The morning after her date with Jude was like that. There was too much panic ricocheting around in her head. She gave in to the urge and, for a little while, it felt good. Later, though, when she was back in her apartment with her aching feet and her shame, her anxiety was just as strong as before.

What had she been *thinking*?

She had planned to stay professional. But sometime during the waltz, all of Kat's resolve had melted away. Jude had bought her a plate of pancakes, and in return, Kat had spilled her guts. She'd told Jude things she'd never said out loud to anyone before. Things she couldn't afford to have leaked to the public. All during her run, Kat's brain had kept up a steady rhythm of *What if she tells, what if she tells.* If Kat was smart, she would cancel tonight's date and never see Jude again.

But Richard Gottlieb had explicitly invited both of them to the party. And, if Kat was being honest with herself, she *wanted* to see Jude again. Spending time with Jude was exciting. When was the last time Kat had actually been excited about something?

Besides, wasn't the whole point of this to get queer dating practice? There was still so much she had to learn. She would go on a few dates with Jude, boost her confidence a little, then walk away. And if she had some fun along the way, even better. Right?

■   ■   ■

Richard Gottlieb lived in a brownstone on the Upper East Side, near the park. A server in a black vest and bow tie opened the door and took their coats as they passed through the hall into a huge living room with gleaming hardwood floors, glass doors open to a large back garden, and a spiral staircase leading to the upper floors.

"I didn't realize theater paid so well," Jude said in an undertone as they made their way through the crowd toward the bar in the back of the room. She was wearing a white button-down and black sweater over gray dress pants, and every time their eyes met, Kat felt a little zing up her spine.

"It doesn't," Kat whispered back. "His grandfather founded Gottlieb & Grove."

"The publishing house?"

"Mm-hmm." Kat took her drink from the bartender: sparkling water with bitters in a tumbler, so it looked like she was drinking but she could keep her wits about her. "They're a very wealthy New York arts family."

Jude craned her neck to look around, staring at the floor-to-ceiling bookshelves on one wall of the living room. "Oh my God, I think those are all first editions."

Kat shrugged. "Probably." She let her eyes rove over the crowd, her spine relaxing as she confirmed that Madelyn wasn't there. She spotted Richard Gottlieb in the far corner, but he was deep in conversation with someone. She would wait to make her move until she was sure they could have a full conversation in peace.

Instead, Kat tugged Jude over to greet his husband, Ashton. She was half convinced he wouldn't remember who she and Jude were, but he greeted them warmly and urged them to check out the library upstairs, since he knew they were "book people." Kat had never been described as a book person in her life, but she accepted the descriptor cheerfully. New York Kat was different from L.A. Kat. New York Kat was well-read and sophisticated, interested in contemporary art and experimental theater. She wasn't the same Kat who'd made a career out of pratfalls and running into cakes.

Across the room, Kat saw Richard Gottlieb disengage from his conversation partner and head for the spiral staircase.

"Can you entertain yourself for a few minutes?" she whispered to Jude, who nodded. Then she counted to fifteen and slipped up the stairs after him. It felt a little rude to go upstairs at a house party, but Ashton *had* specifically told her that she should check out the library.

She climbed the tight spiral staircase. It deposited her in a stunning room: dark wood floor-to-ceiling bookshelves, illuminated by lights on the undersides of every shelf. Gorgeous leather furniture. A bust of someone smart-looking in one corner. Art on the wall in gold frames. A bar cart full of expensive bottles. A sliding glass door leading to a dark balcony. It was beautiful. And it was empty.

That was fine. Kat knew how to wait.

She positioned herself in front of one of the shelves, cocking her head as if deep in contemplation of the titles.

She didn't have to wait long. Richard appeared after a few minutes, adjusting the tuck of his button-down shirt.

Kat turned as if startled. "Oh! I'm so sorry to intrude. Your husband told me it would be okay if I checked out your library."

"Not at all, not at all," Richard said graciously.

Kat looked up at him bashfully through her lashes. "It's gorgeous. Have you read all these books?"

It worked. Instead of heading for the staircase, Richard turned and considered the shelves.

"Not *all* of them, but most." He lifted his hand and ran a finger along some of the matching leather spines.

"Wow. I'm impressed with your dedication." It was a slight gamble. Some people would shy away from this level of blatant flattery. But Kat got the sense that Richard Gottlieb was a man who liked to be complimented.

She turned out to be right. Richard stroked the slight mustache above his lip, as if trying to hide the quirk of his mouth. "When I was young, I made a vow to dedicate myself to a life of literature and art," he said. "It hasn't always been easy, but the internal rewards have been very rich. Reading the classics allows me a certain . . . insight into the human condition."

It took all Kat's professional training not to roll her eyes. How much could this man have struggled to pursue the arts, when he had inherited hundreds of millions of dollars?

Instead, Kat turned slightly so she was facing him, leaning in a little. "And what have you learned?"

"Ah," Richard said, shaking his head slightly. "Life is nasty, brutish, and short. But art, true art, makes it worth living."

"I completely agree," Kat said, shifting her tone from simpering to serious to match Richard's. "That's how I feel about acting. Dissolving into a character, making something bigger than myself . . . that's the only time I feel like I know who I am. When I have a part, everything seems clear and meaningful and ordered. When I'm in real life . . . well, everything else falls short, doesn't it?"

Richard turned and studied her for a moment before responding. "And would you consider the kind of acting you've done to be true art?"

Kat dug her teeth into her cheek to avoid grimacing at the insult. "No," she said. "But making any art, even low art, is better than making no art at all."

Richard hummed thoughtfully in response. She added, "And I hope to make more meaningful art in the future, as my career evolves."

One side of his mouth turned up. "You know what, Miss Kelly? I believe you'll be very successful here in New York." He held out his hand. "I hope I'll see you around more often."

Kat shook it. "I hope so, too."

"Enjoy the library." He started for the spiral staircase. "And bring your girlfriend up to check out the balcony. It's very romantic." He winked and gestured toward the sliding glass door.

His head disappeared down the curve and Kat closed her eyes.

She'd done it. She hadn't mixed up her words or come across as a dumb Hollywood bimbo. He'd literally told her that he thought she'd be successful in New York. This couldn't have gone better.

She wasn't a failure. She wasn't going to spend the rest of her life appearing in listicles called "Ten Child Stars Who Faded into Obscurity." She was going to keep impressing Richard Gottlieb, get this role, and get her career back. She was going to *act*.

Kat laughed out loud. She couldn't help it. Then she took several deep breaths, shaking out her arms, before skipping down the stairs to look for Jude.

CHAPTER 11

JUDE

"Wow."

Jude couldn't help saying the word out loud as she bent over the glass-enclosed bookshelf at the back of the Gottliebs' living room. No one else in the crowded room seemed to care, but Richard and Ashton had a *shockingly* good collection. The Next Chapter didn't deal in rare or collectible books, but Jude had some sense of how much a first edition could go for, and the bookcase in front of her held easily half a million dollars' worth of books. *Moby-Dick, The Adventures of Tom Sawyer, The Great Gatsby, To Kill a Mockingbird, The Grapes of Wrath, Atlas Shrugged* . . . It seemed like they had practically every classic American novel, many with the original dust jackets still intact. Jude wished she could examine them, but she didn't dare open the glass doors.

"Go ahead," a woman's voice said. "No one's watching except for me."

Jude straightened up, startled. The voice belonged to a white woman in a long purple shift dress covered in elegant blue, green, and gold beading reminiscent of a peacock. She had gray hair and a kind smile on her face.

"I was just admiring their collection," Jude said, feeling awkward about being caught.

"I think it's a travesty," the woman said. "All of these famous books, locked up where only two people can see them. And they never take them out, either. They just like the having of them."

"Well, I suppose they're a little too valuable to read," Jude said, eyeing the cracked brown spine of *The Scarlet Letter*.

"I think books are meant to be read and shared, don't you?"

"Definitely," Jude said. "I've never understood the point of buying books just to collect them. I love the way well-read books look on a shelf."

"I agree. I love a torn, waterlogged paperback the best." The woman smiled. "I'm Nina Maguire. I run the Gala Literary Foundation."

Jude actually gasped. Gala was *the* queer literary organization. "You're kidding!"

Nina laughed. "People don't usually get that excited about literary foundations."

"The work Gala does is incredible. Anytime I see a Gala Award seal on a book, I know it's going to be phenomenal. The book that won the literary fiction category last year? I think about it constantly. The way it interrogated the intersection of gender and longing . . . That book changed me."

Nina nodded seriously. "The committee debated about that for a long time. Half the people wanted to give it to that book about the gay businessman. But I fought tooth and nail."

"Are you *on* the *committee*?" Jude was standing in a room full of famous theater people, but this was the best celebrity sighting yet. "As your actual *job*?"

"Well, not every year. It rotates. Most of my job is fundraising. But I'm always surrounded by books, which makes it worth it."

Jude shook her head. "That is so cool."

"And what do you do?"

Jude told her about The Next Chapter and the foundational

queer texts display she'd just finished putting up. Nina seemed delighted and promised to come by the store to see it.

"And are you a bookseller for life, do you think?" she asked.

"Oh. Well. I don't know. I, uh." Jude paused. "I never meant to be. But I love The Next Chapter."

Nina nodded kindly. "Well, I probably shouldn't be saying this, but the director of our emerging writers grant program is leaving us soon. We're planning to start looking for her replacement in a few weeks. It's not a glamorous position—a lot of paperwork, a lot of slogging through applications. But the director helps pick which new queer writers we give the grants to."

"Wow," Jude breathed. "So many of your recipients have gone on to become incredible novelists."

"Exactly." Nina winked at her. "Maybe you should apply for the job."

"Me?" Jude nearly laughed. "But I have no nonprofit experience."

Nina shrugged. "You know the queer literary world. That sounds like plenty of experience to me."

"I— Wow. I don't know what to say."

"Think about it." Nina reached into her purse and pulled out a business card. "If you decide to apply, send me an email when you see the job listing go up. I'll make sure you get an interview."

"Thank you. Thank you so much."

Nina smiled at her, then melted off into the crowd. Jude stared down at the business card in her hand, trying to convince herself it was real. Had she actually just been offered a chance at a job at the biggest queer literary organization in the United States?

Not that she could take it, of course.

She couldn't leave The Next Chapter. Abandon Rhys and Talia and L.J.? Abandon her mother's dream? Let the store become another cookie-cutter Book City with all the personality of an airport newsstand? It was out of the question.

Still, she tucked the card carefully into her wallet. It was nice to be asked, even if she couldn't do it. Nice to imagine other possibilities, just for a little while.

She had just finished putting the card away when someone grabbed her arm. She spun around and found herself face-to-face with Kat, who was beaming and flushed, her eyes glinting gleefully.

"Come on." She wrapped their fingers together, the touch of her skin making Jude's melancholy mood burn off like a morning fog. "I want to show you something."

CHAPTER 12

KAT

Kat felt *expansive*. That was the word that kept coming to mind. Like her insides were bigger than her body, pushing the boundaries of who she was and could be. Jude's hand in hers made her skin spark, sending little race cars of electricity up and down her skin, leaving goosebumps in their dust.

"Where are we going?" Jude asked as Kat pulled her through the party.

"You'll see." Impulsively, Kat swiped a bottle of champagne off the bar as they passed. She pressed a finger to her lips as she looked over her shoulder at Jude, then led them up the spiral staircase, through the beautiful library, and out the glass door onto the balcony.

"Look," she said.

Beyond the balcony's brass railing, the back garden shone with fairy lights strung between the trees. Partygoers drifted underneath them, turned beautiful by the small shimmering lights.

"Wow," Jude said. "This is gorgeous. I mean, mind-boggling that anyone has this amount of space in *Manhattan,* but gorgeous."

"Will you do the honors?" Kat held out the bottle of champagne.

"I'd be delighted." Jude twisted off the cork with a loud pop that made several people below look around wildly. "Cheers." Jude lifted the bottle to her lips for a swig, but the liquid foamed up, exploding around her mouth. Kat laughed.

"You try! It's hard!"

Kat took the bottle and raised it delicately, but it foamed up into her nose, making her sputter.

"Okay, lesson learned," Kat said, wiping her mouth with the back of her hand. "Champagne is *not* easy to drink from the bottle."

"Karma for being a bottle thief," Jude said. "How did it go with the director?"

"*So* well." Kat spun in a little circle, just because she could. She was being *silly*. Kat was never silly. But she felt almost high on happiness and relief. "I think he likes me."

"How could he not?" Jude said, and Kat ducked her mouth to the bottle to hide her blush.

"I'm just relieved. I wasn't sure if I'd be able to pull off impressing him. I mean, he writes these really smart plays, and I was worried he'd see right through me."

"See right through what?"

"That I'm not very smart."

"What makes you think you're not smart?"

Kat shrugged. "I didn't go to college. I didn't even finish high school. I paid some sketchy guy five hundred dollars when I took the GED test and he ensured that I would pass. Lord knows what my actual score was. But the director of *P.R.O.M.* told me to do it if I wanted to get hired—so I could work more hours, because I wouldn't be legally mandated to have on-set tutoring."

Jude frowned. "That's awful."

Kat shrugged again. She leaned against the wall, looking out over the garden, and held the bottle out to Jude. "It was fine. But now I'm a little screwed. The lack of education kind of limits my non-acting job prospects."

Jude leaned beside Kat. Their sides were touching. Kat's veins felt pleasantly fizzy—was that the champagne? Or was it the heat of Jude's body beside her?

"Not having a good education doesn't mean you're not smart," Jude said.

"Yeah, but it's intimidating when I try to talk to people like you."

Jude snorted. "You find me intimidating?"

"Of course I do. You seem to have read every book ever, and you can talk about them so easily. You even understood Richard Gottlieb's play, and that thing made no sense to me."

"Okay, that play made no sense to anybody. Plus, using fancy words or bullshit critical analysis isn't what's important when you talk about books or plays. What's important is how they make you *feel*. Those books I recommended—did you *enjoy* them? Did they make you feel something?"

"I loved them," Kat said, and her voice came out oddly hushed. "I thought about *Mrs. S* for days. The way the narrator feels so out of place, so unsure, moving through a world with rigid rules. Full of longing for something else but not sure what it is they're longing for . . ."

"That's most people's early queer experience, I think," Jude said. "Knowing *something* is different about you. Knowing you want *something* besides what you see in front of you. But also being frustrated because you don't really know what that is."

"That's how I feel," Kat said. "I know I want something different from the life I've been living. I know I want to *be* different, more fully myself. But I don't know who *myself* is, and I don't know how to start figuring that out."

"I think that's a really good place to start, actually," Jude said.

"You have to recognize that you don't know something before you can start learning it."

Kat wanted to shake Jude by the shoulders and beg Jude to tell her how, exactly, she was supposed to start learning these things about herself. But that was too embarrassing. Instead, she took a big sip of champagne and asked, "How are you single?"

"What do you mean?"

"I mean, I can't believe you're not already taken," she said. "What's your dating history like? Have you ever been in love?"

She felt Jude's shoulders tense slightly against hers. "Once."

"What happened?"

Jude picked up the champagne, managing to take a sip without foaming it over this time. She stared at the bottle, turning it in her hands.

"Her name was Becca," she finally said. "We met in college. At Northwestern, in Chicago. We started dating junior year, but when my mom got cancer, I transferred back home. After graduation, Becca moved to New York. We were planning to move in together, but with my mom so sick, it just didn't make sense. And then, when my mom . . ." Jude's voice cracked, and she let the end of the sentence fall away. "Becca was there for me. She kept me from falling apart. And I thought that was *it*. I thought she was the one."

Kat nodded, trying not to reveal the surprising amount of jealousy she felt, hearing Jude talk about *the one*.

"About a year after my mom died, Becca came by the store while I was working and said she needed to talk to me later. But I was so worried, I begged her to just tell me. So she did." Jude let out a sound, something strained that sounded like she'd intended for it to be a chuckle. "She'd accepted a spot at a law school in California. She hadn't even told me she'd applied."

"I'm so sorry," Kat said softly.

Jude's voice had gone hard now. "I think that's the worst thing you can do in a relationship. Hide things from each other. Because if you can't communicate, then you can't do anything."

The champagne suddenly felt sour in Kat's stomach. She'd been hiding things from Jude since their first date.

"So we broke up," Jude said. "That was two years ago."

"That's awful."

"It was really rough. Especially coming right after my mom died. It kind of . . . destabilized my world for a little bit."

"Having someone you love treat you like that . . . I know how painful that is." Kat reached out and put a hand on Jude's arm. Jude leaned into her touch.

"What about you?" she said. "Have you ever been in love?"

Now it was Kat's turn to reach for the champagne bottle. She took a long sip, buying herself time. Was she actually going to share this? It was definitely a bad idea. But Jude had just been so vulnerable . . .

"Once," Kat said, her mouth making the decision before her brain had.

"With that guy from your show? The one you dated?"

"Frasier?" Kat snorted. "God, no. That guy is a piece of shit."

Jude grinned. "I am not *entirely* surprised by that. Knowing literally nothing about him but how punchable his face is."

"Ugh, right? He's like a smarmy, smug Clark Kent."

"No one with a jawline that pretty could *also* be a nice person. It would break the space-time continuum."

Kat laughed. Then she leaned back against the wall. Waiting for the inevitable.

"So, if it wasn't him, then . . . ?" Jude trailed off. "You don't have to tell me. If you don't feel comfortable. I'm sure it's complicated for you. Telling people things. But I promise I would never . . . anything you tell me stays with me."

"Her name was Madelyn," Kat said. "She played my sidekick in *P.R.O.M.* From the very first chemistry read, she told me we were going to be friends. I thought she was just sucking up to me, but she meant it. Once filming started, she was always dropping by my trailer or asking if I wanted to get dinner. And not just me, either. The whole cast.

"Honestly? It was magical." Kat blinked hard, the fairy lights swimming in front of her eyes as she remembered those first few seasons. "I hadn't really had friends since I started acting. Normal kids seemed so young to me. They didn't have jobs. They didn't have responsibilities, or families waiting on their paychecks. And other kid actors were my competition. But on *P.R.O.M.* . . . Madelyn made all of us into a group. She set this tone of friendship from the very beginning and found a way to make us watch out for one another, instead of compete. We were all friends. But Madelyn was my *best* friend."

She glanced over to see if Jude understood what she was saying. "It felt like such a relief to have a friend who *got* it. Who wouldn't call me ungrateful for complaining about how sick I was of signing autographs. Who was on the same crazy restrictive diet I was on. Who I could go to and say, Hey, did that sound guy touch you too much when he was mic'ing you up? and we could talk through whether we thought it was a problem or not.

"We started spending all our time together. Sometimes we would be together all day on set and then I'd call her as soon as I got home. It was the first time in years I didn't feel lonely. I thought about her constantly. I wanted to know everything about her."

Kat stopped to take a breath. She didn't like remembering what their friendship had been like. It made her too sad.

"And then we kissed," Kat said, pushing through. "Just once. But I told her I was straight. Even though I *knew* I liked her like that. I was too worried about people finding out."

"I can imagine that was really stressful as a public figure."

"And afterward—"

Kat cut herself off. What was she doing? She couldn't tell

Jude what had really happened with her and Madelyn. She was being reckless already by sharing this much. Telling the full story was a step too far.

"And then she stopped being my friend," Kat finished abruptly. Another lie she'd told to Jude. She could add it to the quickly mounting tally.

"I'm so sorry," Jude murmured.

Kat knew she had made the smart decision by not sharing the story's real ending. So why did she feel so disappointed in herself?

She put the champagne down. These dates with Jude were supposed to be strictly business. But maybe she didn't *want* this to be strictly business. There was just something . . . nice about Jude. Something sincere and open, something that made talking to her feel easy.

Maybe that was what motivated her to reach up and run her hand through Jude's hair. She'd wanted to touch those rumpled blond strands since the first time she saw Jude. They were just as soft under her fingers as she'd imagined. But she hadn't imagined the way Jude's gray-green eyes would widen as Kat's hand made a slow arc toward the back of her head. Or how Kat's breath would catch in her throat as they leaned toward each other.

Slowly, Jude ghosted a hand over Kat's arm. She ran it upward until it settled behind Kat's neck, pulling her closer. Kat could still hear the murmur of partygoers chatting and laughing in the garden beneath them. But they were alone, shielded from sight, surrounded by the cool night air. She let Jude's hand guide her forward until their lips found each other. Jude tasted like champagne and smelled like cinnamon, and Kat's head spun like she was ten times drunker than she actually was.

After a few seconds, she pulled back, feeling so giddy that she laughed. Jude laughed back, her eyes twinkling like the fairy lights in the garden below.

"We should probably head back downstairs," Kat said reluctantly.

"Okay." Jude led the way back inside. Kat took a second to steady herself before following Jude back down the spiral stairs.

The first girl she'd kissed had ruined her entire life. She could only hope the same didn't happen with the second one.

CHAPTER 13

JUDE

The morning after the party, Jude slept in.

Usually, some strange, restless anxiety compelled her out of bed around 7:30, even on her days off. But for once, Jude felt like something inside of her had quieted down enough to let her stay in bed, wrapped in a warm haze of blankets and daydreams.

When she finally did get up, it was nearly nine. She dressed without showering and went outside.

The West Village was beautiful in the mornings. Even though the streets were filled with greasy paper pizza plates and crushed beer cans from the night before, the sunlight glinting off shop windows and beautiful brownstones made Jude feel like the main character in a movie. The sidewalks were deserted—nine A.M. on Sunday might as well be dawn in the West Village.

Jude walked uptown to the better bagel place, Murray's, and ate her bacon-egg-and-cheese in Washington Square Park. It was warm enough not to wear a jacket but cool enough to make Jude's skin tingle. She felt *alive*. Had the fountain ever leapt so joyfully? Had the big white arch at the park's entrance ever been this beautiful in the morning light?

She was still smiling to herself as she went back into her

building, scooping up a few packages waiting in the lobby and dropping them at various apartments as she made her way up to the fifth floor. Jude had lived in this building since she was thirteen, and while most of the renters moved out after a year or two, several of the tenants had been there for decades. Vera, the old woman across the hall, liked to invite Jude over for tea, and Joe, a tall man with a bushy mustache who was usually smoking outside the front door, had helped Jude install a new faucet last year. In return, Jude carried up everyone's packages and lent Vera books and fed Joe's cats when he went away on vacation. It was special to live in a community where people cared about one another, especially in New York where so many people didn't know their neighbors.

Jude climbed the last flight of stairs to the fifth floor, where a gray-haired man was climbing down from a ladder, lightbulb in hand.

"George!" Jude called out. "Didn't your wife tell you not to climb ladders alone anymore?"

"Pah!" George dropped the lightbulb in a cardboard box. He had a slight stoop to his stance that put his eyes just below Jude's. "Someone's got to climb them."

"I've told you a million times," Jude said, "when you need to change the lightbulbs, just call me and I'll do it for you."

George waved his hand and mumbled something dismissive. He was far too proud to call Jude to help change the lightbulbs, but whenever Jude caught him at it, he could be convinced to let her take over—as long as she consented to having him shout up "helpful" advice from the base of the ladder.

"All done today," George said. "Only had a few to do."

"Let me carry the ladder down for you." George made a brief show of protest before consenting to follow her down the five flights of stairs to the basement, urging her at every corner not to scrape the walls.

"How's your son?" Jude asked. "Still liking college?"

"Pah!" George said. "He changed his major again. Now he wants to study biology."

"Well, that sounds useful, at least."

George made another dismissive noise. "It won't stick. First math, then English, then drama. Mind like a goldfish, that boy. Besides, what good is a biology degree for running a building?"

"Let Ivan decide what he wants to do for himself." Jude tucked the ladder into the storage room and dusted off her hands. "Anything else I can help you with while I'm here?"

"No, no." George ducked his head and shuffled his feet around a little. "Look, hon, I've been meaning to talk to you."

"What's up?"

"Look, I like you, and you're a sweet girl."

Jude resisted the urge to raise her eyebrows. With her short haircut and men's clothing, it was hard to see herself as a "sweet girl." But George was a good guy, so she didn't let it bother her.

"But costs of everything are up right now, and we need to fix the boiler before next winter. It barely made it through this one." George did the weird foot shuffle again, and Jude's stomach twisted in on itself. "I've been trying to give you a pass. I know how hard it was on you when your mom was sick, and now, with you not having any other family . . . I didn't want you to have to leave the place. But it's been six years since I raised the rent."

Jude tried to control her face, but she could feel her horror showing through. George avoided her eyes.

"I'm sorry, sweetie, I really am. But I've got four rent-controlled units in this building. And with the NYU students these days? I could be getting double what I charge you for that apartment."

"Double?"

"I won't do that to you." George patted her arm and Jude resisted the urge to yank it away. "You're a good kid. But I gotta raise it at least a little."

"How much is a little?" Jude dug her nails into her palms as she waited.

"A thousand," George said.

"A thousand dollars a year?"

"A month," he said grimly.

Jude stared at him. She didn't say anything. She couldn't. A thousand extra dollars a month? How could she ever pay that?

"When?" she finally croaked.

"You've got four months until the lease is up," George said. "Plenty of time to figure this out, right? You'll be okay."

"Okay," Jude said automatically. "Thank you."

She stepped around him and headed back up the stairs. She lifted her hands as she climbed to inspect the five deep white crescents pressed into each palm. Her head felt like it was floating above her numb body.

When she opened the door to her apartment, it looked different than it had earlier. The morning light splashing through the window no longer felt cozy and warm. Instead, it felt like a spotlight, shining invasively down on Jude's life.

She sat on the couch and stared around her. The living room was cramped: a squishy pale blue couch with one arm faded almost to white from the sun, next to a small rainforest of potted plants. A clunky TV that was many years out of date. A tall wooden bookshelf that Jude's mom had painted with sunflowers, stuffed with books. A small table with two chairs shoved against the wall. The turntable Jude's mom had loved so much, next to two wooden crates full of records. Framed Beatles posters on the walls, adding pops of color to the already bright room.

Jude stood up and picked out a record from the second crate. The first crate held mostly Beatles records, and Jude didn't play those. Without her mom singing along, they made the apartment feel too empty.

She put on Simon & Garfunkel's *Bridge over Troubled Water*. Their soft voices filled the apartment as Jude walked through her room and opened the closed door to the railroad-style second bedroom.

It didn't smell like her mom anymore. That was the first thing Jude noticed. She didn't think it had been that long since she'd last been inside, but sometime between then and now, the rosewater scent of her mom's favorite perfume had faded. Jude had braced herself for the scent, for the way it conjured the softness of her mom's cotton sundresses against Jude's cheek when they hugged. The absence of the smell she'd been expecting felt so much worse, somehow.

She was really gone.

Jude sat down on the bed. Dust had settled on the dresser, coating the jewelry box and the bottles of perfume. It covered the desk crammed into the corner and frosted the stack of books on the bedside table. Jude wanted to sit there, not moving or thinking or feeling, until the dust coated her, too.

She'd been living alone in a two-bedroom apartment for three years because she couldn't bring herself to dismantle her mom's room. It would be financially smarter and probably emotionally healthier to move out. Jude's mom would never have expected her to keep all her stuff in place like some kind of shrine.

But if Jude *did* move out, then she would never be able to come home again.

Kids were supposed to grow up and move out and go places. But they were supposed to have a home to come back to. If not a place, then a person. A family.

But Jude was alone. Her grandparents were dead. She'd never known her father. This apartment was all she had.

She couldn't move out of here in four months. She wasn't ready. She needed more time.

Which meant she needed a *lot* more money.

Jude got up, shutting the bedroom door behind her, then went into the living room and threw herself onto the couch with a groan.

She could get a roommate. But in a railroad apartment like this, she'd have to find someone she didn't mind traipsing through her bedroom every time they wanted to go in and out of theirs. And the thought of watching someone else move into the room that had been her mom's . . . that felt worse than leaving.

That job at Gala Literary would probably come with a huge pay bump. Maybe if she took it, she could afford to stay in this apartment.

But if she took that job, she'd be giving up her chance to buy the bookstore back. Either way, she'd lose something. Why was it that no matter how hard Jude tried to hold on to things, she was always being forced to let go?

This day had started out so well. She'd actually felt happy for a moment, before life had yanked her right back down like it always did. Being with Kat had made her feel hopeful. Like maybe she was the kind of person who could add good things to her life, instead of just losing them all the time.

She'd liked the way that had felt.

She would figure out what to do about her apartment later. For now, she took out her phone and texted the number Kat had given her last night:

So when do I get to see you again?

CHAPTER 14

KAT

Kat was not very good at shopping.

When she was growing up, someone had always dressed her. At first it had been her mom, laying out the right outfits for each audition on a hotel bed the night before. Her mom hadn't understood anything about dressing for a certain part. She'd only wanted Kat to look respectable, and not give them any reason to feel less-than in front of the rich TV people. And so Kat had shown up at the Disney Channel and Nickelodeon to audition for the roles of sassy preteens while wearing frilly pink church dresses with tights.

Once Jocelyn had entered the picture, she told Kat's mother what to buy: black leggings and neon sweatshirts and long-sleeved T-shirts full of funky patterns and artful rips. She'd sent an assistant to Hot Topic to buy Kat an armful of bracelets—brightly colored plastic ones, fake leather bands with white-and-black checkerboard patterns, chunky ones emblazoned with emojis and phrases like BFF and LOLZ. Jocelyn called it her "quirky but clean-cut tween with perfect comedic timing" costume. Producers had loved it.

Once she was signed on to major projects, stylists had taken over. She'd had the perfect leather jackets for signings in malls, the perfect jean-jacket-and-hat combos for kids' awards shows (why oh *why* had quirky hats been such a thing during those years?), and the perfect athletic clothes for ridiculous televised field days in which she played kickball or Jell-O wrestled with other child stars.

Even after the show had ended, Kat had (at Jocelyn's suggestion) paid a stylist to fill her closet with designer shirts and jackets and shoes, so all Kat had to do was pick one of her prearranged outfits. But all those clothes were meant to make her look like a glamorous straight woman. Which was why phase two of Jocelyn's plan was for Kat to go out and buy some queer-looking clothes.

Normally, Kat would have paid a stylist to do that for her. But stylists were expensive, and their taste in clothes tended to be as well. With a rental in New York, a mortgage on her apartment in L.A., and no income for the past two years, Kat needed to save wherever she could. So, for the first time in over a decade, Kat had to actually buy her own clothes.

She invited Jude to go with her. When Jude had texted asking if they could see each other again, Kat had been filled with a giddy rush. She'd smiled at her phone like a fool as she asked Jude to meet her in SoHo on Tuesday afternoon. She didn't tell Jude that she was trying to piece together a new look, but still, the thought of changing up her wardrobe felt less intimidating with Jude by her side.

Unfortunately, so far, the trip had been a total disaster. Kat had felt a little cool the first time she'd pressed a discreet button and they'd been buzzed into a hidden upscale shop, where a manager had pressed champagne flutes into their hands as they browsed. But after visiting four of the ten stores on Jocelyn's list, Kat had bought nothing.

The problem was that Kat had no idea what she was looking for. When she thought of queer-looking clothes, she could only imagine the kind of clothes that Jude wore—men's buttondowns and suits—which didn't feel like her style. If she wasn't butch, how was she supposed to signal her queerness through her fashion?

"This is terrible," Kat groaned as they left the fourth store, her head fuzzy and her mouth sour at the edges from champagne. "I'm sorry I dragged you along on this."

Kat scrolled through the list of stores on her phone. None of the names inspired confidence. When she'd pictured this date, Kat had imagined the two of them laughing their way through SoHo, weighed down by designer shopping bags. She'd imagined herself trying on clothes while Jude turned into the literal definition of the heart-eyes emoji. She'd imagined feeling cool and confident and *more* secure in her queerness, not less. But she'd forgotten how soul sucking trying on clothes could be. The way the lights showed off every flaw of her body. The way stylists, or in this case salespeople, pursed their lips as if the clothes weren't wrong—she was.

Kat had a sudden strong memory of being trotted out of a dressing room so the showrunner could make a call on whether she should wear a bikini during a Jet Ski scene. It had been for *Pag-Agent,* a blatant tween knockoff of *Miss Congeniality* that had flopped at the box office, largely because no one could pronounce the name. It had featured an extremely serious and uptight tween spy (who secretly had a heart of gold) who was forced to work with a quirky, unintelligent tween beauty pageant star (who secretly had a heart of gold) in order to stop a crime syndicate from stealing the head judge's famous jewels.

Kat must have been thirteen at the time. She could still remember the showrunner's cold stare. She had fought the urge to cross her arms and hide as he assessed her body, his lips pursed, before finally shaking his head and saying to the stylist, "No. It won't work. Change her back into the wetsuit."

It was one of those memories that just wouldn't go away. Eleven years later, Kat still caught herself wondering what, exactly, hadn't been working. If her thirteen-year-old body had been more appealing, could it have saved *Pag-Agent* at the box office? Could it have saved her career so she wouldn't be in this whole mess, doing every desperate thing possible to scrape up a role?

She wondered sometimes if that had been the root of it all. The restrictions and the overexercising had started around then. Had that been the moment that flipped the switch in her brain and set her up for the next seven years of constant calorie counting?

It was impossible to say. There were too many memories just like that one. No one moment had caused anything—it had been the atmosphere, the unapologetic scrutiny, the dismissive way people shrugged and said, "That's just Hollywood, kid."

"Uh-oh," Jude said. "I know that face. Come on."

She put her hand lightly on Kat's shoulder and steered her down a side street.

"Where are we going?"

"Clearly, you are having a shopping-induced blood sugar emergency," Jude said. "We need cupcakes."

Jude held open the door of a bakery with a pink neon sign. Kat started to protest—eating baked goods during a shopping trip? Right before she would have to try on clothes and look in mirrors? But then she caught a whiff of melted chocolate and frosting, and she closed her mouth.

Jude bought them a Brooklyn Blackout and a raspberry-lemon cupcake and led Kat out the back into a small courtyard, looped with fake but appealing strands of ivy. She found them a table tucked up next to a soothing little fountain.

"Here." Jude cut the cupcakes in half and pushed the chocolate one across the table. Kat took a bite and moaned. Jude smiled. "My mom used to take me here whenever I'd had a bad day. Mostly when I got bullied at school. She always said there was no problem a cupcake couldn't fix."

Kat finished her cupcake halves with alarming speed. She was surprised to find that she felt better almost immediately. More alert, less grumpy. Less full of existential shopping despair. "You know what? I think she might be right."

"So, are you looking for anything in particular from this shopping trip?" Jude asked as she chewed.

Kat bought herself some time by taking the knife Jude had used to cut the cupcakes and licking it clean, determined not to waste any of the precious frosting. Surely it couldn't be bad to admit she was changing her look, right?

"I've been feeling like I want to dress a little differently lately. More"—she paused, the word feeling unfamiliar and potentially offensive in her mouth—"queer."

"Do you have any idea what kind of style you want to have?"

Kat winced, then shook her head. She should have prepared for this more. She should have looked up queer celebrities online and taken notes or made some sort of vision board of how she wanted to look. But that hadn't even occurred to her. After all, she was supposed to be figuring out her own *personal* style. Shouldn't she just know what it was when she saw it?

Instead of scoffing at her like she deserved, though, Jude grinned. "I have an idea."

CHAPTER 15

JUDE

Kat did not seem particularly impressed by Jude's brilliant idea.

"Your idea is . . . Old Navy?" she said, shading her eyes to look up at the store in front of her.

"Yup," Jude said cheerfully. "There's a Uniqlo near here, too. We can go there next."

Kat's eyes darted to the sign in the window offering fourteen-dollar jeans. "Look, Jude," she said, as if choosing her words very carefully. "I really appreciate the help but I'm not sure those stores convey the exact . . . glamorous vibe that I'm going for."

Jude grinned. "That's the whole point," she said. "In those high-end stores, everything is so stylized. There's no room to figure out what your new look is going to be, because someone else's vision has already informed all of those clothes."

Kat hesitated.

"You don't have to even buy anything," Jude said. "Think of it more as an exercise in starting to figure out what you like. They have so many different options in this store, you can consider a bunch of styles at once."

Kat pursed her lips as if she was considering it. "I don't know," she said finally. "It looks crowded."

"If anyone recognizes you, they'll just be really excited that you're shopping at the same place as them," Jude said gently. "You'll probably get a spread in *People* magazine: 'Katrina Kelly—She's Just Like Us!'"

Kat lifted her hand to her sunglasses, nudging them farther up her face. "Okay. Let's do it."

The inside of the store was enormous. Kat hesitated for a second before heading for the nearest display of women's clothes. Jude followed. Kat flicked through a couple of racks without enthusiasm, biting her lip. Then she turned to Jude. "I don't really know where to start."

"Well, what kind of clothes do you like?"

"I don't know." Kat ducked her chin, the way she always seemed to when she thought her face might give away some emotion. "Usually, a stylist tells me what to wear."

"So why did you decide not to hire a stylist now?"

"Because my parents burned through my salary when I was a kid, and now I'm running out of money faster than a Marvel movie runs over budget." She said it like a joke, but there was bitterness under her airy tone. Jude decided not to push.

"Well, maybe just browse around. Try to figure out what you like."

Kat flicked through a few more racks, then said, helplessly, "But how do you know when you like something?"

Jude frowned at her, confused. "What do you mean?"

"I mean, people always say you should *trust your gut*. But what does your gut feel like? What if mine is broken?"

"Hmm." Jude leaned against a shelf full of sweaters. "I don't think your gut is broken. But maybe you never listen to it, so it's gotten quieter and quieter over time. Maybe you just need to practice paying attention to it."

Kat looked up at Jude, her eyes big and shining. "How?"

"Well." Jude considered the issue for a few seconds. "I think you have to just pick something. Anything. Look around, see what catches your eye, and try it on. If you feel good when wearing it, then that's a good sign." She put her hand lightly on Kat's shoulder and steered her over to the shirts section. "Here. Just pick a shirt."

Kat looked skeptically at the three-for-one-special sign. "What if I pick a really ugly shirt?"

"That's okay. That's great, actually. Wearing ugly clothes is part of figuring out your style. If you're too worried about picking clothes that other people think look good, you'll never figure out what you actually like. So go ahead. Pick a shirt, any shirt. The uglier the better."

Kat rolled her eyes, but her mouth turned up a little at the corner. She flicked through the shirts, glancing at each of them and then dismissing them one by one, for long enough that Jude started to worry she'd given bad advice. But then Kat paused for a moment, staring at one shirt longer than the others. After a few seconds, she held it up to Jude for inspection. It was a blue-and-white-striped T-shirt with a round crew neck and rolled sleeves.

"What about this one?"

Jude held up her palms. "Don't look at me. Your opinion is the only one that matters here."

Kat stuck her tongue out at Jude. "Okay, fine. This one. It's tomboyish, but it still has a feminine cut. I could wear it under a black blazer or a bomber jacket or something."

"Then it's perfect," Jude said. "I mean, it's not nearly ugly enough, but I'll let that slide. Come on. Let's look at jackets."

"Are you going to march me around to every section of this store and make me choose something?" Kat said, slowing as they walked so their fingers brushed together. Jude's heart leapt inside her chest like it was on a moon bounce.

She opened her mouth to reply, but before she could, a girl came up to Kat's other side.

"Excuse me?" the girl said. She looked no older than fourteen, with braces on her teeth and a furious blush on her face. "Could I take a photo with you?"

"Um." Kat's eyes darted around the store. "Okay." She leaned her face next to the girl's and smiled, her mouth melting into cheerful nonconcern as the girl took her time holding up her phone and snapping selfies. "Have a great day," Kat said, her voice straining as she straightened up. The girl opened her mouth as if to say something else, but Kat took Jude's elbow and started pulling her toward the checkout counter.

"We need to leave," she said in an undertone.

"Why?" Jude looked back. The girl was looking through the photos on her phone, not following them or doing anything weird.

"Just trust me," Kat said.

"Oh my God!" a woman said from a couple feet away, her voice so loud she was practically yelling. "Are you *Katrina Kelly*?"

"*Shit*," Kat whispered. Her grip on Jude's upper arm tightened suddenly. She dropped the T-shirt on the nearest display and waved at the woman, then started marching Jude over toward the doors.

But it was too late. At the woman's shout, everyone in the store had looked up. Faster than Jude would have thought possible, people started to gather around them.

The woman who'd shouted ran over, pushing her way to the front. She grabbed Kat's free hand. "Katrina!" she said. "I love you. I've seen every one of your movies. I've watched every episode of *P.R.O.M.* like six times." Her voice reached a frantic pitch, like she was on the verge of tears. "I've been having a really hard time lately and I just feel like—I feel like me seeing you is a sign and—"

"Thank you so much for being a fan." Kat tried to pull her hand away, but the woman was holding on too tightly. Other people had started to press in close to them, their phones raised to snap photos. Behind them, Jude could see more people coming over, their necks craning as they tried to figure out what was going on. There were now at least two dozen people between them and the exit.

"Katrina! Can I have a photo?" someone shouted, but Jude couldn't tell who. There were too many people holding out their phones.

"Excuse me!" Jude tried to yell. "We need to get through!" But her voice was swallowed up by the noise of the crowd.

"My husband left me," the woman still holding on to Kat's hand said. "And I've been so depressed, but now—"

"Could you *please* let go?" Kat said, her voice forceful now. Her smile was fading, her teeth gritting together. She dropped Jude's hand to try to gently push the woman away.

"Ma'am, please back up." Jude tried to get between them, but someone in the front of the crowd got shoved by someone in the back and went knocking into Jude, sending her crashing painfully against a table of corduroy pants. She cursed and rubbed her hip. When she looked up, people had filled the space between her and Kat, pressing in so tight that they could no longer see each other. She could hear Kat's voice over the crowd, saying desperately, "I'm afraid I don't have time to take photos right now, but thank you all so much for being fans. If I could just get through—"

But no one was listening. Jude tried to get back to Kat, but the crowd wouldn't part. She shoved at shoulders, but people shoved her back and the motion rippled through the crowd, making people less civilized, more unruly, more willing to push to get toward the front. Someone knocked over a mannequin in a floral dress and it crashed onto the ground, its head rolling away from its body. Everyone was reaching out, trying to tap Kat's shoulder to get her attention, trying to make her hear their request for a selfie, trying to get closer. She would be crushed.

"Kat!" Jude called desperately, cupping her hands over her

mouth. She looked around wildly. Was there another way out?

"Kat!"

An earsplitting noise filled the air in two sharp blasts. Jude's hands jerked to cover her ears as she looked around wildly for the source, finally locating a short, stout woman in an Old Navy polo shirt, holding an air horn over her head. The crowd fell silent, and the woman pushed her way through.

"This is a *store*," the woman yelled, shaking the air horn. "Please resume your shopping or leave."

The shocked crowd let her through as she authoritatively shouldered her way through until she reached Kat. Jude could see several people holding up phones, filming the whole thing. The woman walked Kat as fast as possible toward the back of the store and a door marked Staff Only. Jude scrambled to catch up and the woman whirled around, brandishing the air horn at her as if it were pepper spray. Jude hurriedly held up her hands.

"She's with me!" Kat said.

"Okay. Get in here." The woman held open the door and ushered them through. Inside, it was blessedly quiet. Jude and Kat both gasped, breathing hard.

"There's an exit in the back," the manager said. "Do you have transportation?"

"I'll call a car." Kat took out her phone. Her hands were shaking so badly that it took her three attempts to unlock it. Jude held out her own hand to check—it was shaking, too. She could feel painful bursts of adrenaline spiking through her body with every heartbeat. Her chest felt so tight she could barely breathe.

The woman stood in front of the door as if guarding it while Kat stared at the app, muttering, "Come on, come on" to herself as the car got closer. Finally she looked up and said, "It's outside."

"Okay. Quickly." The woman swept them through a concrete room full of shelved boxes and to the large cargo doors in the back. She typed in a code and pushed them open.

Kat turned to the woman. "Thank you. Really, I don't know how to thank you enough for—"

"Just *go*," the woman said, and Kat nodded, scurrying down the concrete steps. Jude followed, turning her head to both sides to make sure no one was following them, and then they both collapsed into the waiting car.

CHAPTER 16

KAT

It had been seven hours since they'd escaped from the crowd in Old Navy, and Kat hadn't heard a word from Jude.

That wasn't necessarily unusual. So far, they'd only texted each other to make or confirm plans. It wasn't like they messaged back and forth all day long. But still, it felt odd that Jude wouldn't check in *at all* after they'd been nearly crushed to death against a rack of discount sweaters.

Unless, of course, the whole incident had made Jude realize just how big of a mistake dating Kat was.

In the car afterward, they'd barely said a word to each other. Kat had told the driver to drop Jude off at home, and Jude hadn't protested. She'd only asked if this kind of thing had happened before, and Kat had shrugged and said yes. Then Jude had nodded and stared out the window while Kat watched the side of her face.

It had not looked good. Kat would have bet money that it had been the face of someone realizing that dating a famous person was, in fact, a huge pain in the ass. Being famous wasn't just galas and parties and fancy outfits. It was everyone feeling like they owned a piece of her. It was never being able to relax, because she never knew when someone might take a photo. It was back entrances and not going to the supermarket even though she *really* needed that one thing, because then she'd have to pretend to be ecstatic to meet some fan who cornered her in the toothpaste aisle. It was hiding in her house. It was chewing the insides of her cheeks until they bled against her teeth. It was trying to juggle recovering from an eating disorder with staying fit and thin, because her entire career depended on her body. It was eyes on her all the time.

Jude didn't deserve that. Jude was a nice, normal person with a nice, normal life, and she was probably sitting at home realizing that Kat was a wrecking ball who would crash right through that life and take all the nice, normal parts of it away.

She was probably sitting at home realizing that Kat wasn't worth it.

Kat threw herself onto the hard leather couch in her living room. Would Jude text to explain her decision? Would she insist on one more date, so she could do the right thing and let Kat down in person? Or would Kat just never hear from her again?

Kat should let her go. She had been supposed to go on only a handful of dates with Jude before she moved on to someone famous. Now she wouldn't have to break up with Jude. She should be relieved.

She wasn't. Somewhere in there—was it in the diner? On that balcony, kissing over a stolen bottle of champagne?—Kat had started having fun. *Real* fun. Paired with *real* feelings.

She liked Jude. No, she *like* liked Jude, as if she were in junior high or something. She'd been walking around for days replaying their kiss, and the way Jude's lips had felt on that balcony, getting a little electric shock in her stomach every time.

Jude was different from anyone else in Kat's life. She took listening very seriously, really stopping to think about what Kat said before she responded. It made Kat feel as if what she had to say might actually be important. It made her want to talk.

Now Jude was one more thing that Kat's career had taken from her.

Kat groaned into her hands, then got up and forced herself to do a yoga video to stretch some of the tension out of her body. She'd already gone through her usual postdisaster procedure: updating Jocelyn on the situation, showering for half an hour to try to scrub off the memory of that woman's grip, exercising furiously for way too long, showering again, staring at her ceiling while dissociating. The whole routine.

She tried to take deep breaths as she shifted into downward dog, but her phone lit up with a reprimand from Jocelyn: *What were u doing in an old navy anyway??? V bad for ur brand!!*

Kat let out a sigh that was closer to a scream. Photos and videos of the incident were circulating the internet, and some reporter named Ned Edwards at the *New York Host* had already run a scathingly satirical article about it, implying that the whole thing had been a publicity stunt to try to make a clearly irrelevant actress seem relevant again.

Kat switched into a plank, even though she'd already done her designated core workout for the day. This was exactly why she needed to do whatever it took to get her career back. So she wouldn't be a punchline in some hack's headline.

Her phone lit up again and Kat considered throwing it across the room. But she'd already caused enough stress for Jocelyn today. She unlocked her phone without releasing from her plank.

It was a message from Jude.

Kat's core gave out, and her knees thunked to the mat. She opened the message.

If you're free, can I come over? I want to talk about earlier.

Apparently, Jude was an in-person breakup kind of person. Which made sense—Jude was too kind for anything else.

At least she wasn't leaving Kat waiting. She didn't have to spend days dreading the inevitable.

But goddamn, Kat wished they could have had more time.

With numb hands, Kat responded and went to touch up her makeup. She could at least look hot while she got broken up with. But the doorman called only a few minutes later—Jude must have already been nearby when she texted.

Kat's throat felt tight as she waited for Jude to come up in the elevator. She would be cool and calm the whole time. She wouldn't make a scene. She'd just accept Jude's decision and shove any feelings way, way down.

When she opened the door, Jude gave her a hug, but it felt strained. She was holding a plastic shopping bag in one hand. They went into the living room and sat down on the couch, but on opposite ends, turning awkwardly so they could face each other.

"How are you doing?" Jude asked. She looked uncomfortable.

"Fine."

"Really? If I were you, I'd be struggling. That was terrifying."

Kat shrugged. If Jude was breaking up with her, she wasn't going to share anything personal. "It's happened before."

"Right." Jude shifted the bag awkwardly from hand to hand, then put it on the floor. "Well, that's kind of what I wanted to talk to you about."

She hesitated. Kat dug her teeth into the inside of her cheek, trying to resist the urge to chew. No emotion. She couldn't let Jude see that this hurt.

Jude rubbed the heels of her palms together, like she was cold. Finally, she said, "I just wanted to say that I'm really, really sorry."

"It's fine," Kat said. "Really. It couldn't last forever, right?"

"What?" Jude said, her eyebrows hunkering down over her eyes. "No, I'm really sorry that I forced you to go into that store. You didn't want to, and I pushed you. I thought you were concerned about looking cheap or something for shopping there. You *said* it looked crowded in there and you weren't sure about going in. I should have listened. And then"—Jude shook her head, her jaw just as tight as her eyebrows now—"I was totally useless. I should have helped you more, held that woman off. But all I did was make things worse. If that employee hadn't helped us, I don't know."

Kat stared at her, waiting for the rest. The *It's not you, it's me* part.

"I'm also sorry that I didn't realize before what your life is like," Jude said. "You live under a microscope, and there are a lot of things you have to think about that I've never had to think about before. Which is on me, for not understanding that."

Here it came. The *It's just too much, I can't handle this*. Kat sat up straighter, bracing herself.

"I promise I'll be more thoughtful in the future," Jude said, those earnest green-gray eyes focused directly on Kat now. "So you don't always have to be the only one dealing with those extra pressures."

Wait. That didn't sound like a breakup line.

Jude reached down between her legs and picked up the plastic bag. She held it out to Kat. "I got you something," she said, flashing a hint of that one-dimple smile.

Kat took the bag, still not quite sure what was going on. She opened it and lifted out a blue-and-white-striped T-shirt.

"I know you never got to try it on," Jude said. "But even if it doesn't fit, I hope it's a reminder that you can learn to trust your gut as long as you remember to listen to it."

Kat pressed her lips together, hoping to hide the slight tremble running through them.

"You went back to the store for it?"

"I actually went uptown to the other Old Navy. I was too scared to go back to the one downtown."

"Jude, I . . ." Kat stared at the T-shirt in her hands. "I thought you were going to say you didn't want to see me anymore."

"What?" Jude moved closer to her on the couch and put a hand on her knee. "Why?"

"Because my life is fucked up." Kat was horrified to discover that her voice was thick with tears. "Because it's not all galas and glamour."

Jude's arms fell around her like a summer rain, warm and soft. Coating her in their protection. She pulled Kat's head to her shoulder. Now that her face was unobserved, Kat started to cry for real. Why was she being so embarrassing? She'd known Jude for less than two weeks.

"Kat," Jude said tenderly. "You are so worth any inconvenience your situation might bring."

Kat heaved out one humiliating sob. Then she clamped her teeth down and forced herself to pull it together. Jude let her stay like that, hiding her face in the safety of Jude's sweater, until her breathing slowed and calmed.

"Okay," Kat said when she could trust her voice to come out evenly. She pulled away from Jude, standing up and turning around in a quick motion so she could wipe her eyes without Jude seeing. "Do you want tea or something?"

"Tea sounds great."

Kat hurried into the kitchen, pressing her fingertips under her eyes in hopes of reducing any puffiness. As she turned on the electric kettle, she heard Jude come into the kitchen behind her and stop near the counter.

"Can I ask you something?" Jude said.

"Of course."

"Why did you ask me out again, after we went to drinks? You seemed so upset when I told you I wasn't the one who sent the DM. I thought I'd never see you again."

Kat froze with her hand halfway toward a cupboard. "I wasn't that upset."

"Yes, you were. It really hurt your feelings. I could tell."

Kat pulled out two mugs slowly, trying to buy herself a little time to think. She should just tell Jude the truth: she'd needed a date to the gala so she could get photographed with a woman.

Maybe Jude would understand. But Kat had already lied about that at the diner. And Jude had said she thought lies were the one thing a relationship couldn't recover from.

The kettle clicked as it began boiling.

"How do you take your tea?" Kat asked.

"With as much honey as it can handle, usually."

Kat paused. Madelyn used to drink her tea like that. Kat would make fun of her for piling in honey until the liquid was almost thick. It was one of the rare indulgences Madelyn allowed herself despite the strict diets they were both on, because she said it made her voice smooth and sweet, even during long days on set. Kat didn't like the taste, but she'd kept bottles of honey in her trailer for whenever Madelyn visited.

This small reminder of happier days made Kat realize how foolish it would be to tell Jude the truth. Sure, Jude seemed trustworthy—but Kat had thought that about Madelyn, too, hadn't she? And she'd known Madelyn for four years, not two weeks.

If this story got out . . . Kat would be ruined. She'd be even more of a laughingstock than she already was.

Besides, Kat had already thought she was losing Jude once today. She couldn't handle thinking that wasn't true, only for it to happen for real a few minutes later.

"Okay, I was really mad." Kat turned around. "But mostly because I was embarrassed that I was making it clear that I was into you and you didn't do the same."

There was a scene in *P.R.O.M.* Season 2 when Lily Carlson confesses that she's been in love with Jackson Messier since the first time she saw him at a football game sophomore year. Jackson had only been in one season, as a way of introducing tension into Lily's perfect relationship with Frasier's character, Lance, but many fans considered Jackly the best ship of the entire show.

Kat didn't exactly make a decision to copy the script. The lines just sprung into her head, as clear as the day she'd memorized them. The words felt *right* in this moment somehow. They felt like hers.

Kat stepped forward, looking directly into Jude's eyes, watching the way they widened in response.

"I asked you out again because I felt like our story wasn't over yet. I could tell that underneath that shy exterior"—Kat switched the words *bad boy exterior* for a more appropriate epithet here—"there was something else, longing to come out. From the moment I saw you, something about your soul just hooked into mine."

Jude's breathing had gone shallow. She leaned in toward Kat, as if she couldn't resist the pull.

"Me too," she whispered. "I, um. I felt the same way. When I saw you in the store." She paused, and then repeated in a wondering tone, "Your soul just hooked into mine." Her eyes started to shine and Kat stepped forward to kiss her, ignoring the sudden nausea that twisted through her stomach.

CHAPTER 17

JUDE

"And then she said that she asked me out again because she felt like our story wasn't over yet. And because 'something about your soul just hooked into mine.'" Jude tried to repeat the words casually, but it was hard to hold back the big, goofy smile that kept wanting to fill her face.

Rhys wasn't fooled. He smacked her on the arm with the advance reader's copy of a horror novel he had just finished pulling out of their pile of unopened mail. "Dude! She likes you!"

Jude let the smile out, cheesing like a fool. "She likes me."

"I'm so happy for you," Rhys said.

Jude leaned against the wall next to the rickety ARC shelf in the bookstore's back room and sighed at the fluorescent lights. "She's so interesting. And unafraid. Like, if she wants something, she just *goes* for it. It's very inspiring. And she's under all this scrutiny all the time, but she still manages to be so kind. She could totally be a dick, being that famous, but she's not at all."

"Uh-oh," Rhys teased. "It sounds like someone's falling hard."

Jude shrugged but didn't deny it.

"Speaking of dating . . ." Rhys's ears turned slightly pink as he shelved some more ARCs. "I was thinking of maybe asking L.J. out."

Jude's happiness vanished, erased in one swipe like a whiteboard. "Really?"

"Yeah." Rhys shrugged. "I've had a crush on them for a while. And we've been texting a lot lately. And the other day, when we were doing globe bar and they said the thing about being inspired by me . . . I don't know, I kind of thought maybe it seemed like they were into me."

"Huh." Jude felt like someone had taken a corkscrew to her insides, twisting her stomach into a tight, sickening knot. She was already going to lose her apartment. How could she handle losing her two best friends at the same time?

"What do you think?" Rhys said.

"About what?"

"Do you think they were flirting with me the other night?"

"Well." Jude picked one of the ARCs up off the shelf and turned it idly in her hands. "Honestly? No. I thought they were just being friendly."

"Oh."

"And you know how L.J. is," Jude continued. "They're always hooking up with someone. Do you really think they'd commit to a relationship? It's probably not worth damaging your friendship over what would end up being a casual fling, right?"

"Yeah. I guess you're right." Rhys picked up his cane and gathered the empty packing material into a pile but didn't move to throw it away. Jude felt a twinge of guilt at the disappointed look on his face. But she wasn't wrong. L.J. *did* hook up with a lot of people. If Rhys and L.J. dated, they would fracture the friend group when they inevitably broke up in two months. Jude was just saving her best friend from future heartbreak.

"Here. Let me." Jude took the pile of packing material and

shoved it in the trash can. Just then the door opened, and Stephen's furious face appeared at the crack. "What are you doing back here? I'm not paying you overtime to open mail."

Jude's stomach started inch-worming up into her throat for an entirely different reason. For a moment she'd almost managed to forget that tonight the author of *Liberal Snowflakes* was giving a talk in the store, and Stephen expected her to introduce him.

Jude had introduced authors at events before, but speaking in front of crowds still made her nervous. Especially this time, when she'd be speaking to a bookstore full of rich conservatives, rather than their usual supportive queer readers.

She pulled the notecard out of her pocket, muttering the words to herself, making sure she could pronounce the name of every conservative think tank in the author's bio. Outside, she could hear a crowd gathering as L.J. and Talia checked tickets at the door. To Jude's dismay, the talk had sold out—apparently people were very invested in the weakening of America's youth. They could only fit thirty chairs in the bookstore at once, but still. Jude would have to stand up in front of thirty people and form coherent words without tripping over her own feet or throwing up.

"Right." Jude moved her eyes over the words one more time, as if a final read through could save her from public humiliation. Then she put the paper in her pocket and followed her friend into the store. Rhys thumped her back encouragingly as they went.

Jude stopped for a moment behind the desk. Surely this couldn't be just thirty people. The store was completely packed. Stephen was in his element, greeting people, shaking hands. He seemed to know half the people there.

Jude cleared her throat, hoping to corral people to their seats. Inside her pocket, her fingers traced over the piece of paper as if she might memorize the words through osmosis. Finally, Stephen nodded at her and she trudged to the front of the room.

She felt like she was moving through Jell-O. Every step took twice as much effort and concentration as usual, like in one of those horrifying dreams where you forget how to run. She reached the front of the room. Remembered to switch on the microphone—a good start. She pulled out the card with numb fingers. Her wrists were tingling now, and she tried to stretch them out, but everyone was looking at her and there was no subtle way to do it. Her vision seemed slightly wavy, the way heat lines look coming off a road. Her chest was tightening, tightening, tightening. She couldn't breathe. She looked out at the sea of conservatives in fancy clothes, their faces hard and expressionless as they waited for her to speak.

Oh God. Jude was going to have a panic attack in front of a room full of people. While holding a microphone. Why hadn't she asked someone else to do this? What had she been thinking?

Everyone was looking at her. People were shifting in their seats. She had been silent for too long. She had to say something.

She lifted the index card to eye level and said into the microphone, "Thank you for coming." Her voice boomed out of the speakers, making her flinch. She tried to speak the next line at a more normal volume, but it came out closer to a whisper. "The Next Chapter bookstore is very . . . excited to host"—her tongue felt thick, and the words came out strangled—"Eric St-Stockton."

A couple of audience members exchanged glances. Others stared fixedly at the bookshelves over her shoulder. Behind the last row of chairs, Stephen stood with his arms crossed under a furious glower.

Her stomach lurched. She was going to throw up.

Why couldn't she do this? What was wrong with her?

A hand closed over hers. She looked up in surprise as L.J. plucked the notecard from her hand.

"Thank you for introducing the store for us, Jude," L.J. said, beaming into the microphone like the MC of a comedy show.

"I'm L. J. Jeong, and I'm the events coordinator here at TNC. We have a very, uh, *interesting* talk planned for you tonight. Now, Eric Stockton is currently a professor at MIT, where he holds . . ."

Jude couldn't follow the words. As L.J. read the prepared bio, she swayed on her feet next to them, trying her best to smile at the audience like this had been planned. Finally, the audience started clapping, and L.J. pulled Jude to the back of the room. Jude was grateful—black sparks had started to eat at the sides of her vision. As the author began talking, Jude stumbled behind the counter and through the door back to the staff room.

Once inside, she collapsed against a wall, sliding down it until she could rest her head between her knees. She felt sick. Her heart was beating hard. Surely it wasn't safe for her heart to beat this hard for this long. It would give out. She would die here, having only ever worked at one place, having done nothing with her life.

Oh God. She really was going to throw up.

The door opened. A few seconds later, something cold and wet trickled down the back of her neck. She gasped, eyes flying open to find Rhys kneeling beside her.

"It's ice," he said. His voice was calm. "I'm holding a handful of ice to the back of your neck. Focus on it. Think about how cold it feels." He pressed the ice in a little tighter. Jude felt it drip down the back of her shirt, cold drops rolling the length of her spine. "You're okay," Rhys continued. "You're having a panic attack, but you're okay. I'm here. You're safe. Nothing is wrong. Just think about the ice."

The cold seared through her panic, an icy sword that cut away the worst of her nausea. She focused on the painful freezing sensation. Gradually, her heartbeat started to slow.

Finally, Jude took a deep, hitching breath and looked up at Rhys.

"Thank you," she whispered.

"It's nothing." Rhys got up and dumped his handful of ice in the sink, then sat next to her. Jude took deep breaths. She could breathe. She was fine.

"What happened up there?" he asked.

"I don't know." Shame sluiced through Jude's veins, washing away the remains of the panic, weighing her body down with a different kind of pain. "I thought I could handle it. But it's been a while and I guess, I guess public speaking . . ."

Rhys's hand landed softly on her shoulder. "Has this been happening often?"

"A couple times."

"Maybe you should talk to someone about it."

"I know," Jude whispered. As if speaking quietly might hide how choked her voice had gotten.

Rhys's hand squeezed lightly.

The door opened and L.J. came in, closely followed by Talia. Jude hid her head in her knees again, trying to subtly wipe her eyes.

"Thank you for saving me," she said to L.J. when she could trust herself to speak again. L.J. waved her off.

"No problem at all," they said. "Stephen is pissed, though."

"When is Stephen *not* pissed?" Talia said.

Jude closed her eyes. The heart that had been working so hard before now seemed sluggish, limping along in her chest. "He's going to use this to say I'm not up to managing the store," she said. "He's been looking for an excuse to change how we run it for ages."

And Jude had just given him one. Her little display up there had shown Stephen exactly how incompetent she was.

There was a long, heavy silence. No one contradicted Jude's prediction.

L.J. dropped into the computer chair. "Maybe we should all quit."

"*What?*" Rhys and Jude said together.

They shrugged. "I know we all love this store, but Stephen is changing it piece by piece. He owns the place. We can only fight him for so long. Wouldn't you rather work somewhere where you're valued and get halfway decent benefits?"

"I did practically get a job offer the other day," Jude said, mostly as a joke.

All three heads swung to her at once, waiting for more information.

"It was at that weird theater party I went to with Kat. I met the woman who runs Gala Literary, and she said they're going to hire someone to run their emerging writers grant program in the next few weeks."

"Dude!" Rhys said. "That job would be *perfect* for you."

"You'd meet so many cool writers!" Talia said.

"I mean, it would be totally awesome," Jude said. "But I can't leave the store."

"Why not?" Rhys said. "Maybe L.J.'s right. Maybe it's time."

"This is my mom's store," Jude said. She expected that point to end the conversation, but they just stared at her, waiting for more. "If I quit, I'll be giving up the chance to buy the store back. That was the deal Stephen and I struck. I can buy the store back at market rate as long as I stay on to run it."

The glance her friends exchanged felt like a betrayal.

"Jude," Talia said, and the gentleness in her tone cut far deeper than harshness. "How are you ever going to get enough money to buy the store back at this salary?"

Jude stood up. She couldn't sit still while having this conversation. "I'll figure it out," she said. "I have to. Because if I quit, there's no way Stephen would ever sell the store back to me."

"Jude. Buddy." Rhys looked up at her. He was still on the floor, his head tilted back so he could look at her, but Jude couldn't meet his eyes. "Are you sure leaving the store wouldn't be best for you? Sometimes I worry that you're a little . . . stuck."

"What do you mean, *stuck*?" Jude crossed her arms.

"Everything with your mom was so awful. No one could

blame you for wanting to stick with the familiar while you got back on your feet. But then Becca left, too, and it was like you . . . I don't know, retreated into yourself. Like you're so worried about losing anything else that you're not willing to try anything new. But you can't just hang on to things forever. Eventually, you have to start growing."

Jude could tell from the synchronized nodding and sympathetic expressions on L.J.'s and Talia's faces that they'd had this conversation before. They'd been talking behind her back about how she was too weak to handle the store.

"I am not *stuck*," Jude said, and her voice came out so loud she was sure the audience in the front of the store could hear it. "And I am not abandoning my mother's dream just because *you're* tired of working here. If you all want to quit, go ahead. I don't need friends who think I'm a failure."

Rhys's face cracked, the careful concern giving way to hurt. Jude had gone too far.

She couldn't stand to look at him. Instead, she pushed open the door and left.

CHAPTER 18

KAT

Kat was a complete failure.

Two days after her shopping date with Jude, she spent the morning with an acting coach named Wallace, going through the script for Richard Gottlieb's new play. Usually, Richard kept his scripts tightly under wraps. He preferred to get cold reads during auditions for "authentic emotions and reactions." But one of the producers owed Jocelyn a favor, and so the script had arrived in her inbox on Monday morning. At first, Kat had been resentful—she was a good actor. If Richard wanted to see organic reactions from everyone, why not just show up and give it her best?

That was how she felt *before* she read the play. After going through the script, she was ready to accept whatever fucking help she could get.

She had to be missing something. Her terrible education had to be failing her. Or maybe she just hadn't seen enough experimental theater to get what Richard was doing. Because right now, the script was completely incomprehensible.

The play followed a college student who seduced an esteemed male philosophy professor, beloved by both faculty and students.

The young woman was pretty but insecure, desperate for the validation that attention from authority would bring her. She came on to the professor at every opportunity, wearing down his resistance over time. Then, when he seemed to be getting tired of her neediness, she turned on him, presenting herself as a victim to the university and causing him to lose his job, his wife, and his family.

That part was straightforward enough, although Kat had some issues with the main character. Why, exactly, was she so hell-bent on seducing this professor? Her motivation was never explored, except for vague hints at trauma in her past. She was a bold character, sure, but she seemed oddly one-dimensional. Kat also could have done without the long monologues about cancel culture that muddled up the play's end.

The parts that didn't make any sense were the scenes when the ghosts of various famous philosophers appeared and held long debates about the play's actions and morals. At first, Kat had assumed they were figments of the professor's imagination, but then the other characters had started talking to them, too. But those scenes weren't *nearly* as bad as the drawn-out sequence halfway through in which the professor spoke to living representations of every vagina he'd ever been in, starting with his mother's and ending with his wife's and the student's.

"Think of it as representing the circle of life," Wallace the acting coach had said, tapping his hand emphatically on the script. He'd filled his copy with notes and circles and underlines in red pen. Kat's copy was just filled with question marks. They were sitting in Kat's living room, and he was wearing a black turtleneck with black jeans, because of course he was. "We spend so much time trying to get back to where we started—the security and wholeness of our mother's womb. That's why men are so obsessed with sex."

Kat was sure there was *something* wrong with that statement, but she didn't have any better interpretations to offer. So she went along with it, trying her best to act like the main character becoming a personified vulva. After about fifteen minutes of the acting coach telling her she wasn't channeling the right "energy," she threw her script on the floor.

"Isn't Richard Gottlieb gay?" she asked. "Why isn't he writing about personified dicks?"

Wallace sniffed. "His outsider perspective allows him startling insight into the power dynamics of men and women." He paused for a moment. "That's what *The New York Times* said about his last piece, anyway."

By the time Wallace finally left, Kat felt like her brain had been scrambled with an eggbeater. He had picked apart every single thing she'd done. Her gestures were too big, her facial expressions too exaggerated, her displays of emotion not subtle enough.

Maybe she wasn't cut out for Broadway. Maybe she was only right for movies with big explosions and pop-heavy soundtracks.

Kat lay down on the couch with a groan. She should really start getting ready for tonight's networking event—*another* play, this one hopefully with no talking genitalia. Richard Gottlieb had tickets, and Jocelyn had strategically purchased Kat a ticket two rows ahead, to make sure Richard would see her appreciating fine art.

She couldn't bring herself to get up. She took out her phone instead, getting a little ding of happiness when she saw she had several messages from Jude about the new lesbian romance she was reading. Kat responded, then turned her attention to the texts she had from Jocelyn: a link and the message *Am I good or what???*

The link took her to an *Entertainment Daily* article with the headline "New Love Interest for *P.R.O.M.* Star Katrina Kelly?"

Kat dropped her phone on her face in surprise.

When she picked it back up, she studied the photo under the headline. It was the one from the Stars for Sound gala, with

Jude's arm wrapped around her. Kat was posing for the camera. Jude had her eyes on Kat, her cheeks pink and a small, pleased smile across her face.

It was an adorable photo. Kat just wished she wasn't seeing it for the first time under a headline.

She skimmed the article, her eyes catching on certain lines: "The *Spy Pigs* star was seen getting cozy with an individual who *Entertainment Daily* has identified as Jude Thacker, the manager of The Next Chapter, a queer and feminist bookstore in the West Village." Then, a little farther down: "Katrina Kelly's last known relationship was with her costar Frasier Pierce, but they broke up several months after *P.R.O.M.* was canceled. Frasier Pierce could not be reached for comment." She couldn't concentrate enough to read the rest of the article. Instead, she held her breath as she opened her Instagram to the *Entertainment Daily* page. Sure enough, they'd posted the photo from the gala there, too. Kat scrolled down to the comments.

The first comment was innocent enough. Just an omg they look so good together and a 🔥 emoji. She started reading through the rest.

omg that chemistry tho 🤤

is she gay?? I had the biggest crush on her in middle school

no way she's gay. they're clearly just friends

omg I cannot believe katrina kelly is queer! PROM was my favorite show growing up and I didn't realize it at the time but I had such a big crush on her. It means so much to me that she's out now #representation #pride

gross 🤮

I'm disappointed. Katrina kelly makes wholesome family movies and now this corrupting influence? My family and I will never be watching one of her movies again no way she's gay look at her body language. She's probably just faking it cause her career is over lol

Kat put her phone down. She bit the inside of her cheeks.

She started counting her breaths. In, out, one. In, out, two. She tried to clear her mind, to focus on breaths and numbers. A kind publicist had taught her this tactic to use before interviews. She'd also advised Kat to come up with an inspirational mantra. Before every interview, Kat would stare into the mirror, take deep breaths, and whisper to herself: *I am lucky to be here. All my dreams are coming true. I am lucky to be here.*

She wished they hadn't mentioned Frasier in the article. It had been three years since they'd broken up. If she'd had a normal life, he would be a footnote in her memories, a bad-boyfriend story she would pull out when bonding with other women. Instead, she could never seem to shake him. Her name was paired with his constantly. There were several paragraphs about him on her Wikipedia page, next to a photo of her crying in her car in an In-N-Out parking lot after one of their fights, clutching a milkshake in one hand and ragged tissues in the other. When she officially came out, Frasier would probably sell his side of the story to some magazine.

Would Jude do the same one day? When Kat was hopefully even more famous than she was now, back in L.A. starring in an Oscar-nominated film and dating some insufferable lesbian singer in a flat-brimmed hat, would some reporter call up the bookstore to ask Jude for a comment on Kat's new relationship?

Kat got up to get a glass of water, feeling slightly sick. What kind of comment would Jude make?

She had the glass halfway to her mouth when she almost dropped it. She'd been so wrapped up in her own reaction that she hadn't even thought about Jude.

God, how selfish could Kat be? This article felt intrusive and uncomfortable to Kat, but she'd had articles published about her private life for years. Whereas Jude . . .

They'd mentioned Jude by *full name* in that article. They'd said where she worked.

Jude had absolutely no idea what was coming.

CHAPTER 19

JUDE

Jude spent the morning in the storeroom, packing up books to return to publishers. She was too distracted for anything that required brainpower, so she let Rhys handle the front-of-store. Things were tense between them. Jude couldn't stop turning over his comments in her head. Was she stuck? Clinging to the fantasy of saving her mom's bookstore, even though her friends so clearly thought it would never happen?

Rhys was right about one thing. Jude had been a lot less afraid before her mom died. Back then, she'd hungered for new experiences. That was why she and Becca had purchased tickets to backpack across Europe for the summer after their junior year—a trip Becca had gone on without her when Jude realized how sick her mom was. They'd had plane tickets to Paris, a guidebook, and no plans. Jude had been ready to just take things as they came and try to have as many adventures as possible. She couldn't imagine doing something like that now. Where had that person gone?

Jude sighed, stacked the last of the boxes, and threw down the tape gun. She walked into the store. Rhys was sitting behind the checkout counter, staring moodily down at his phone. He had a heating pad wrapped around his left knee—it must have been hurting.

"I'm sorry," Jude said, sliding onto the stool next to Rhys. "I shouldn't have gotten upset with you. I know you were just trying to be helpful."

"I'm sorry, too," Rhys said. "I wasn't trying to gang up on you or make you feel criticized or anything. I just want what's best for you."

"I know," Jude said.

"I don't think you're a failure," Rhys said. "You've been through so much these past few years, and the fact that you're still the kind, openhearted person you are is truly incredible. I'm proud of you."

Tears pricked at Jude's eyes. Rhys was such a good friend. She should tell him that she'd thought things over and decided that she was wrong: L.J. clearly liked him.

Before she could, a group of teenagers let out a collective giggle, and she looked up, trying to see what book was sending them into hysterics—her guess was that they were clustered around a copy of *Fifty Shades of Grey*. But the teenagers were huddled together by the door, not even looking at the shelves.

Jude kept an eye on them, worried they were trying to psych themselves up for a bit of shoplifting. It wouldn't be the best choice, since they had cameras by the entrance, and it would be a simple enough task to email the principal of the nearby high school and ask them to identify some faces. But they didn't make a move toward any of the displays. Instead, one of them took out their phone and angled it toward Jude and Rhys, trying to be discreet but clearly taking a photo.

Rhys looked at Jude, bewildered. She shrugged.

"Hey," Rhys called over. "What are you guys doing?"

The kid with the camera flushed red, and the whole group dissolved into laughter. They ran out, the bell over the door tinkling wildly as they fled the store.

Jude watched them run away. "Well, that was weird."

"Seriously," Rhys said. "At least they didn't steal anything."

"Hey," Jude said. "L.J. really saved my ass the other night. And I was thinking that maybe I was wrong to—" But just then, she was interrupted by a young woman looking to check out, clutching the latest Emily Henry novel. Jude moved over to the register.

"You're going to love this one," Jude said, taking the book from her hands.

The woman blushed furiously. Was she embarrassed to be buying a romance? As Jude scanned the barcode, she said, "Um. I just have to ask. Is Katrina Kelly as nice in person as she seems?"

Jude froze with the scanner in one hand and the book in the other. "What?"

"It's just, she's, like, my role model from when I was a kid. I watched *P.R.O.M.* every day. I wanted to be her."

"Um." Jude liked to think she was quick on her feet, but her brain was coming up absolutely blank. "Cash or credit?"

The woman tapped her credit card, then craned her neck, looking around the store as if Kat might be hiding behind one of the shelves. "Does she ever come here?" she asked. "I've been wanting to meet her forever."

Jude thrust the novel back at the woman. "Here's your book. Have a nice day."

The woman lingered for a moment, disappointed, then grabbed her book and left.

Jude scanned the other customers milling around the bookstore. Was it just her imagination or were they . . . staring at her?

"Hey, Jude," Rhys called. He was reading something on his phone. She could tell immediately from his tone that something was wrong. "I think you should check your phone."

Jude grabbed her phone and took it off Do Not Disturb. Instantly, text messages and Instagram notifications started flooding her screen, one after another, so fast that she couldn't read any of them.

"What is this?"

"Here." Rhys handed over his phone. "L.J. texted it to me."

Jude paused for a moment before she took the phone. Then she looked down to see her own face, plastered underneath a headline on *Entertainment Daily*.

"It came out, like, an hour ago," Rhys said.

Jude skimmed the article. She handed back the phone, feeling lightheaded.

"Okay," she said. "Well. That's not so bad, right?"

"Right," Rhys said, but he didn't sound convinced.

"Um, I'm sorry to interrupt." A woman leaned over the counter to speak to Jude. "But could I, like, take a photo with you?"

Jude stared at Rhys, wide-eyed.

"No," Rhys said firmly. "There are no photos allowed in the bookstore. Please buy a book or leave."

The woman held up her hands defensively. "I was just asking. Jesus."

Rhys glared at her until she walked away.

"Thanks," Jude muttered. "How many people do you think have seen this?"

"Um." Rhys made a face like he was about to lie. "Not that many? She hasn't been in a movie for a while, so maybe people don't care that much?"

A tall man in a black sweater strode up to the counter. "Hi," he said, flashing Jude a huge smile. "My name is Ned Edwards, and I'm a reporter for the *New York Host*. I was wondering if—"

"Out!" Rhys bellowed, interrupting the man midsentence. "Anyone who isn't in this store to buy a book, get out now!" He glared around the store, then half turned to Jude. "I'll handle this. Go home. Leave through the back door."

Jude hurried into the back room, slamming the door behind her. She leaned against it and took a deep breath. What was happening?

She'd expected people to find out that she was dating Kat. She was famous, and they weren't exactly being discreet. But she hadn't realized it would be front-page news.

Jude's phone rang and she jumped. She went to put it back on Do Not Disturb but stopped when she saw who was calling.

"Hello?"

"Oh, thank God." Kat sounded relieved. "I've been calling you for the last twenty minutes. Where are you?"

"At the bookstore, but Rhys just told me to go home. It's . . . a little wild over here."

"Ah. I'm really sorry about that." There was a long pause, and then Kat sighed. "Can I come over?"

■　　■　　■

The one benefit of being a homebody with a very limited social life was that Jude's apartment, with the exception of her mother's dusty room, was usually clean. So at least Jude didn't have to frantically sweep and mop while she waited for Kat to arrive.

Instead, she surveyed her apartment, desperately looking for anything embarrassing. She took a framed photo of a teenage Jude with a buzz cut off a bookshelf and tucked it into a drawer. She swept the half-read comic book off the coffee table and replaced it with a collection of essays by Sartre. Then, after staring at it for a minute, she decided that was *too* pretentious and replaced it with *My Autobiography of Carson McCullers* instead. Just the right amount.

The buzzer rang, making her jump. She pressed the button to let Kat in and then ran to the bathroom to smooth her hair down and quickly rub on more deodorant. Just as she finished, there was a knock at the door.

"I am so sorry," Kat said as soon as Jude opened the door. "I am so, *so* sorry."

"Whoa, whoa, hey." Jude stepped aside to let Kat in. "It's okay. Take a beat. Deep breaths."

Kat strode past Jude into the living room. "What happened at the store?"

"Um." Jude followed her. "It filled up with a lot of people asking questions about you."

Kat groaned and flopped down on the couch. "I'm so sorry," she said again.

"It wasn't so bad." Jude sat down next to her. "Just a few people asking for photos and one reporter."

Kat sat up very quickly. "Which reporter?"

"Some guy from the *New York Host*."

"What did you tell him?"

"Nothing. Rhys told him to get out and then I snuck through the back exit."

"So you didn't talk to him only because Rhys wouldn't let you?"

"What? No. Why would I talk to him?"

Kat studied Jude, her forehead furrowed. There was a divot in her cheek, like she was biting the inside. Finally, she dropped back against the couch with a long sigh.

"I'm really sorry you had to deal with that."

"Please stop apologizing." Jude put her arm around Kat's shoulders.

"I should have warned you."

"You didn't know they'd run this article," Jude said.

Kat bit her lip. She swallowed a few times and then said, "Of course someone would report on it eventually. That's how my life works."

Jude turned to face her, letting her palm trail across Kat's back as she shifted. "That must be really stressful."

Kat's big eyes blinked up at Jude, and for a second Jude

thought she was going to lean in for a kiss. But instead, she held out her hand. "Give me your phone."

Jude handed it over and tried to pay attention to Kat's words, not her lips, as Kat talked her through basic security measures. Making her Instagram private and closing her DMs. Making sure her email wasn't listed anywhere. She even made Jude sign up for a service that would scrub her phone number and address off any public-listing websites and then insisted on paying for it.

"Are you sure this is really necessary?" Jude asked as she typed her signature into a consent form.

"Yes. Trust me." Kat took the phone back, hit Submit on the form, then got up and put her phone back in her purse. She paused, looking around her. "So this is your place, huh?"

"This is it." Jude surveyed her apartment, trying to see it through Kat's eyes. It wasn't exactly glamorous.

"Big Beatles fan?" Kat asked, studying the framed posters on the wall.

"My mom was," Jude said, going over to stand beside her. "Hence the name."

"Right. That makes sense."

Kat turned to face Jude. "I really am sorry about the article," she said softly. "But it's good to see you again."

"It's really, really good to see you." Jude let her hands rise up to brush Kat's arms, trailing the softness of her skin as lightly as she could.

Kat looked up at her, and Jude's breath stuttered in her throat. She'd endure a hundred tabloid articles just to be here, right now, touching this wonderful person.

Jude smiled, and Kat smiled back, a little shyly, ducking her gaze down. Jude reached out and gently used two fingers to tilt her chin back up. Then she leaned in and closed the space between them.

CHAPTER 20

KAT

Jude's lips touched her own gently, pressing so lightly that Kat's skin prickled. She wrapped her arms around Jude's torso, feeling the reassuring solidity of her body combined with a heat that made Kat's hands want to explore. When Jude pulled back, Kat didn't let go.

"Hi," she said.

Jude cupped her hands to either side of Kat's face, stroking her thumbs over Kat's cheekbones. Her touch felt so good that Kat wanted to lean into it and purr like a kitten. "Hi," Jude said back in a low, seductive tone.

Then Jude pushed back Kat's hair, tucking a loose strand behind her ear. It was like she'd revved an engine—Kat could feel her body warming up, starting to hum. Her breaths came shallower. Her fingers twitched, longing to dig into Jude's skin. Her stomach tightened and her lungs shrank and her skin seemed to become twice as sensitive, so that every place Jude touched her felt almost unbearably good, a pleasure so sharp it bordered on pain.

Kat pressed against Jude's front and let her hands roam over the strong and soft curves of shoulder, hip, and stomach. She squeezed Jude's arms, feeling the muscles she'd only previously allowed herself to eye.

I want to lick those muscles. The thought surprised her so much she briefly froze. She'd never had eager, dirty thoughts quite like that one—in the past, she'd kept her licking to the designated licking areas. But now she wanted to drag her tongue over every contour of Jude's skin, to taste her sweat, to make her moan, to make her shiver.

Whoa, she thought. *I am* definitely *into girls.*

Jude leaned down to kiss her again. Kat didn't let Jude set the pace this time. Instead, she kissed hard and fast as she ran her hand through Jude's hair. Shocked by her own boldness, Kat gathered some of it into a fist and tugged, making Jude gasp. The sound made Kat even more eager, and she slid her tongue into Jude's mouth.

Jude made a hungry noise deep in her throat, like a growl, and backed Kat up until she was against a wall. She pinned Kat against it with her hips and Kat bucked up against her, letting friction build between them, her back arching. She slipped her hands under Jude's shirt, running her nails over the warm skin hidden beneath.

She wanted to touch Jude, wanted no barriers between them. She tugged Jude's shirt off, revealing a black sports bra. Before she could reach inside it, Jude pulled off Kat's own shirt and pressed against her. Kat dug her nails into Jude's back, wanting her closer, closer, closer still.

Jude put her hands on Kat's shoulders, stepping away while leaving Kat pinned to the wall. Kat moaned in protest and Jude smirked that sexy one-sided smirk, but she didn't come back. Instead, she let her eyes travel over Kat's body.

Jude slid her hand under one bra strap, slowly pushing it down Kat's arm as she leaned in to kiss the tender skin underneath. Then she did the same on the other side. Kat tried to press against her, but Jude held her back, kissing her collarbones softly, taking her time.

She moved lower, her tongue dipping below the edges of Kat's lacy black bra. Her hands stroked Kat's sides, and Kat ached for them to cup her. She arched her back, moving her nipples toward Jude's mouth, and Jude reached back and unclasped her bra with one deft twist, letting it fall away to the floor.

Kat started breathing hard, practically panting as Jude's hands drifted lightly, teasingly, up her ribs, brushing the sides of her breasts until she squirmed. The delicate stroking made her nipples harden and stand, begging to be touched. Every part of her, reaching for Jude.

Jude lowered her mouth once again, and Kat braced herself for the sensation of a mouth closing around her nipple. But instead, Jude started kissing slow circles around them, taking her time as she pressed her mouth to every inch of skin. Her nails scratched softly against Kat's back, and Kat arched into her more and more as Jude got closer to finally touching her where she wanted to be touched.

At the last minute, though, Jude reversed again, retracing her earlier path, her tongue swirling. Kat made a moan of protest and Jude bit down, just a little, the sensation cutting Kat's moan off with a sharp gasp. She ran her hands through Jude's hair urgently, trying to convey how desperately she needed this.

"Please," she panted, hooking her fingers into Jude's sports bra to tug her closer. "*Please.*"

Jude looked up with a cocky gleam in her eye. "Please what?" she asked. Kat pretended to smack her, and she laughed, a deep, throaty laugh, huskier than usual.

"Please touch me," Kat said, her words strangely breathless. "I need you to touch me. Please."

"Good girl."

The praise turned Kat's entire body to water. It was something about the confidence in Jude's tone, or the way her voice had gone into a lower register, or how her eyes had gone dark with longing. Whatever it was, Kat wanted to hear her say it again and again and again.

Jude dipped her head again, and this time her tongue brushed up against the edges of Kat's areola, teasing the sensitive bumps and ridges. Kat squeezed her hips forward, unable to sit still. And then finally, finally, Jude's tongue curled around her nipple. Softly at first, just teasing, then slowly turning to flicking and swirling, her entire mouth sucking until Kat thought she might scream.

She needed to scream. She needed to move. She needed to writhe and dig her nails into Jude's skin and throw her head back against the wall. Because she had never, ever been touched like this. So deliberately and teasingly, this mix of soft and hard. Kat could feel the sensation lightning-forking through her body, making her clit swell and her legs tense and her hands curl into fists. It was almost terrifying, to feel this good. She had a strange urge to push Jude away, even as she heard her own voice begging Jude not to stop.

Kat grabbed Jude by the hair and hauled her up, pressing their mouths desperately together. Jude closed all the space between them, pulling Kat flush against her from top to bottom, the pressure of her warm skin sending another rush through Kat's sensitive nipples. Kat grabbed at every part of Jude she could reach. One hand closed around Jude's ass and squeezed.

"I need you." Kat's voice sounded unfamiliar in her ears.

Jude kissed Kat again before taking her by the hand and pulling her into the bedroom. Kat looked around, curious to see this new part of Jude's life. There was a full bed against one wall, under the window, with a light blue comforter on it. There was a small desk shoved in one corner next to a closed door, and a bookshelf so overflowing that a stack of loose books had begun sprouting up next to it. Over the desk was a corkboard, stuffed with Polaroids and ticket stubs and a small queer flag.

The brief pause in action seemed to cool Kat's overheated body slightly, and instead of heading for the bed, she walked over to the corkboard to peer at the photos. The most adorable of them featured a tiny kid with a tangled cloud of bright blond hair. She saw a few shots of a teenage Jude with the coworker she'd seen at the bookstore, although he looked very different now. He was trans, Kat realized after studying the photos for several seconds.

Her attention caught on a poster. It was a painting of a kitchen table, covered in half-eaten platters of food and glass cups of tea. Sunlight came through the window, highlighting a magazine with a name in Arabic, laid open on the table, and a red scarf left draped over a chair. The colors were soft, fading into one another, giving it the atmosphere of a dream. It looked cozy and comfortable, as if the people in the painting had just gotten up to get dessert and would be back at any moment, but something about it made Kat's chest ache.

"What is this painting?" she asked.

Jude came up behind her. "It's by my favorite artist," she said. "Fatima Halabi. She's a Syrian artist who lost her home and most of her family in a bombing early in the war. Now she does these gorgeous paintings, all of different homes."

"Wow." Kat lifted her fingers to the poster. That explained the aching in her chest. Every brushstroke of the painting seemed infused with longing.

Jude stepped closer and kissed the back of her neck. Kat arched into her touch, but she suddenly felt very aware of being half naked in an unfamiliar apartment. It was like opening the door to the bedroom had opened the door on the real world again, and suddenly she could feel all her insecurities and worries flooding back in. Namely, one big, pressing insecurity—the fact that she'd never had sex with a woman before.

Kat could feel her heart rate picking up and her breath going shallower, but this time it wasn't with desire. What if she was terrible? What if Jude laughed at her? What if she hated the taste? What if Jude went to *Entertainment Daily* and told them that she was bad in bed? The whole thing seemed so much more complicated than sucking a dick or letting some guy pump away. What if she absolutely humiliated herself? What if she got down there and realized mid-act that she wasn't actually gay and didn't want to do this? She would have to tell Jude and then tell Jocelyn and they would have to come up with an entirely new plan for saving her career and then—

"Hey." Jude's voice was gentle against Kat's ear. She'd stopped kissing her neck. "How are you doing?"

"I'm fine," Kat said automatically. She turned around and leaned in to kiss Jude, but Jude pulled back.

"You got really tense all of a sudden," Jude said. "Do you want to take a break?"

Kat looked down at her feet so Jude wouldn't see the tears welling up in her eyes. Why was she crying? What was wrong with her? She nodded, not trusting herself to speak.

"Can I hug you, or would you rather have a minute to yourself?"

"Um." Kat's mind spun, trying desperately to make this simple choice. "A minute to myself, I think." She crossed her arms as if that would help her disappear into the fiery hole of humiliation that was currently filling her entire brain.

"That is totally fine," Jude said. "I'm gonna grab you a shirt and some water, okay?"

"Okay." Kat sat down on the bed, keeping her arms crossed over her bare chest. She tried to take deep breaths. What was wrong with her? Why had she frozen like that? Why couldn't she just have sex like a normal person?

Jude came back in and held out a large flannel shirt. Kat put it on and instantly felt better. The fabric was soft, comforting and warm, and she felt steadier now that she wasn't exposed.

She took a few deep breaths, then took the glass of water Jude offered her.

"I am so, so sorry," she said as soon as she felt she could trust her voice again.

Jude sat down next to her on the bed, not touching her. "You have nothing to be sorry for."

"I just—got a little in my head, I think. Froze up."

"That is so normal." Jude's voice was so kind that Kat could almost believe her. There was a pause and then Jude added, a little hesitantly, "Is this your first time with a woman?"

Kat flushed. She turned away slightly so Jude wouldn't see. "Uh. Yes."

"Then it makes total sense that you'd be a little nervous. It might even be weirder if you *weren't* in your head. But I don't mind taking things slow. Really."

"What if I'm terrible at it?" The question tore itself from Kat's throat before she could stop herself.

Jude shrugged. "What if you are? Isn't hooking up with someone new for the first time always pretty awkward? You don't know what that person likes or how to touch them, so you're just kind of guessing. But we'll talk. I'll tell you what I like and you'll tell me what you like. We'll get better."

Kat leaned her head against Jude's shoulder. "You make it sound so simple."

Jude put her arm around Kat. "It kind of is that simple," she said.

Kat turned her head toward Jude, burrowing deeper into her. Then she pushed back, taking a deep breath. "I should probably go."

"You could go," Jude said slowly. "*Or* you could stay, we could order takeout, and we could watch all eight episodes of a Netflix show where amateur chefs have to make elaborate wedding cakes while completing an army-level obstacle course."

Kat could feel her cheeks stretching before she even realized she was smiling. "Wait, wait, wait. Do they do the obstacle course before they make the cake, or after?"

"No, no," Jude said seriously. "You don't understand. They do both *at the same time*."

"Well, in that case," Kat said, widening her eyes as if deeply impressed, "I think I'd better stay."

Jude beamed down at her, her boyish grin lighting up her face, her cloud of blond hair sticking up in every direction thanks to Kat's wandering hands.

"I think you'd better."

CHAPTER 21

JUDE

They made it through four and a half episodes of *This Takes the Cake* before Kat's eyes started to close.

"You're gonna miss it," Jude said. "Gavin just completed the pull-up challenge, so now he gets to sabotage Amy's cake."

"Describe it to me," Kat said sleepily. They were on the couch. Jude had put her arm around Kat two episodes ago, and now Kat nestled closer, moving her cheek against Jude's chest in adorable little burrowing motions.

Jude shifted her arm so that Kat could recline more fully against her. She felt unbelievably warm and cozy against Jude's side. "Amy tried to earn a defense card by swinging across the giant monkey bars over the pond of sludge, but she fell in."

"Oh no," Kat said, her voice barely audible against Jude's shirt. Her cheek was all smushed to one side, and Jude had to resist the urge to kiss her on the temple.

"Uh-oh. Gavin pulled a picky-eater sabotage. Now Amy has to make her cake vegan *and* gluten free."

Kat didn't respond. Jude looked down. Kat's jaw had slackened, and one loose fist was gripping the fabric of the sweatshirt Jude had put on. She was asleep.

Jude strained her free arm and was just able to reach the remote to turn off the TV. Then she shifted to make herself as comfortable as possible and leaned her head against the top of Kat's.

Had cuddling someone ever felt so good? Even with Becca, Jude didn't remember it being quite like this. Every inch where they touched felt sparkly, like that experiment in seventh grade science when they'd all held hands in a circle and passed an electric shock between them. Jude's side was already cramping, and her arm was well on its way to falling asleep, but she didn't care. She would stay up all night if she had to, just to keep Kat this close.

She loved watching Kat's face finally relax, her guard at last fully down. It had to be so hard living in the public eye. Fans stopping you on the street and strangers leaking photos of you to the press. It seemed exhausting.

For some reason Kat had chosen Jude to let her guard down around. That wasn't a gift that Jude intended to take lightly.

Uh-oh. You're in trouble, a voice in her head whispered. It sounded suspiciously like Rhys.

The voice was right. Jude liked Kat a *lot*. A scary amount. A potentially-life-shattering-heartbreak amount. And it had only been a few weeks. They hadn't talked about the long-term at all.

But this felt *good*.

Jude was tired of playing it safe. Rhys was right—she'd been living life defensively for the past three years, playing goalie against anything that might hurt her again. But she didn't want to be stuck anymore.

Jude leaned down and pressed the ghost of a kiss against Kat's warm hair, trying her best not to wake her up. She felt a swell of something in her chest, as if each heartbeat was pumping a little more happiness into her body.

"Your soul just hooked into mine," she whispered, echoing Kat's words from the other night, feeling the same caffeinated thrill she'd felt when Kat had said them the first time. How had she found someone so romantic? Someone who could use words in such beautiful ways? Who knew exactly what to say to make Jude feel special?

That gave Jude an idea. A good idea. No, a *genius* idea. She smiled to herself as she thought through the logistics. Then, as carefully as she could, she pulled her phone out of her pocket and opened the bookstore group chat, The Next Chatter.

What are you guys doing tomorrow night? I need your help with something.

CHAPTER 22

KAT

Kat hadn't meant to sleep over, but when she woke up pressed between the couch cushions and Jude's warm body, she felt no regret, even though she had a killer crick in her neck. They'd stayed wrapped around each other until the last possible second before Jude had to go to work, unwilling to leave the warm cocoon they'd created.

Kat smiled into her coffee cup as she walked the twenty minutes uptown to her apartment, remembering the feeling of Jude's mouth covering her skin in small, tantalizing kisses until she begged for more.

When Kat had stopped things, she'd expected Jude to be annoyed or hurt or angry. That was how Frasier had reacted when Kat hadn't been in the mood during their relationship. It had always become a big song and dance of comforting and reassuring that ended up being more exhausting than the sex she'd been too tired for in the first place. But Jude had acted like it was the most natural thing in the world to not be ready. To take their time.

Kat replayed the memory of Jude's husky voice saying *Good girl* over and over in her head, feeling a little buzz between her legs each time she did. Holy *shit,* last night had been hot. Had anyone ever made her vibrate in her skin like that? And Jude hadn't even seemed to care that she'd never slept with a woman before and had no idea what she was doing. She'd said they would figure it out together.

Jude made Kat feel comfortable. She felt like she could actually trust Jude. Which was rare. Working in Hollywood, Kat was used to being told she could trust people. Older male costars who said she could always talk to them, then invited her to their hotel rooms for late-night drinks they hoped would lead to more. Producers and directors who talked a big game about trust and accountability, then dismissed her concerns. Stunt coordinators who told Kat to just trust them as they rigged together some extremely rickety-looking equipment. PAs and makeup artists who told Kat they were a safe space, then ran to the director with her secrets. The only person Kat had been able to consistently trust in her career was Jocelyn.

Kat's smile faded as she thought about Jocelyn, who she was supposed to meet at her apartment in ten minutes. Surely, Jocelyn had seen an early draft of the *Entertainment Daily* article. So why hadn't she stopped them from printing Jude's full name and workplace? She should have known it would send people scrambling to the bookstore to disrupt Jude's life.

Kat's phone buzzed as she nodded to the doorman of her building and headed to the elevator. A text from Jocelyn, asking where she was.

"Finally!" Jocelyn called from the sofa as Kat unlocked the door.

"Sorry, sorry," Kat said, even though she knew from the text that Jocelyn had only beaten her by two minutes.

"We need to keep this quick. You have that theater luncheon at noon."

Kat made a face. Any event that called itself a "luncheon" was guaranteed to be a nightmare. She still had two and a half weeks left until the audition, and she was already sick of theater events. Hollywood might be more toxic, but damn, these Broadway people loved to show off how smart they were.

Jocelyn started by running down a list of people who would be at the luncheon and who she should talk to. Kat fidgeted uncomfortably, waiting for her to mention the article so she could bring up her complaints.

"How's it going with the acting coach?"

"Oh, fine." Not exactly the most accurate word to describe the amount of progress they were making on deciphering the impenetrable script, but at the moment, Kat had more important bones to pick. "Why didn't you review the *Entertainment Daily* piece before they printed it?"

"What?" Jocelyn frowned. "Of course I reviewed it."

"Then why did you let them print Jude's full name? And where she works?"

Jocelyn stared at her for a moment, her mouth pursed thoughtfully, and then she shrugged. "I didn't even think about it. The whole point of this is to draw attention to who you're dating."

"I know, but—" Kat cut herself off. "What if some crazy stalker who thinks I'm the love of his life decides to show up there and kill her?"

"You're spiraling," Jocelyn said, her tone firm.

"People are going to bother her, though. A reporter already showed up at the store and asked her for an interview."

"That's a good thing," Jocelyn said. "This is exactly the kind of attention we were hoping for from phase one. If people are going to show up at a bookstore to talk to someone you were photographed with once, then they'll show up to see you on Broadway. Which reminds me—I've arranged for you to be at Richard Gottlieb's table today. Maybe you could work the article into your—"

"I don't want to mess up her life," Kat said quietly.

"Fame comes with a price," Jocelyn reminded her gently. It

was a mantra she'd repeated to Kat often over the years. "If someone wants to date a celebrity, they have to be able to handle a little scrutiny."

Kat didn't respond. She knew this relationship would put Jude in the public eye—that was literally the whole point. But when they'd discussed phase one, Kat hadn't known how sweet Jude was. She hadn't known how Jude rumpled her hair back to front when she felt unsure or how she snorted when watching a ridiculous TV show or how her arms felt wrapped around Kat's waist while they slept on the couch.

Now that she had a real person in front of her instead of just a theory, this whole plan felt so much worse.

Jocelyn sighed. "Don't get too attached to this girl, okay? You can't date her forever."

Kat's stomach started to churn.

"Anyway, as I've been trying to say, we need more photos," Jocelyn said. "Explicit ones."

"*What?*" Was Jocelyn asking her to do porn? Kat would do a lot of things to save her career, but she didn't think she was ready for that one.

"Have you looked at the comments lately?" Jocelyn nodded toward Kat's phone, and she opened Instagram to the *Entertainment Daily* photo. The supportive comments had been overtaken by people leaping to Kat's "defense" by saying the photos were clearly taken out of context and Katrina Kelly couldn't possibly be queer.

Kat bit her lip as she read them. It was just as she'd expected. People thought she was faking it. She didn't look or act queer enough.

"We need to give them the money shot," Jocelyn said, leaning forward. "You and the bookstore girl, locking lips on some dark street corner. But we can't be too obvious about it or everyone will think you're trying to play this for points." She paused. "I reached out to a discreet contact at *Sundial*."

Kat groaned. *Sundial* was a grocery store checkout tabloid, full of pregnancy scandals and cheaters caught in the act and "Celebs! They're Just Like Us!" spreads of flustered people getting photographed coming out of drugstores. Engineering her own scandal release in *Sundial* was a new low.

"I know it feels beneath you," Jocelyn said. "But everyone does this. Next time you meet up with bookstore girl, text me the location and get her outside. I'll coordinate with *Sundial*. And then, *boom,* you lay one on her."

Kat bit her lip again, harder this time, as the realization of what she would have to do sunk in. Letting Jocelyn leak some photos was one thing. But leading Jude to a specific location, pretending they were having a private moment, and then acting horrified when they were ambushed by paparazzi? That was . . . bad. That was really bad.

"I don't know about this," Kat said.

"Look, Kat," said Jocelyn, "I know that all of this scheming and doing whatever it takes to get a role isn't glamorous. I know it's the last thing you want to be doing. You just want to act. And that's what I want, too—for you to be able to act. But in order for that to happen, you have to be willing to do all this icky stuff. I wish it was different. Believe me, all I want is for you to be happy and have a good career, and if I could make that happen without putting you through all this, I would. But this is just how the game is played, okay?"

Kat hesitated.

"How long have I been your manager?" Jocelyn said. "Thirteen years? I got you *Spy Pigs*. I got you *P.R.O.M.* I protected you when your parents were spending all your money. I got you through your scandal in the last season. I've only ever wanted what's best for you. And I think I've proven that by uprooting my whole life to come to New York to help you orchestrate your comeback. I've always put you first, Kat. And have I ever led you wrong?"

Kat twisted her hands together, trying to think as quickly as possible. Jocelyn was right—she had gone above and beyond to guide Kat's career. She hadn't abandoned Kat, not even when it seemed like her career was over.

Kat didn't want to hurt Jude. But . . . she and Jude had been kissing anyway. They could be photographed at any point. How was this any different?

"Okay," she said. "I'll do it."

Jocelyn smiled and patted Kat's knee. "Good girl," she said.

It couldn't have felt more different from the way Jude had said it last night.

CHAPTER 23

JUDE

Jude fidgeted on the corner of Bleecker and Seventh, putting her hands in her pockets and then taking them out again, her head swiveling every few seconds to check if Kat was coming down the sidewalk.

She hoped this would work. And that it wasn't overly cheesy. And that Kat didn't hate it. And that she didn't get upset that Jude had done this without asking. And—

Nope. It was too late. She'd already asked Kat to meet her here, and she couldn't back out now. Thankfully, she spotted Kat turning the corner at that moment, which spared her from further spiraling.

"Hi!" Jude opened her arms and Kat stepped into them, but Jude could feel tension in her shoulders.

"Hi there." Kat smiled, but it didn't fully reach her eyes. "So, what's this mysterious date you have planned for us?"

"You'll see." Jude gestured for Kat to follow. As they walked, she asked Kat about the luncheon and her meeting with Jocelyn, but Kat seemed distracted. Jude wondered if her manager had been upset about that photo of them at the gala leaking to the press. She really hoped not. She didn't want their relationship to make Kat's life more difficult.

When they turned the corner to The Next Chapter, Kat rolled her eyes.

"Okay, I know I like books and all, but I don't think going to the bookstore where you work counts as a romantic surprise date."

Jude turned her head to keep her smile from giving something away. "Just wait and see."

Jude unlocked the front door and ushered Kat in, then locked it behind them again. The lights were off except for the under-the-shelf ones they kept on all night to deter potential break-ins, filling the store with shadows as she led Kat through to the back. She paused in front of the door to the storeroom, trying to think of something to say that wasn't overly earnest.

She settled on: "If this is weird, just let me know." Kat gave her a confused look, but she went ahead and knocked on the door—three times fast, then three times slow, as prearranged.

The door creaked open just a little bit, making Kat jump.

"Password."

Jude leaned in and whispered, "Marsha P." The door swung open. Jude held it for Kat so she could walk in first.

Kat looked around, her mouth slightly open. "What is this?"

Jude cleared her throat. "Um. When we were at the diner, you said you wished you could go to a queer bar but you're too afraid of getting recognized. And I really wanted you to have that experience. So . . ." She gestured around the storeroom. "Welcome to Kat's."

Jude had spent most of the day transforming the storeroom. She'd swept and de-spiderwebbed the whole space, then used the boxes of books to form a makeshift bar, which she'd covered in a dark red tablecloth and lined with string lights. She'd placed a few stools on one side and installed L.J. on the other, dressed in suspenders and a white button-down shirt.

In front of the bar she'd set up a few small tables, where Rhys and Talia were waiting. She'd set a lamp on each one to give the dingy storeroom more romantic lighting. She'd covered the walls with large pride flags in every variation she could find and framed photos of historic lesbian bars from around New York: from long-closed ones like Meow Mix and the Sea Colony, to the currently operating ones like Ginger's and Scissors. Over the bar she'd hung a large paper banner painted with the words "Kat's Queer Speakeasy."

Kat turned back to Jude. "You put all this together?"

"Yeah." Jude shrugged, as if she turned her workplace into a code-defying speakeasy all the time. She ran her hand through her hair. This was too much. She'd gone too far. She had weirded Kat out by being too intense and—

Kat reached out and grabbed Jude's hands. Her eyes were shining. She squeezed once, then didn't let go.

"Thank you," she said softly.

Jude beamed at her. Suddenly the bar didn't look like an embarrassing mess anymore. Suddenly the lighting actually felt romantic. Had she gotten taller in the last few seconds?

"Would you like a drink?"

Kat laughed and shook her head, gazing around at all the decorations. "Yes, of course."

Jude led her over to the bar.

"Hi, welcome to Kat's queer bar," L.J. said in a resentful monotone. "What would you like to drink?"

"L.J. is playing the role of the hot bartender who's far too cool to care about you or your friends," Jude said to Kat. "But also, they're just kind of like that."

L.J. flipped Jude off, and Jude winked.

"Kat's is a divey queer bar, so there are no cocktails. Just well drinks and beer," Jude explained.

"Okay. I'll take a vodka soda, then."

L.J. turned to the globe behind them, popped it open, and got to work. Kat leaned into Jude slightly, her shoulder brushing against Jude's side and sending a little sizzling thrill through her entire body. "Who are these people?" she whispered.

"They work at the bookstore with me," Jude said. "But they're like my family. They promised me they won't tell anyone about this. And we all left our phones in the other room so you don't have to worry about pictures. I want you to be able to enjoy this."

Kat bit her lip and looked like she was about to say something, but she was interrupted by L.J. handing over her drink. She said thank you and took a sip, then gagged.

"Oh my God. This is, like, all vodka."

Jude laughed. "That's the queer bar way. Straight vodka in a plastic cup."

Kat eyed her doubtfully, making Jude laugh again. "Come on," she said, putting her arm around Kat's shoulders. "Let me introduce you to the rest of the gang. Here we have Rhys, who has chosen the role of 'old butch who is always at the bar, no matter what day or time you come.'"

Rhys had really committed to the bit, with a short-sleeve button-down and a bow tie. He'd even put in gray hair dye. "Come sit by me later and I'll tell you stories about going to West Village queer bars back when it was illegal," he called.

"And finally, we have Talia, who has chosen to portray 'the high femme so hot and glamorous you feel deeply insecure and briefly consider leaving the bar altogether.'"

Talia stood up and curtsied. She'd done her makeup to the nines and borrowed a long, glamorous wig to compliment her red dress. "I may look intimidating, but I'm secretly a sweetheart," she whispered. "Also, I'm a top."

Jude glanced down at Kat, hoping she wasn't overwhelmed. "Of course, if this was a *real* queer bar, we'd also have two people you've kissed before, someone you saw on TikTok once, four people you've swiped left on on dating apps, one person you swiped right on and then had a weird conversation with, and one really hot person who you'd make eye contact with all night and then never actually speak to." She dropped her arms. "However, we had limited resources here, so we're making do with what we have. Also, Rhys said we couldn't invite anyone who doesn't work at the bookstore, because we're 'operating an illegal speakeasy without a liquor license.'" She made her fingers into air quotes. "And could 'get a huge fine.'" She looked back at Kat. "So . . . what do you think?"

Kat didn't respond. Instead, she squeezed Jude around the middle so tight she may have damaged some sort of crucial organ.

Jude didn't mind. She put her arms around Kat and squeezed, too.

"This is so thoughtful," Kat said, her voice muffled into Jude's chest. "No one has ever done anything like this for me before. Thank you." Then she reached up and kissed Jude hard.

When she pulled back, Jude blinked at her, feeling dazed. Her cheeks already hurt from smiling, and the night had barely begun.

"Seriously," Kat said. "Thank you."

Jude kissed her again. Just because she could. Just because she had this gorgeous girl in front of her and Jude had made her happy and Jude got to kiss her whenever she wanted.

At the bar, L.J. turned on the speaker and "Like a Prayer" started blasting through the room.

"Hey! Young 'un! Come sit next to me and hear about the time I rode my motorcycle all the way to California and then went straight to a sex club!" Rhys called.

"Not before she hears about the time I killed a man with nothing but a tube of lipstick and a set of keys," Talia called in a high falsetto.

"Hey, keep the rowdiness down in here. I run a respectful

establishment." L.J. glowered at them all. "Don't make me get the bat out from under the bar. I played D-1 softball in college, you know."

Jude rolled her eyes. "Everyone took fleshing out their backstories a little too seriously," she said. "So if you don't ask them a hundred questions about their characters, they're all going to be deeply offended. But also dyke drama at the queer bar is a big part of the experience, so please feel free to offend them."

Kat laughed, a deep unselfconscious laugh that Jude had never heard her use before. Her eyes sparkled, and her smile filled her entire face. She looked positively giddy. She grabbed Jude's hand and pulled her over to the others.

"Well, we have to make my first queer bar experience memorable, right?"

CHAPTER 24

KAT

Kat wasn't sure she'd ever had a better night in her life.

She'd been a little nervous at first about whether she could trust Jude's friends. But the bookstore crew didn't ask her any intrusive questions about being famous or pull out any cameras for a sneaky selfie. Instead, they were just having *fun,* all clamoring to one-up each other with outlandish details from their made-up backstories. All of them asked her to dance—Talia cheekily flirting with her, Rhys twirling her around the floor like he was her dad, L.J. pulling out a surprisingly spot-on electric slide. She couldn't finish even half of her disgusting vodka soda, so Jude whipped up a Shirley Temple with extra cherries. The combo of sugar and cheesy music and people who seemed so gosh darn happy made the night feel like a cheerful, blurry rush, even without alcohol. Especially when Jude pulled her close during "Fast Car" and they swayed, pressed together. Next to them, Rhys and Talia giggled their way through a two-step with their arms fully extended like they were at a middle school dance. Halfway through the song, L.J. tapped Talia on the shoulder and asked to cut in. Rhys blushed as L.J. put their arms around his waist, pulling him close.

"Ain't No Sunshine" by Bill Withers came on, and Kat laid her head on Jude's shoulder as they danced. The warmth coming through Jude's shirt made her feel strangely soothed. Like she could relax for once in her life and just be a normal person having a good time.

And then her phone buzzed in her pocket.

For a moment, she'd actually managed to forget. She should have texted Jocelyn the address hours ago.

Kat pulled away from their dance abruptly, leaving Jude looking startled. "Be right back."

She wished more than anything that she could ignore her responsibilities and stay pressed up against Jude's shoulder. But instead, she hurried out of the fake bar and into the store's bathroom.

She had half a dozen increasingly impatient texts from Jocelyn. Kat's stomach twisted up so tight she thought she might vomit. She quickly texted Jocelyn the bookstore's address and several apologies.

Her chest ached as the three dots indicating typing showed up. She held her breath until the text came through. *Out front. Twenty minutes.*

She exhaled. Jocelyn wasn't mad at her. The pain in her chest briefly eased, but then she remembered that she had to lure Jude outside. She groaned.

What was she doing? Jude had planned this incredible date for her, and this was how Kat was repaying her?

The choice felt impossible. Let down Jude or let down Jocelyn. But she barely knew Jude, while Jocelyn was the person who'd guided Kat's entire career. She'd taken care of Kat when her parents couldn't—hell, Kat was closer to her than to her actual parents, who she hadn't even texted in months. How could she stop listening to her now?

Besides, her career needed this.

Maybe . . . could she just tell Jude she needed some photos? See if she'd cooperate?

But what if she was disgusted that Kat would pull such a ruse? What if she thought Kat was fame hungry and pathetic? What if she put the pieces together and realized their whole relationship was supposed to be a photo op? What if she ended things? What if she called that reporter from the *Host* and told him everything?

Kat tucked her phone back into her pocket and washed her hands. No, she couldn't tell Jude the truth. She would just have to find a way to get Jude outside.

When she left the bathroom, Jude was waiting for her in the store, leaning over a table labeled "Oscar Obsessed," adjusting the stacks of books. She straightened up as Kat came out and gave her a guilty grin.

"Can't help myself," she said. "Even when I'm off the clock."

Kat walked over to stand next to her, trying to ignore the queasy feeling building in her stomach. There were little cards with movie posters on them, so readers could pick a book based on their favorite Oscar nominee for Best Picture. "That's a cool idea for a table."

"Thanks." Jude ducked her head and smiled an adorable little shy smile. It made Kat want to reach out and kiss her, but her stomach gave a guilty squeeze and she clasped her hands together instead. "I came up with the idea last year and it sold so well we decided to do it again."

"That's awesome." Kat was trying her best to act like a real person, but it seemed extremely obvious that she was faking it. "You're really good at coming up with clever ideas to promote the store."

Jude shrugged self-deprecatingly, but a little rosy blush colored her cheeks. How could a person be this sweet and sincere? Why had Kat ever decided to get her horrible, fame-obsessed, Hollywood-monster self involved with a person like this?

"Do you want to sit out here for a second before we go back in?" Jude asked. "You seem like you could use a beat."

Kat tried hard to act natural. Could it really be this easy?

"Actually, what if we got some air?"

"Sure." Jude smiled at her guilelessly, and Kat had to swallow down a shot of sudden anger. Why was Jude so trusting? Why did she have to be so damn thoughtful and innocent? She was practically *asking* to get hurt.

Jude locked the door behind them, and they stepped out into the night. The cool air felt refreshing after the fake bar. Big, loud groups of girls in tight skirts and guys in button-down shirts swarmed up and down Bleecker Street, crowding the sidewalks in front of the restaurants. The Friday night air held a barely suppressed feeling of potential, of thousands of people out looking for possibilities.

Jude led them down the street to a small park with benches and fountains. It was the same park where Kat had sat and had a meltdown after Jude hadn't asked for her number.

"Do you want to sit?"

"Yeah." Kat chose a bench far from a streetlamp to minimize her chances of being recognized. Then she pulled out her phone and quickly texted Jocelyn her new location.

"Sorry," she said, turning back to Jude. "Just my manager checking in."

"No worries. I know you're really busy with work stuff."

Jude's hand found Kat's on the bench between them. Kat tucked her fingers through Jude's, amazed at how good skin-on-skin could feel. Holding hands had never made her heart race like this, or her entire body buzz with pleasure. Was that because she'd never been with a girl before? Or was it because of Jude?

"Thank you for this date," Kat said. "It was really magical."

"You deserve magic," Jude said, and Kat looked away.

"You seem really close with the bookstore crew," she said, desperate to distract herself from the shame creeping through her veins.

"They're the closest thing I have to family since my mom died."

Kat squeezed Jude's hand. "This was your mom's store, right?"

Jude nodded.

"It sounds like you guys had a really amazing relationship."

Jude let out a long, slow breath. "Sort of."

"What do you mean?"

"We actually fought a lot," Jude said. "And she never really stopped treating me like a little kid. Even when I got older."

"What do you mean?"

"When she got breast cancer . . ." Jude hunched down over her knees. "She didn't tell me. I was away for school and she didn't want me to worry. I came home the summer after junior year and found out that she'd been going to the hospital *alone* while I was partying and making friends and just living my life. And she hadn't said anything.

"I was supposed to spend the summer traveling with Becca. But I couldn't leave her. So I canceled my trip. And when the end of summer came and she wasn't any better, I transferred to a school here. So I could be where I needed to be."

"Oh, Jude." Kat shifted closer, pressing their sides together. "You're a really good daughter."

"She didn't think so," Jude said. "She was furious. She didn't want me to change schools. She didn't want me 'wasting my life' taking care of her. All I wanted was to be there for her, and she was so bitter about it. So angry that she needed to be taken care of. She didn't understand that"—Jude's voice cracked and she paused to compose herself—"that I would never forgive myself if I *wasn't* there, you know?

"After a few months, things seemed to get better. It seemed like she'd be okay. Her hair grew out, her appetite got better. And then the cancer came back a year later, aggressively this time. She died six weeks later."

Kat rested her hand on Jude's shoulder. "I am so sorry."

"I couldn't believe it. Even when the doctors told me, I didn't believe that she was really going to die. And those last few weeks, when I should have been—should have been . . ." Jude's voice gave out, and she lowered her head. "We fought all the time. She wanted to sell the bookstore. We needed money to cover the hospital bills, and she didn't want me to be stuck with the debt if she—if she didn't make it. But I refused. I told her that I loved the store, too, and she couldn't make that decision for me. And finally, she agreed. We wouldn't sell the store. We'd find some other way to pay the bills."

Jude stared out into the dark park, her eyes shining, and Kat's stomach twisted with dread.

"Two days after she died, Stephen showed up. My mom had sold him the store without telling me." Jude laced her hands together, squeezing until her fingers mottled white and red. "I didn't believe it at first. And then, when I saw all the paperwork . . . My mom was *dying,* and the last thing she did was lie to me. *That* was the memory she decided to leave behind."

Kat's heart wrenched. She knew what it was like to have your parents let you down. But Jude spoke so fondly of her mom, she'd assumed they had some perfect *Gilmore Girls*–style relationship. Kat thought about telling Jude that she felt that same mix of anger and grief about her parents, but she couldn't find the words. Skirting around that part of her life was too ingrained, a habit that felt impossible to break.

"But you decided to stay?"

"I'd just lost my mom. How could I lose the store, too?" Jude's voice trembled on the last words. "This place is my home."

Kat put her arm around Jude's shoulders, leaning against her. Trying to convey that she wasn't alone. Even though Kat was a coward who couldn't give Jude that same vulnerability back.

"Thank you for listening." Jude squeezed Kat's hand, then took a long, steadying breath. "You make sharing things like this feel easier."

"Only because you're brave enough to share them," Kat said.

Jude's smile hooked a tiny bit higher. "How did I get this lucky?" She leaned in until their foreheads pressed together. Kat could feel a tender, overwhelming feeling building inside her, threatening to crash and pull her under.

"I'm the lucky one." Kat's hand lifted to Jude's face. Jude put her hand over Kat's, pressing it tighter to her skin.

"Your soul hooked into mine," Jude said, eyes twinkling now.

Kat winced. To cover it, she said the words back. "Your soul hooked into mine." She was about to lean in for a kiss when her phone buzzed in her pocket. A spike of panic went through her chest.

"Sorry," Kat said, fumbling for her phone. "One second."

She tilted her phone away from Jude while she looked at the screen. Two texts from Jocelyn: *Stand up and get her under a streetlight.* And then, simply, *Now.*

Kat's mouth went dry. Her entire *body* seemed to go dry, shriveling up into itself, becoming smaller and smaller with each breath. But she stood up and put her phone in her pocket. She felt disjointed from her body, trying desperately to tug on the strings connected to her limbs to get them into natural formations.

"Should we head back?"

Her voice sounded like a cartoon mouse, all squeaky and fake.

Jude looked momentarily surprised by the sudden shift in tone, but not suspicious. She stood up. "Sure," she said, and started walking back toward the store.

Kat's heart thudded. Her vision had become a tunnel, and each heartbeat seemed to shake the walls, a mini earthquake destabilizing her entire world. There was a streetlight right ahead of them, at the corner of the park. They were only a few steps away. Once they got to the other side, the photographer should have a clear shot from any angle. She could do this. Was she going to do this? She just had to reach out and stop Jude in three, two, one—

Kat's hand closed around Jude's wrist. She tugged lightly to pull Jude to a stop.

"Hey," she said, and Jude turned, the skin around her eyes tightening a little in confusion, and then Kat used her grip to tug Jude closer still, and her expression melted into warm, hungry desire.

Jude put one hand on Kat's back and one in her hair. The cinnamon scent of Jude's cologne surrounded Kat as their lips met, mouths already open.

Kat's already heightened nervous system sprang to life. Every movement of Jude's lips seemed to flood her with some desperate feeling, a tsunami of desire rushing through every cell. Her heart had already been racing, but now it thundered. Her breath had already been shallow, but now she was gasping, more eager for Jude than for air. Her skin prickled and rose, every brush of Jude's fingers filling her with longing.

Then there were several flashes in quick succession, bursting orange across her closed eyelids.

Jude looked around wildly for the source of the flash. As soon as she pulled away, a sinking horror smothered all of Kat's sexy feelings.

She looked to her right, and there he was. Across the street, stepping out of the shadowed awning over a cupcake store, a large camera raised to his face. As soon as Kat turned toward him, the camera flashed again.

"Hey!" Jude shouted, starting toward the photographer.

"Don't do it." Kat caught Jude's arm. Her voice sounded heavy and hollow in her own ears. Resigned. "He'd love some photos of you looking threatening."

"So we should just let him get away with—"

"Yes." Speaking took so much effort. Her whole body felt heavy. She was exhausted. All she wanted was to lie down and forget this entire night. "We just let him go."

Jude looked furious, but she stayed put. Across the street, the photographer lowered his camera and hurried away.

CHAPTER 25

JUDE

"Here. Drink this."

Jude placed a glass of water on the coffee table in front of Kat. After the photographer, the streets had felt too exposed, so Jude had hurried them back to her apartment, messaging the Next Chatter group text that they'd had to leave. Kat was on the couch, alternating between texting her manager and staring into space. "Are you sure you won't eat something? It might help with the shock."

Kat shook her head. Jude hovered for a moment, battling the urge to fetch more things, then sat down. She waited to see if Kat would say anything, but Kat just stared at the glass of water as if it were some peculiar regional delicacy.

"I'm so sorry that happened," Jude said. "I should have been more careful."

"What?" Kat looked up, seeming startled.

Jude shook her head. "We started kissing and I just lost track of where we were. I should have been aware that we were on the street. I shouldn't have put you in that position."

"No!" Kat's voice was loud. She shook her head rapidly. "No,

I kissed *you*. This is on me. This is not your fault. Not at all, okay?" She sounded desperate.

"But you're the one who has to deal with the consequences," Jude said. "With public scrutiny and people examining your personal life and making assumptions. I can't imagine how hard that is." She reached out and took Kat's hand. "I want to protect you from that kind of stress, not make it worse."

Kat stared at Jude. She looked mildly horrified. Jude dropped her hand. She was being too much. Too serious, too intimate, too needy. They'd only known each other for a few weeks.

But Kat reached out and caught Jude's hand before she could pull it away. She swallowed a few times. When she finally spoke, her voice was choked. "You're too good for me."

Jude felt her pulse leaden, beating heavily against her skin. Was Kat about to break up with her? Give her some sort of *It's not you, it's me* speech and send Jude packing?

But Kat hung her head, studying the water glass again. "I'm sorry I'm making your life complicated."

"Life is always complicated," Jude said.

"Yeah, but these photos . . . People will keep bothering you."

Jude shrugged. "People bother you all the time. I can deal with experiencing a little piece of that. It will help me understand your life more. Besides." Jude reached out and tilted Kat's chin up so they could look at each other. "You're worth it."

Kat's eyes softened, some of the tense lines that had been hovering around them finally melting away. Her expression was so vulnerable it made Jude's chest ache. She wanted to wrap her arms around Kat and protect her from all of Hollywood, all of America, all of the world. She wanted to tell Kat how incredible she was over and over again, until Kat started to believe it.

She leaned in and kissed Kat. Just a peck, to show her she meant what she said. But when she went to lean back, Kat's hands caught her, pulling her closer. Their lips met again. Jude could feel warmth spreading through her body as they kissed, an urgent tide sweeping away her insecurities and worries, until she could only think about the here and now, the feeling of Kat's lips against her own, the sparks that trembled through her when their tongues brushed together.

Kat swung one leg over Jude's lap and straddled her, settling her hips over Jude's. She leaned forward, shifting her weight in a way that made Jude's brain briefly black out, and pressed their mouths together with a more urgent pressure.

Jude managed to restrain herself from grabbing Kat's ass and pushing their hips closer together. Barely.

"Are you sure?" she asked. "After what just happened, maybe it's not—"

"I don't want to think about it." Kat lowered her mouth to Jude's neck, kissing lightly along her jawline. Jude groaned. "I don't want to think about anything. I just want to focus on being here with you."

"Well, if it starts to feel like too much, just say so and we'll—"

Kat bit down on the delicate skin under Jude's ear. "Stop being so fucking nice," she said.

The jolt from the bite ran through Jude's body, lighting up her nervous system, making desire flood through her. Jude reached out, took Kat's ass in both hands, and stopped being so fucking nice.

She sat up, putting Kat off-balance, so only Jude's arms kept her from falling. She dug one hand into the denim of Kat's back pocket, squeezing to feel the shape underneath as she pressed Kat's hips back down against hers, grinding up until the friction sent a shock of sparks through her. Kat gasped, tilting her head back, and Jude took the opportunity to fist her hair and tug backward until Kat's neck arced in front of her, exposed. Kat's chest rose and fell as Jude took her time leaning in, letting her lips just barely skim the pale, soft surface beneath them.

She started with Kat's shoulder, pushing aside the fabric of Kat's shirt to kiss the skin underneath as lightly as she could.

She felt Kat shiver as she kissed her way up. She kept her touch featherlight at first, soft enough to raise goosebumps, until she couldn't resist the urge to taste.

Kat started to squirm, thrusting her hips forward each time Jude's tongue flickered across her neck. Jude pressed their bodies together so that each reaction from Kat sent her grinding up between Jude's legs. She continued until tiny moans grated out of Kat's throat, each sound only making Jude hungrier.

She pulled off Kat's shirt, then couldn't help herself and unclasped Kat's bra, too. She could feel her clit aching and her stomach clenching as she stared at the pale triangles of skin over those smooth, small breasts.

She put her hands under Kat's ass and lifted, turning her until she was flat on the couch cushions. Jude settled over her and lowered her head to lick one of those hard, delicious nipples. Kat gasped, and the sound urged Jude on. She sucked lightly, making Kat arch underneath her, pushing herself deeper into Jude's mouth.

"Oh my God," Kat whimpered. She clenched Jude's shoulders so hard her nails dug in, then she scratched downward, leaving burning lines along Jude's back. Jude let out a low, deep groan. Kat tugged at Jude's shirt and sports bra, and then Kat's hands were on her, cupping and teasing, eyes hungry with desire.

"You are so fucking hot," Kat said in Jude's ear.

The words made Jude flush with longing. She pressed her mouth back onto Kat's hungrily, desperately. As they kissed, Kat reached her hand down and traced the zipper of Jude's jeans.

Jude couldn't take it anymore. She stood, pulling Kat with her, meaning to take her into the bedroom. But Kat's hands caressed Jude's sides, distracting her, and suddenly the bedroom seemed too far to travel. Instead, Jude pressed her up against one of the living room walls. They kissed fervently while Kat undid the button of Jude's pants, then slid her hand inside, cupping Jude through her underwear. She started to trace light patterns on the fabric, letting her pressure slowly increase until Jude could feel the cloth turning damp. Jude pressed forward into her hand.

She undid Kat's pants and pulled them to the ground. Kat stepped out of the legs, and Jude threw them to the side, running her hand over the thin fabric of Kat's lacy black underwear. Then, unable to wait any longer, she dropped to her knees.

Kat let out a tremulous *"Oh"* and pressed herself back against the wall as Jude pulled her underwear down a fraction of an inch and kissed the sensitive skin underneath it. She kissed from hip bone to hip bone before she lowered the fabric just the tiniest bit more and kissed that skin, too. She did it again, then again, kissing her way down, then to the sides, coming close but never actually touching her lips to Kat's most sensitive parts. She had almost worked the underwear all the way down when Kat started to tremble. Jude looked up at her. Kat had her hands braced on the wall on either side of her.

"I— I can't," Kat panted. "I can't take it anymore. Please. Please touch me. Please."

The need in her voice pushed Jude over the edge. She pulled Kat's underwear off and let her tongue run over Kat from top to bottom. Then she switched to small, light licks up and down the sides, enjoying the high-pitched whimpers coming from above her. She circled the hole to Kat's cunt, her tongue lapping up the thick, salty wetness there. Then finally, finally, she let her tongue glide over Kat's clit until she reached the top and started to circle, increasing the pressure just a little, keeping up a consistent rhythm. Kat's legs started to shake harder, and she heard a desperate *"Don't stop"* from above as a hand dug into her hair, pressing her closer. Jude moaned in pleasure, cupping her lips around Kat's clit so Kat could feel the vibration, could get off to how much she was turning Jude on.

"Talk to me," Jude said, breaking away, her throat thick with lust and Kat's wetness. "Tell me how you like it."

Kat's back arched off the wall, pressing her clit further into Jude's mouth. "I like that," she panted.

"Like this?" Jude pressed her tongue against the hood of her clit, moving it up and down slowly with her tongue.

"Uh-huh." Kat's voice was high-pitched and breathy.

"What about like this?" She let her tongue approach Kat's clit from the side, rubbing up against it with quick, light strides.

"Yup." Kat's voice sounded strangled now, like speaking at all was effortful.

"Or maybe like this?" She went back to licking circles right above the most sensitive part of Kat's clit—not directly on it, but very close, moving her tongue fast, keeping the pressure firm but not hard. Kat screamed softly, then balled her free hand into a fist and pounded it on the wall beside her.

Jude took that as a yes. She kept going, keeping her rhythm consistent, letting her hands roam up and down Kat's sides as she buried herself deeper and deeper between her legs. She could feel her own wetness soaking her underwear, could feel the uncomfortable hardness of the floor beneath her knees, but she didn't care. All she cared about was the thrusting of Kat's hips as they pressed themselves closer and closer to each other, as Jude picked up the pace slightly, fighting desperately to keep her tiring tongue in the right rhythm. Then Kat screamed a real, loud scream that would surely frighten the neighbors, but Jude didn't care, because she was keeping her tongue going to help Kat ride this wave as long as possible, squeezing Kat's ass and letting herself luxuriate in the wetness that covered her face as Kat came into Jude's mouth, her hips thrusting forward again and again until they finally slowed and she slid down the wall, landing on the floor and pulling Jude's forehead against her own.

"Oh my *fucking God,* Jude," she said.

Jude opened her mouth to respond, but before she could, Kat covered it with her own, kissing Jude's wet lips desperately. She pushed Jude back until they were both lying on the floor, then hooked her hands into the waist of Jude's pants and tugged. Jude lifted her hips obligingly, and then Kat's naked body pressed down against her own, making her gasp.

Jude gripped the back of Kat's head as they kissed, moaning when Kat's fingers moved down and dipped into her wetness. Kat broke away and kissed a path down Jude's body until she settled between her legs. Jude moaned again as Kat's tongue ran along the seam between her lips, then parted them and moved inside.

"Will you talk to me?" Kat said, pulling back a little. "Tell me what you like?"

"Of course," Jude said, then groaned as Kat's tongue started moving over her body again. "That feels amazing. I love it when you tease me like that. What you're doing right now, just licking around my clit? That feels incredible. Except— Oh my God, I can't take it anymore. Please lick my clit. *Please*. Yes. Like that. Right there. Oh my God. A little to the left. No, a little less. *Yes*. There. Right there, Kat. Please don't stop. I need you, Kat." Saying Kat's name felt incredible, each repetition driving her closer to the edge. "Now a little harder. Yes, yes, yes, Kat. Like that. Please don't slow down. Please keep going. Oh my God, Kat, you feel incredible. Yes, yes, *yes*."

Jude lifted her head, and Kat looked up, her eyes sparking as they met Jude's. The sight of Kat, with her hair messy and her tongue working over the swollen redness of Jude's clit, was more than Jude could bear. She came, tossing her head back as waves of pleasure made her thrust forward again and again until she finally gasped and tugged Kat back up to collapse on top of her.

She put her arms around Kat and pulled her so close that Jude could feel both of their heartbeats, shuddering irregularly against each other. When she could breathe again, she kissed Kat, deep and slow.

"Whoa," Kat said.

"Whoa," Jude agreed. "That was— Wow."

Kat snuggled her head into Jude's chest, almost shyly. "Did I do an okay job?" she asked, her voice muffled.

"You did an *incredible* job," Jude said. Kat laughed, and Jude squeezed her a little tighter. She felt like her heart had expanded inside her body and was now pushing painfully at her chest. She wanted to pull Kat as close as possible and never let go.

But she was also lying on the floor with Kat on top of her, driving her elbows into the hard floor and making her neck ache.

"What if we moved to the bed?" Jude said, and Kat laughed.

"I guess," she said, pretending to be reluctant. Jude kissed her again before they got up, then kissed her in the hallway, then kissed her again once they settled in bed. She never wanted to stop kissing Kat. It made her feel full and desperately empty at the same time.

"I don't want to stop kissing you," Jude admitted as she pulled the covers around their naked bodies.

Kat rolled off her side and onto Jude, settling her weight on top of her once again and grinding her hips forward until Jude gasped. She leaned down and ran her tongue over the curve of Jude's ear.

"Then don't," she whispered.

CHAPTER 26

KAT

As she surveyed the picked-over cheese platter in the lobby, Kat decided that there was nothing worse than a bad musical.

A bad play was one thing. You could cover up bad writing with good acting. But once tunes (or a lack thereof) got involved, it was impossible to hide the true quality of a work. Suffering through a full six (six! Just in the first act!) meandering songs was a level of pain Kat had never previously imagined. The actors were doing their best, but Kat was developing a strong suspicion that Kafka's *The Metamorphosis* just hadn't been meant for a musical format.

And she still had another act to go. Kat moved to get in line at the bar, to receive a free plastic cup of the same cheap wine that seemed to be served at every single staged reading—early performances without costumes or sets, intended to convince producers to invest in bringing the show to a real theater. Kat had been to five since she moved to New York, some for networking purposes and some for the sole purpose of becoming a known entity in the theater scene. She wished Jude was with her—this would be a lot more fun if they could giggle through it together.

"Miss Katrina Kelly!" Richard Gottlieb joined her in the line for the bar, greeting her with an air kiss on each cheek.

"Richard! I didn't realize you were here." Kat infused the lie with a healthy amount of surprised delight. "How have you been?"

"Excellent, excellent." They accepted their plastic cups of wine, then Richard pulled her over to a secluded corner of the lobby and leaned in furtively. "What do you think of the show?"

"It's definitely . . ." Kat tried to remember if Richard was friendly with the playwright or director at all. "A daring attempt."

Richard snorted and raised his eyebrows as he sipped. "That's certainly one way to say it. That song about being a bug? I wanted to dig my eyes out with my program."

"No, don't go for the eyes," Kat said. "It's the ears that were really assaulted."

"True, but it's much harder to take off an ear with a piece of paper."

Kat nodded gravely. "Yes, but worth the effort in this case, I think."

Richard snorted. "Oh, you're bad!" He lifted his cup of wine. "Drink up. That's the only way we'll make it through the second half."

"Cheers." Kat held out her cup, and they clinked them together. She expected Richard to melt back into the crowd to schmooze with someone else, but instead he stayed, narrowing his eyes at Kat studiously as he sipped.

"I see you everywhere these days, don't I?"

Kat felt a little *zing* up her spine. "Well, I'm really enjoying exploring the theater world."

"Mm-hmm." Richard sipped again. "And I suppose there are no *other* reasons that I happened to run into you twice a week?" He raised an eyebrow.

Kat knew what she should say. She should recite the lines Jocelyn had given her about her passion for experimental theater. But strangely, it wasn't Jocelyn's voice she heard in her head at this moment. It was Jude's, saying, *Why the hell not? Why not just put it all out there?*

She remembered Jude in the Old Navy, saying her gut wasn't broken, she just needed to listen to it more.

Kat always listened to Jocelyn. They strategized together, planned things out in advance. But just this once, Kat could feel her gut saying that being strategic wasn't the right play here.

Should she listen to it? Trust herself over Jocelyn's instructions?

She rolled back her shoulders and looked Richard in the eye. "I want the lead role in your new play."

He didn't look surprised. "And why should I give it to you?"

"I have name recognition and a following," Kat said. "A dedicated one. I can send you a list of publications that have reported on me in the last month alone, and I don't even have a movie to promote right now."

"If you're so famous, why do you need this part?"

"You know why." Kat took a deep breath. Again, she was going against the Jocelyn code by admitting this and making herself seem desperate, but Richard already knew that her career was floundering. *Everyone* knew it. "I need a breakout role to help transition my career. Force casting directors to see me as a serious, adult actor and not just a kid. This play can get me there. And in exchange, I can fill your theater. We can help each other."

Richard gave her a sly little smile. He was about to say something when the lights flickered, beckoning them back to their seats.

"Well, you've certainly given me a lot to think about," he said instead. He swiped two more cups of wine off the bar. "Here. You'll need this."

"Thank you." Kat felt slightly stunned as she accepted the drink and followed him back into the theater. Sitting in the dark, clutching her plastic cup, Kat barely heard a word of the second act. Which seemed like a blessing—the song about Gregor dying went on for a truly *unfathomable* length of time. Instead, she thought over her conversation with Richard in minute detail, trying to remember every single twitch of his expressions and word of his responses. Had it gone well? She couldn't tell. Did he think she was a pathetic failure for being honest? Had she just blown everything that she and Jocelyn had been working toward these past few months? What would Jocelyn say when she found out that Kat had gone rogue? What had Kat been thinking?

When the lights finally came up, to a collective sigh of relief from the audience, Kat decided to hurry out. She didn't want to face her failure quite yet. Unfortunately, everyone else in the audience seemed just as determined to leave before they came face-to-face with the playwright, and so Kat found herself stuck at the back of a desperate scrum.

"Miss Kelly." Kat's heart sunk as Richard tapped her on the arm. "I hope you enjoyed the second act?"

They were surrounded, very likely by people who had been involved in getting this work as far as it had gotten. "Oh, very much."

Richard's eyes twinkled in response. He pressed something into her hand. "A souvenir, to remember this lovely night."

Kat looked down. He'd given her his program. She started to ask him why, but when she looked up, he had walked over to a man in a velvet suit. "Isaac!" she heard him say, throwing out his arms. "That was your best work yet!"

Puzzled, she rejoined the line of people shuffling for the door. It wasn't until she made it outside to the safety of the sidewalk that she flipped the program over and noticed the words scrawled on the back:

It's yours.

CHAPTER 27

JUDE

On her way out of the subway, Jude raised her fingers to her eyes for a third time, exhaling in relief when they touched plastic. She felt a little ridiculous wearing sunglasses at night, but taking them off made her feel much worse.

In the past two weeks, Jude had been recognized by strangers on the street five times. *Five* different people had come up either for a photo or to ask invasive questions about her relationship with Kat. Jude felt like an asshole, but she'd refused every time and then fast-walked away. And those were just the people who actually spoke to her. How many people had recognized her as she walked by and not said anything?

Ever since the paparazzi photos of them kissing had been released, things had changed. Kat had gained five hundred thousand Instagram followers practically overnight, and her days were suddenly busy with interviews and podcast recordings. People weren't just interested in Kat, either. They were also interested in who she was dating.

Jude had told Kat she was worth it, and she meant that, but it was unsettling. She felt *watched* all the time. Buying groceries or walking through Washington Square Park, she couldn't help imagining how she looked from the outside. She held herself differently, standing taller and monitoring her facial expression, and she dressed more carefully in the mornings. Even when she was by herself, it was hard to turn off. She caught herself posing a little as she cut open boxes in the empty storeroom. Like part of her was always acting.

She couldn't imagine *growing up* with this pressure. Always feeling watched, always needing to perform to other people's expectations. How could you form a sense of self under those conditions? How could you know who you were when you were alone if you could never *be* alone, even in your own head?

Kat was hard on herself for not knowing she was queer for so long. But under those conditions, Jude was impressed that she had figured it out at all.

Jude double-checked her sunglasses as she headed to the corner of Thirty-fourth and Madison. Kat had told Jude to come there after work for a "surprise."

Once she arrived, Jude shifted awkwardly on the sidewalk, checking for anyone looking at her. Maybe she was being paranoid, but Rhys had already chased another reporter away from the bookstore. At first, Jude had hidden in the back, busying herself with inventory and unboxing. But when Stephen had stopped by the store and caught her skulking, he'd ordered her to work the front desk. If people wanted to come take photos of her, he said, then she would let them—provided they bought a book while they did it.

"Hi, cutie," a voice said in Jude's ear, causing her to jump. She whirled around, but it was just Kat, laughing delightedly at Jude's startled expression. Jude smacked her playfully on the shoulder and Kat laughed again, then gave Jude a big, squeezing hug. She didn't let go afterward, just kept her arms around Jude's waist and pulled back far enough to give Jude a kiss.

"You look happy," Jude said.

Kat beamed. "I am."

Jude grinned back, feeling her tension wisping away under the force of Kat's smile. "So, what's this surprise?"

Kat threaded her fingers through Jude's and tugged her up the street. "You'll see when we get there."

Jude let herself be led. Two blocks later, Kat paused. "I hope you like this," she said. "If you don't, that's totally okay. But you making the bar was so sweet, and I just . . . wanted to try to do something for you. As a thank-you."

"A thank-you for what?" Jude asked, but Kat just smiled mysteriously.

"Come on." Kat tugged Jude up another half block to a huge, ornate stone building.

"The Morgan Library?" Jude said. "Is that where we're going?" The Morgan Library had once been the private library of J. P. Morgan before being turned into a museum where ordinary people could gawk at the beautiful shelves and first editions.

Kat led Jude up the stone ramp to the modern wing. "Have you been before?"

"My mom took me when I was a kid, but I don't remember it much. Are you sure it's still open? It's already 7:30."

Kat gave her a mysterious smile. "Why don't we find out?"

Sure enough, when Jude pushed on the glass front door, it was locked, and the interior only lit by a few shadowy lights.

"Well, we can always come back another day," Jude said, trying to sound cheerful.

Kat reached out and pushed a buzzer next to the door that Jude hadn't noticed. A few seconds later, to Jude's surprise, the door unlocked with an audible click. Kat pushed it open and gestured for Jude to go first, laughing at the shocked look on her face.

"Are we allowed to be here?" Jude whispered as they walked into the shadowy lobby. "Am I committing a crime right now?"

Kat laughed. "One of the producers of *Spleen Girls* is on the board here. I made a few calls."

"Wow." Jude gazed around the empty lobby. She'd never had a museum all to herself before. This was definitely cool.

"Come on." Kat strode toward the stairs.

"I think the library is the other way," Jude said, but Kat just shot her a mysterious glance and started downstairs. Jude shrugged and followed.

"Wait," Kat said suddenly as they reached the bottom. "Close your eyes."

Jude obediently closed them. A second later, she felt Kat come up behind her, reaching around to cover Jude's eyes with her hands.

"Step forward slowly," Kat said, and her voice tickled Jude's ear, sending a shiver up her sides and making the hair prickle on the back of her neck. She took a few cautious steps. "Now turn to the left. A little more. Good. And keep walking." Kat hovered behind her as Jude walked uncertainly, her eyes still squeezed shut. Was it weird that this was turning her on?

"Okay," Kat breathed softly into Jude's ear. Jude was pretty sure she was doing it on purpose this time. "You can look."

Jude opened her eyes. They were in an exhibit room, with shining wood floors and white walls hung with paintings. The paintings were beautiful, done in soft, dreamy colors with an oddly familiar style.

"Wait. Are these by Fatima Halabi?"

Kat wrapped her arms around Jude from behind. "You said she was your favorite artist. When I saw she had an exhibition here, I decided we had to come. But I thought it'd be a little more romantic if we did it after hours, when there are no crowds."

Jude twisted around to gape at her. "I can't believe you remembered that."

"Of course I remember," Kat said.

Jude wrapped her arms around Kat and kissed her hard.

"This is incredible. Thank you."

"It's actually also a thank-you for *you*." Kat bounced on her feet. "I got the role!"

"*What?*"

"I saw Richard Gottlieb at the reading yesterday, and he asked me why he'd been seeing me around so much lately, and suddenly I just heard your voice in my head. You've been urging me to listen to my gut more, and my gut was telling me to go for it. So I told him that I wanted the role in his show. And he said *yes*."

Jude picked Kat up and swung her around in a circle, making her feet flare out. They stumbled into each other dizzily, laughing. "That's my girl!" Jude said. "I'm not surprised at all."

"It's thanks to you," Kat said.

"That was all you."

"No." Kat steadied herself from the spinning and took Jude's hand. "Really. With you . . . I feel different. Like what I feel and think actually matter. You're pretty magical that way."

Jude felt something shift inside her—whatever walls had still been protecting her heart giving in, letting her feelings flood through every last inch of her body.

She was Kat's. Completely. Thoroughly.

She picked Kat up again, but instead of spinning her, she kissed her.

When she pulled away, Kat laughed breathlessly. Then she swatted Jude on the shoulder. "You have to actually look at the paintings!" she said. "That's the whole point of the date."

Jude leaned in and snuck one last kiss before putting her down. "I can multitask," she said, and felt a rush of satisfaction when Kat laughed again.

They held hands while they studied each painting carefully. The exhibition was called *Home*. Fatima Halabi had painted domestic settings, but in vivid, otherworldly colors. A blue-toned painting of a dusty, old-fashioned living room with plastic covers that made Jude want to weep. A crowded apartment entryway, bursting with vivid pinks, filled with piled shoes, tiny hats, and tossed toys. A beautifully tiled courtyard with a fountain in the middle. A cardboard box with a sleeping bag, done in vivid swirls like the northern lights. An ice-fishing cabin, lit by the glow of a lamp. There were dozens of different kinds of homes, and you could feel each one—the loneliness or happiness or grief that infused each place.

"These are absolutely beautiful," Kat said as they made their way through the exhibit for a second time.

"They're even more powerful in person," Jude said. "I've only seen one of her paintings before."

"This is her first major exhibition, apparently," Kat said. "You have good taste."

"Her work always reminds me of my mom," Jude said. "How our apartment growing up seemed so warm and full, because of her. And now . . ." she trailed off.

Kat squeezed her hand. "It makes me wonder what my painting would look like," she said. "A cold prefurnished rental, probably. Empty and sterile."

"What about where your parents live?"

Kat's hand pulsed in hers, just once, like an uncontrollable twitch. "I haven't been back there in four years."

"Because of the money thing?"

"Sort of." Kat studied one of the paintings in front of her, but Jude was pretty sure it was just an excuse to avoid eye contact. "When I was young and making a lot of money, my parents asked me if I was okay with them giving themselves salaries. After all, my mom had given up her job to move to L.A. with me. Of course, I said yes. They bought a big house, in a great neighborhood. And then they bought new cars. And the salaries just kept getting higher, and then . . ." She sighed. "Jocelyn sat me down when I was sixteen. Legally, they had to put fifteen percent of my savings into a trust that I could access when I turned eighteen, but otherwise . . . there was almost nothing left. Jocelyn advised me to get emancipated so I could control my own money."

Kat dropped Jude's hand and ran it through her hair instead. "My mom took the emancipation very personally. She told me that if I severed legal ties to her, I was severing all my ties with her. But I did it anyway."

Jude took in a sharp breath. Losing her mom at twenty-two had been horrible. To have your mom cut ties with you voluntarily at sixteen? She couldn't even imagine.

"That's an awful thing to say to your kid."

"Yeah. It hurt." Kat pursed her lips. "After that, we didn't talk for a long time. Now we text every few months, but I haven't seen them in years."

Jude studied Kat's profile as she stared at one of the paintings. "I'm so sorry."

Kat shook her head, as if shaking off the memory. "Where did you even come from?" she asked, taking Jude's hand again. "How do you get me to admit these things I've never told anyone before?"

"I think you mean where did *you* come from?" Jude said. "We're literally standing in a museum after hours looking at paintings by my favorite artist."

"Well, that's not the last surprise."

"It's not?"

"Come on." Kat led Jude upstairs. She made Jude close her eyes again before walking into the library room, where a round table with a white tablecloth was sitting, cluttered with rose petals and electric candles and two covered plates.

"I wanted real candles, but obviously the museum wasn't into that idea," Kat explained as they walked inside. "You know. Hundred-year-old books and all that. Jude?" She turned, realizing that Jude had stopped in the doorway. "Are you okay?"

"It's just . . ." Jude swallowed down the words *really romantic*. "It's really, really special."

Kat walked over and took Jude's hands. "You deserve to feel special," she said. "You deserve this and so much more."

Jude blinked rapidly. She wouldn't cry. She couldn't. She kissed Kat, trying to convey her thanks with her touch, because she didn't trust herself to speak. Because she was pretty sure that if she did, the only words out of her mouth would be *I love you*.

CHAPTER 28

KAT

When Kat showed up at the CTA office for her morning meeting with Jocelyn, the smarmy assistant at the desk showed her to a conference room right away. One of the big conference rooms near the entrance, with cushy leather chairs and a little tray of organic snacks. *And* he brought her a coffee when she asked. At long last, Kat was back on CTA's priority list.

"How's my favorite superstar doing?" Jocelyn called as she walked in. "The numbers on your video just keep getting higher."

Kat squirmed in her cushioned chair. Thinking about the video she'd posted to her socials after the paparazzi photos made her feel slightly nauseous.

"You knocked it out of the park." Jocelyn strode around the room, apparently too excited to sit down. "Talking about how upset you were about your privacy being invaded. I nearly believed you myself. You can really act, kid."

"Thanks." Kat took a sip of her coffee, but her stomach had tightened, and swallowing it suddenly felt impossible. She subtly spit it back into the cup.

"Six million views." Jocelyn gazed contentedly out the window. "And now public opinion is on your side. Have you been reading the comments?"

"Trying not to."

"Everyone is furious that you were forced to come out. They're trying to organize a boycott of *Sundial*."

Kat raised an eyebrow. "How does *Sundial* feel about that?"

"Any press is good press for that rag," Jocelyn said. "They're used to it." She turned away from the window. "Anyway, everyone is proud of you for being so brave and open with your fans." She winked.

Jude had also been proud of Kat. She'd sent a heartfelt text message after the video went up, saying she knew how challenging this must be, but that Kat's coming out was certainly inspiring thousands of people out there to embrace their real selves. She'd wanted to take Kat out for a celebratory dinner, too, but Kat had pretended to be busy every time she brought it up.

Kat couldn't help thinking that her parents must have also seen the video, or at least heard about it by now. But she hadn't heard a word from them.

"You even got offered the lead role in a movie the other day," Jocelyn said. "Some independent gay film. Not big enough for us. But I'm going to forward you the script. Maybe you could do an event with the director or something, build a reputation as a supporter of queer art."

"Sure. Okay."

Jocelyn finally sat down, spinning triumphantly in the rolling chair before pulling up to the table. "Phases two and three are complete," she said, leaning over her elbows eagerly. "You're back in the public eye and more popular than you've been in years. Now we need to translate that to ticket sales."

Kat nodded wearily. She wished she could just focus on acting for a while instead of constantly scheming.

"I chatted with Madelyn's agent. Here's the plan. Three weeks before the first night of previews for the play, you're seen around town together. Then, the week of, you post on Instagram. A photo of you kissing her cheek and a vague caption. Something like 'Finally found my way to you' and a sparkle emoji. Fans will go wild. The speculation! Your costars-turned-lovers story! Every media outlet in town will want an exclusive interview. And then we'll give them one—the day before opening night." She snapped her fingers in the air triumphantly. "They'll sell out every performance."

"Wait. You talked to her *agent*?" Kat said, horrified. "Why would you do that?"

"To set up your relationship."

"I told you not her! Anyone but her. I specifically said that." Kat could hear panic in her own voice. "What if she goes to the media and tells them I'm setting up fake relationships?"

Jocelyn batted a dismissive hand. "If she goes to the media, we'll say she's making it up out of jealousy. A public feud would be just as good for your popularity as dating her." She paused, considering. "Maybe we should orchestrate a feud after you date. Get the best of both worlds."

"I am not dating her!" The words came out louder than Kat had intended, but she didn't care. How could Jocelyn have gone behind her back like this?

Jocelyn sighed. "I thought you'd have come around on this by now."

"Why would I have come around on this?"

"You're always hesitating these days," Jocelyn said, frustration leaking into her tone. "You hem and haw about every decision, but eventually you realize that I only have your best interests at heart. The way I have for the past thirteen years."

"I won't do it." Kat crossed her arms. "Not her."

"Then who?" Jocelyn said. "Tell me, which other New York–based lesbian with at least three million followers do you think would be a good fit for this?"

"Why do I need a famous girlfriend anyway?" Kat said. "I already have the role. Why can't I just stay with Jude?"

"Ah." Jocelyn gave her a sad smile. "So that's what's going on."

"What do you mean?"

"You fell for the bookstore girl."

Kat studied the table and didn't respond.

"It feels nice, doesn't it?" Jocelyn said gently. "You go to her apartment and you can pretend that you're a normal girl for a little while. Away from all the pressure, away from all the fans. I get it. You've been under so much scrutiny since you were a little kid. No wonder you want a break! You deserve one."

She reached out and squeezed Kat's knee under the table. "I've seen this happen a hundred times with a hundred clients. You're just playing house. Hiding from reality. But you and this girl, you live in different worlds. You will always have to put your career first, ahead of anything else. She won't understand how this industry works. Eventually, it will be too much for her. And if you try to keep her happy, you'll end up holding yourself back."

"She . . ." Kat's tongue felt thick in her mouth. Her brain seemed to have slowed down, gotten gummed up with something sticky that kept it from working. "I don't want it to end."

"Sweetheart." Jocelyn took Kat's hand. "I know. She sounds like a nice girl. And I wish you could have this, I really do. But I need you to decide which is more important to you: this girl you've known for six weeks, or your entire career."

Kat didn't respond. A thick numbness had crept over her, and she couldn't seem to hold thoughts in her head anymore. She felt strangely like she was floating over her body, watching herself talk to Jocelyn from a distance.

Jocelyn patted her hand twice and then dropped it. "Think about that."

CHAPTER 29

JUDE

The Gala Literary job had been posted.

Jude's throat encountered a sudden drought as her phone slowly loaded the post on the store's shitty Wi-Fi. She'd been checking every couple of days, just out of curiosity, and now here it was. Manager, Emerging Writers Program. Not that she was going to apply.

Even if things had been particularly miserable at the store lately.

As if proving her point, a woman approached the register, her phone held up to her chin. Jude could tell what she was going to ask before she said it.

"Sure, we can take a picture," Jude said, unable to keep the weariness out of her tone.

Normally, Jude didn't mind working the register. But lately, most of the people she interacted with just wanted to talk about Kat.

The woman held up her phone and Jude leaned over the counter, pasting on a smile. She dropped it as soon as the photo was taken. At first, she'd tried to see these interactions as an opportunity to understand what life was like for Kat, but after three weeks, she had to admit she was tired. She was sick of posing for photos, sick of pretending she was delighted to meet these people who only wanted proof of their proximity to fame, sick of making the same exact small talk over and over while having to pretend it was new.

She was sick of it all. But the bookstore was having its best month ever. Stephen had used the influx of new customers as an excuse to change up their display tables. He wanted more of what he called "mainstream" books in easy reach: the biggest bestsellers, the celebrity memoirs, the thirty-five-dollar cookbooks with glossy photos. The Oscars-inspired table had been nixed, and the staff recommendations had been relegated to a shelf near the back.

Jude swiped open her phone and started reading the job listing. The director role offered good benefits and a much higher salary than what she currently made. But her eyes caught on one item in the list of requirements.

Strong public speaking skills.

Jude put her phone down next to the register.

Well, that was it, then, wasn't it?

She should never have even looked at the posting. She'd only been setting herself up for disappointment.

As another customer approached with their phone hovering at their side, Jude closed out of the tab and put her phone away in her pocket. Then she leaned across the counter and pasted on another smile.

CHAPTER 30

KAT

Which is more important to you: this girl you've known for six weeks, or your entire career?

Jocelyn's words echoed in Kat's head, the way they had for the past two days. She'd hoped that seeing Jude would make the echo go away, but the question had only gotten louder. Now, as she lay on the couch with her head in Jude's lap, it was almost deafening. She wanted to enjoy their time together, but all she could think was that if she listened to Jocelyn, this would be one of the last times she sat in this living room.

She tried to refocus on her phone, where she'd pulled up the independent film script that Jocelyn had sent her. The movie was called *Rom-Con,* and when she could actually pay attention to it, Kat loved it. It was about a woman coming out in her twenties and trying to find a romance like the ones she'd always loved in movies, but slowly realizing that her romance would look different from the ones she'd grown up with. The protagonist's confusion as she tried to figure out who she was and what she wanted was almost a little *too* relatable.

She flipped a page, snorting at a description of the main character trying to figure out how to wear a strap on. Jude lowered the book she was reading and peered down at Kat curiously.

"Having fun?" she asked.

Kat tried to banish any thoughts of Jocelyn's ultimatum and just smile. "This script is really good."

"That's great," Jude said. "Are you going to take the role?"

"This isn't for a role. I'm just reading the script to see if I want to support it. Post about it on social, do an interview with the director, something like that."

"I thought you said they offered you the main part."

Kat extricated herself from Jude's lap and sat up. "They did. But I'm not going to *take* it."

Jude closed her book. "Why not?"

"It's an independent film, not a major studio. It's way too small."

"So?" Jude shrugged. "If you love the script, why not do it anyway?"

Kat grimaced as Jocelyn's voice reentered her head. *She won't understand how this industry works.*

"That's not an option, okay?" she said, her tone coming out more snappish than she'd intended.

Jude held up her hands. "Whoa. Okay."

"I'm sorry." Kat sighed. "Yes, I love the script. But in my business, that's not a good enough reason. They can barely afford to pay me. And there's no guarantee it will get picked up by a distributor. It will probably show at a few festivals, then disappear."

"That's kind of sad," Jude said. "I mean, you don't seem to like Richard Gottlieb's play at all. And now here's a project that you really like, but you're turning it down without a second thought."

Annoyance flashed through Kat. "What about you?" she said. "Are you going to apply for that Gala Literary job when it gets posted?"

Jude's jaw twitched. "It actually got posted yesterday," she admitted.

"And?"

"It's not the right move for me right now."

"Why not?"

Jude reopened her book and held it in her lap but didn't look at it. "It includes a bunch of fundraising and networking and public speaking," she said. "None of which I would be good at."

"How do you know that?"

Jude's face flushed pink. "Because I had to introduce someone at an event recently and I had a panic attack, that's how."

"You did? Why didn't you tell me?"

"Because it's embarrassing."

Kat pulled the inside of her cheek between her teeth. She didn't want to admit it, but that *was* embarrassing. Was Kat really considering sabotaging Jocelyn's plan to save her career for a woman who couldn't even handle an introduction? Kat needed a partner who could handle pressure and scrutiny. She needed someone who could confidently walk a red carpet by her side and handle being asked questions by reporters. What if Jocelyn was right and Jude just couldn't be that person?

"Public speaking is something you can practice, though," Kat said, trying to sound encouraging. "It isn't something that should hold you back from a job you really want."

"It's not holding me back," Jude said, "because I don't want the job."

"Really? You seem so unhappy every time you come home from work."

"It's just a rough patch," Jude said. "I probably need a vacation or something."

"Are you sure you're not just scared of trying something new after being at the store for so long?"

Jude hardened on the other end of the couch, her jaw clenching, her arms crossing. "Are you sure you're not just scared to make a decision for yourself instead of mindlessly listening to what your manager tells you?"

"Okay." Kat's voice cracked. "Not cool."

Jude's expression softened immediately. "I'm sorry," she said. "I didn't mean that. I'm just really tense today. Things at the bookstore have been stressful lately. I shouldn't have said that."

"It's fine," Kat said. "I shouldn't have said what I said, either. I'm just feeling a little off today."

"Hug?" Jude held out her arms, and Kat gave her a squeeze but pulled away quickly. "Do you want to talk about what's making you feel off?"

"No," Kat said. "I think I need to relax a little bit. Let's just read."

"Okay." Jude lifted her book, but her eyes weren't moving. Kat watched her for a few seconds before reopening the script on her phone. She stared at it, but she couldn't take any of it in. Instead, all she could hear was Jocelyn's voice again:

If you try to keep her happy, you'll end up holding yourself back.

CHAPTER 31

JUDE

If one more person asked Jude if they could take a photo with her today, The Next Chapter was going to get a lot more famous, this time as the scene of a brutal murder-suicide.

As the most recent selfie-taker moved away, Jude rubbed her jaw, which ached from clenching all day. Stephen was doing paperwork in the back room, or she would have abandoned the register hours ago.

She'd been in a bad mood for three days, ever since her tense conversation with Kat. It hadn't been a fight, exactly, but Jude had snapped at Kat. She hadn't meant to go on the attack. It just seemed like everyone in her life was questioning her lately, telling her what she should do, urging her to abandon the store. Didn't they understand how important this store was? That behind this register was the only place where Jude still felt like her mom could walk out of the next room at any second? The only place where she felt like she hadn't lost her only family, her entire life, the person she used to be?

Jude checked her phone for the fifteenth time that hour, hoping to see a text from Kat, but there was nothing. They'd exchanged a few messages since their conversation, but the way

Kat was texting felt off. More terse than usual, with long periods of time between her responses. When Jude had asked when they could see each other next, Kat had replied that rehearsals were starting this week, so she wasn't sure.

Was this it? Would Kat slowly pull away until this thing between them died out?

No, she was being ridiculous. One weird conversation wouldn't end things. Couples fought all the time. Not that they'd ever actually had a talk about labels. Were they even a couple? Jude had been thinking of them as a couple, but maybe Kat hadn't. Maybe this was just a fling to her, and now that things had gotten complicated, she would disappear.

"Hey." Rhys came over and slid onto the other stool behind the register. "You okay?"

"Fantastic," Jude said bitterly.

"Yeah." Rhys put his elbow on the counter and slumped over it, his cheek propped up on his fist. "Me too."

Jude turned to examine him. Now that she thought about it, Rhys had seemed off lately, too. He'd been moping around the store and had barely responded in the group chat.

"What's going on with you?" Jude asked.

Rhys let out another sigh, then looked around to see if anyone was nearby. "L.J. asked me out," he said in a low voice. "After that night we turned the back room into a bar."

A trickle of panic ran through Jude's chest. "Isn't that a good thing?"

Rhys shook his head. "I said no."

"You did?" Jude said. "Why? I thought you liked them."

"I do," Rhys said glumly. "But I kept thinking about what you said the other day. You're right. It's so rare for me to like someone, but they're always dating someone and then moving on. I don't want to blow up our friendship when they're just going to dump me in a few weeks."

Jude bit her lip.

"But it messed up the friendship anyway," Rhys said, kicking the toes of his Hokas against the checkout counter. "They've been giving me the cold shoulder ever since."

Jude was such an asshole. It had been obvious during the globe bar night that L.J. really liked Rhys. And yes, L.J. went out with a lot of people, but they didn't normally seem genuinely into the people they dated in this way. But when Rhys had asked her for her opinion, she'd panicked and said the first excuse that came into her head.

Fuck. Maybe Jude *was* afraid. So scared of things changing that she was clinging on to everything too tightly, squeezing the life out of what she had left.

"Rhys," Jude said, turning on her stool so she could face him, "I should never have said that. I'm sorry. I can tell that L.J. does really like you."

Rhys raised his eyebrows without lifting his head off his fist. "That's not what you said before."

"Maybe I was wrong."

Rhys rubbed the back of his neck as he thought. Finally, he said, "I don't think you were. Things probably wouldn't work out between us."

"You don't know that," Jude said. "Maybe you should go for it. You won't know unless you try, right?"

Rhys considered that for a moment. "It's too late," he said. "I said no, and now things are weird between us. I missed my chance." He got off his stool. "I'm gonna go get lunch."

Jude watched him go out the front door, feeling like the world's worst friend. She'd made Rhys doubt himself. All because she'd been selfish and scared.

She looked around the bookstore, her eyes lingering on the framed photo of her and her mom on opening day, with their matching enormous smiles. Her mom looked so happy. She'd loved this store. So why had she been so eager to take it away from Jude?

She rarely admitted it to herself, but she knew exactly why. Her mom hadn't wanted Jude to be stuck holding on to someone else's dream, staying there out of obligation long after it had stopped making her happy.

Was that what she was doing?

No, she loved the store. Of course she loved it.

But . . . did loving the store mean she was happy here?

Jude stared at her mom's smiling face for a few seconds longer. Then she pulled out her phone, navigated to the Gala Literary job posting, and clicked Apply.

CHAPTER 32

KAT

Kat paced around her apartment, ignoring her phone.

Well, trying to ignore her phone. Although at this point, she'd read the message she was trying to ignore so many times that she'd memorized it, and it ran on a constant loop in her head as she turned tight circles around the leather couch in her living room. Which didn't stop her from snatching up her phone as she passed it and staring at the message once again.

Jude: *I just wanted to say that I'm really sorry for getting heated during our conversation the other day. I shouldn't have turned on you like that. I know it's only been two months, but you've become such a big part of my life and I want to keep it that way. I hope we can see each other soon* ♥

Kat sank down on the couch, reading the message again and again. She'd been ignoring Jude for three days. Not fully, but letting hours go by before responding to any messages, putting off making plans, sending short responses. Setting the groundwork for an *I'm just too busy to date right now* conversation. Or, even better, a slow fizzle out with no need for an emotionally draining conversation at all.

There was only one problem: she was miserable.

The last three days had felt excruciatingly long. Kat had reached for her phone a dozen times each day with a thought or joke that she wanted to share with Jude, only to pull her hand away at the last second. Each night in bed, she'd imagined Jude's arms around her, wishing she could relax into their warmth instead of staring at the ceiling for hours, chasing her own thoughts like a hamster running on a wheel. She'd had an interview with *Cosmo* this week, for a cover article titled "Your New Girl Crush!," along with an accompanying photoshoot of her posing in a oversized suit with no shirt on underneath. Kat should have been thrilled, but instead she'd spent the entire photoshoot wondering what Jude would think of her outfit.

Her career was thriving. But at what cost?

Since she was eleven, Kat had prioritized her career over everything else. She'd prioritized it over keeping friendships. Over normal life experiences like going to prom or having a first kiss (which had happened on set during *Agent Princess*, in front of a full crew, with an actor who was later accused of sexual assault by five different women). She'd prioritized her career over her relationship with her parents. She'd certainly prioritized it over her health. Even when she'd gone to the Serenity Center, the goal hadn't necessarily been to heal—it had been to get her shit together so she could get back to work.

She wanted a successful career. But why did succeeding always mean sacrificing something?

What was the alternative, though?

Kat grabbed one of the throw pillows and hugged it to her chest, squeezing it as tightly as she could. Surely Jocelyn could come up with a different plan.

She'd never thought that before. That she could just put her foot down and say no. But this was *her* life. If she didn't want to do something, that was her decision to make.

Maybe it was foolish to upend Jocelyn's plan for someone who could hurt her just as much as Madelyn had. But Madelyn had been the best part of her life for four years. If she was being honest with herself, Kat missed Madelyn so much it ached. She didn't want to feel that same lonely pang whenever she ate cupcakes without Jude, or read a good book and wanted to talk to her about it. She didn't want to miss Jude the way she missed Madelyn. She didn't want to add Jude to the list of things her career had taken from her.

She didn't want to lose Jude.

She tossed the throw pillow to the side, grabbed her keys, and ran for the door.

CHAPTER 33

JUDE

Someone buzzed Jude's apartment three times in quick succession, jolting her away from staring at her phone and refreshing her email, hoping for an update on her job application. She went over to the door and leaned on the speaker.

"Who is it?"

"It's Kat." The speaker crackled, distorting her words. "Can I come in?"

Jude pressed the button to unlock the door. She leaned against the wall next to the buzzer. Was Kat here to fix the weirdness between them? Or end things altogether?

She didn't wait until Kat knocked. When she heard footsteps on the stairs, she opened the door, scanning Kat's face for any hint of how she was feeling. But as soon as Kat climbed the last step, she flung her arms around Jude, squeezing tight.

Jude squeezed back, relief making her body soften into Kat's.

"I have to tell you something," Kat said, and Jude's arms tensed again.

"Okay. Come in."

Kat let go and went inside. Jude followed, shutting the door behind them, her heartbeat fluttering in the base of her throat. They sat down on the couch and Kat took Jude's hand.

"Do you remember when I told you about that girl from my show? Madelyn?"

"Of course."

"Well, I didn't tell you the full story."

Jude's heart started to beat harder. Was Kat still in love with Madelyn? Were they going to ride off into the sunset together?

Kat took a deep breath. She turned Jude's hand over in both of hers, running her fingertips over Jude's palm.

"We kissed when we were twenty," she said. "And then our friendship changed. We were still friendly, but we didn't call each other at night or spend breaks in my trailer anymore. There was a distance between us." Kat hesitated, tapping her fingers nervously against Jude's hand. "I had a problem with eating back then. I mean, we all did. Our contracts with the network required us to stay in a certain weight range, and we were all on really restrictive diets. But after things got weird with Madelyn, mine started to get really bad. I ate pretty much nothing. I could barely stand to drink water. And I was exercising three or four times a day."

Jude squeezed her hand, not wanting to interrupt but wanting to show that she was there, she was listening. Her heart ached for that lonely younger version of Kat and how much pressure she'd been under.

"I started fainting," Kat continued. "Just a couple of times, but one time I fainted during a meeting with the showrunner and hit my head. After that, the network said I had to get things under control. So I went to rehab. Two months of inpatient at the most discreet treatment center we could find. We had to delay the filming of Season 5, but the showrunner didn't tell anyone why. And Jocelyn told me to never tell anyone. She said if I did, they would use it against me. But I told Madelyn. After the weirdness with the kiss, I couldn't handle dropping off the face of the earth for two months and not explaining why."

Kat swallowed.

"At first, everything was fine. I did the treatment, I came back. We started filming Season 5. Everything seemed normal. But then I started dating Frasier. And Madelyn got jealous." Kat's mouth quirked up on one side humorlessly. "So she went to the tabloids. The interview was anonymous, but I knew it was her. She told them about the rehab, and that the filming delay was my fault."

"Oh my God," Jude said.

"It ruined my career. It made me a liability, so directors didn't want to hire me."

"I am so sorry that happened to you," Jude said. She wanted to curse and rage about how awful Madelyn was, but she could tell that wasn't what Kat needed. Instead, she settled for saying, "I can't believe she would do that."

"I wanted to tell you this, because . . . well. Ever since that happened, I've kind of had trouble trusting people."

Jude nodded slowly. "That makes sense."

"But I want to trust you." Kat shifted so that she faced Jude fully. "I want to tell you things. I want to let you in. And . . ." She hesitated. "I really don't want to break up."

Jude laughed, confused. "We don't have to," she said, gripping Kat's hand.

Kat's mouth quirked up again, with a real smile this time. "You're right," she said. "We don't."

"I really like you, Kat," Jude said. "And I promise that no matter what happens between us, I won't do anything like Madelyn did."

"I know you wouldn't," Kat said, her voice quiet. "I trust you."

"Can I ask you something?" Jude said. When Kat nodded, she added, "Is your eating okay now?"

Kat sighed. "It's not the best," she admitted. "I've been really stressed about my career lately, which is bringing up some old habits. I need to be more diligent about sticking to an eating schedule and limiting my exercise. But I promise I'm keeping an eye on it."

"Thank you for telling me," Jude said. "It means a lot to me that you're trusting me with all this. And I'm here if you need support."

Kat's cheek spasmed, as if she'd been about to cry and then suppressed it. She swallowed. "Thank you."

Jude hesitated, not sure if this was the right time, then said, "I applied for the Gala Literary job."

"What? Really?" Kat looked so excited that Jude laughed.

"Really. I thought about what you said, and you're right. I'm scared of leaving my comfort zone. But I know my mom would never want me to stay at the bookstore because of her. That's exactly what she didn't want. So maybe I owe it to her—and to myself—to start thinking about moving on."

Kat threw her arms around Jude. "I'm proud of you."

Jude turned her head, catching Kat's mouth with her own, kissing her hard. She tried to let all her feelings seep into the kiss—how much she'd missed Kat, how empty these past three days had felt without her.

She pulled Kat into her lap and started kissing her neck. Kat tilted her head back, leaning into the touch, grinding her hips forward in just the right way, making Jude's hands dig tighter into her hips. But Jude paused, her lips pressed against Kat's skin.

"Can I ask you one question?"

Kat stilled, her body tensing nervously. "Of course."

"Are you my girlfriend?"

The sides of Kat's mouth rose slowly, building into a grin. Then she fell forward into Jude, tackling her backward onto the couch.

"You know what?" she said, leaning down until her lips hovered right over Jude's. "I think I am."

CHAPTER 34

KAT

Kat smiled to herself as she strode out the back entrance of the theater. Her arms felt loose, her steps were quick, her shoulders were tall. She could feel a rising sensation right under her ribs, and her stomach felt light and airy, not tight or sick. It was a good sensation. Pleasant. It made her want to walk faster and grin at nothing as she went. She'd walked the mile and a half to Jude's apartment every day since rehearsals had started this week. The cast had spent the first few days doing a reading, getting to know one another, and starting to block out the first act. The other actors were intimidatingly theater-y. The woman playing the professor's wife had three Tonys under her belt, and the man playing the professor had spent most of his career doing Shakespeare. The two of them had been friends for years, and they took their dinner breaks together every night, along with three of the actors playing the various dead philosophers. They all clustered together at the beginning of rehearsals, talking and laughing, then falling silent when Kat approached. It stung a little, but Kat got it. They were waiting to see if she was a Hollywood diva who would make their lives more difficult by thinking she was too good for live theater. But she would win them over eventually. She would show up on time, know her lines and blocking, work hard, and prove that she was actually a decent actor, not just a name.

The thought made her grin even wider. Ever since Kat had decided that she wasn't going to end things with Jude, she'd felt *good* in a way that she hadn't in a long time. When Kat had told Jocelyn, she'd sighed and moaned and told Kat that she was making a big mistake. But eventually she'd conceded that they could find another publicity stunt to make sure the play sold out.

Talking to Jude had also made Kat realize that her eating habits had been sliding in a bad direction, so she'd started making sure that she sat down and had actual meals three times a day. It wasn't always easy, but at least her stomach had stopped feeling so twisted and nauseous all the time now that things were more settled. She was taking care of herself, she had the role she needed, her career was coming back, and she had a girlfriend.

A *girlfriend*. The word still made her giddy. She, Kat Kelly, had a girlfriend. And she *was* someone's girlfriend. They were girlfriends, plural. A pair of girlfriends. A matching set. It made something inside her chest flicker and dance like a candle flame.

Kat turned onto Jude's street and let herself into the building—Jude had given her a key earlier that week so she wouldn't have to wait on the street and potentially get recognized. Kat's apartment was bigger, but she preferred how cozy and welcoming Jude's place felt.

As she walked in, Kat looked around at the framed posters and the golden late-afternoon light filtering through the plants by the window, and she felt something in her release—like she'd been tense until she arrived and could suddenly take a deep breath. Filled with an urge to capture her happiness, she lifted her phone and took a picture of the living room. Her mouth curved into a smile as she studied it. It looked like the warmest, homiest place she'd ever been.

"Hi!" Jude shouted from the kitchen. She was chopping a mound of vegetables, a towel thrown over her shoulder and various ingredients piled up on the wooden cart that served as extra counter space.

"Hi, sexy," Kat said. "How did your interview go?"

"Apparently well," Jude said, beaming. "They asked me to come in for another interview next week."

"Jude! You're amazing!"

"I went to the Union Square farmer's market on my way home, and their produce is incredible. Here. Try this." She cut a slice off a large tomato. It was so ripe that juice dripped down her wrist as she held it out.

Kat leaned forward and took the tomato slice with her mouth. Then she touched her tongue to Jude's wrist, tracing it slowly upward, lapping the spilled juice all the way up until her tongue curled around Jude's finger.

Jude inhaled sharply. She slid her finger into Kat's mouth. Kat swirled her tongue over it, sucking her in farther.

"Get in the bedroom." Jude's voice had turned low and rough. "Now."

Kat scurried to obey. As soon as she crossed the threshold to the bedroom, she turned, pressing herself against Jude, her mouth open and her hands diving beneath Jude's shirt, desperate to feel skin. Jude kissed her for a second, then pulled back.

"Clothes off," she commanded.

Kat only hesitated for a moment before undressing, blushing slightly under Jude's unbroken gaze. Once she was naked, she moved back to Jude.

Jude kissed her, walking her backward until her knees found the bed. Jude gave a soft push so she fell back onto the comforter. Kat grabbed Jude's shirt, trying to pull her down on top of her.

"So impatient," Jude chided. She took Kat's wrists and stretched them over Kat's head, pinning them to the mattress.

Then she lowered herself on top of Kat until their faces hovered inches apart. Kat lifted her head, trying to land a kiss, but Jude pulled back, smirking.

"Not yet," she said, pressing down on Kat's wrists a little harder. "We're going to play a game first."

"A game?" Kat's brain seemed to be processing slower than usual. All she could think about was the ache building between her legs and how desperately she wanted to touch Jude.

"A game," Jude confirmed. "These are the rules. I'm going to touch you. And you're going to keep still."

"Keep still?" Kat panted.

"That's right," Jude cooed into her ear with a cocky lilt. "Absolutely still. Because if you move a single muscle, I'm going to stop touching you."

"That's mean," Kat whined.

"It *is* mean," Jude said. "But I think you're going to play with me anyway. Because I think you really, really want me to touch you."

Kat battled her pride for a few seconds, but desire won. She nodded.

Slowly, Jude released her wrists. "Now, are you going to keep absolutely still for me?"

"Yes," Kat said, pouting to make her feelings clear.

"Good girl."

Jude sat up, kneeling with a leg on either side of Kat's body. She started running her hands over Kat's chest and arms, so gently it made Kat want to squirm. She managed to stay still, barely repressing a shiver as Jude's fingertips traced ever so lightly across her skin. They ran up her throat, into her hair, across the line of her jaw, and with each stroke Kat could feel the pressure building between her legs, making her want to writhe and grab and scream. Instead, she closed her eyes, trying to keep her breathing regular, focused on keeping her outstretched hands from twitching.

Jude's hands roamed lower, tracing the shape of her breasts, teasing lightly. Then they closed on her nipples, twisting them lightly between her fingertips. Slowly, the pressure increased, until Kat let out a long, low moan.

"Careful, now," Jude warned. Her hands trailed lower. She caressed Kat's thighs, stroking closer and closer before finally moving her hand between Kat's legs.

Kat's hips jerked forward before she could stop herself. Instantly, Jude's hands disappeared. Kat let out a strangled whine.

"None of that, now," Jude said. "I made the rules very clear. It's not my fault you couldn't follow them."

"*Please*," Kat moaned.

Jude's half-hitch grin was cockier than Kat had ever seen it. "Please what?"

"Please touch me again."

"Are you going to stay still this time?"

Kat tossed her head back, bouncing it off the bed as she groaned. Finally, resentfully, she muttered, "Yes."

"You'd better," Jude said. "Because now I have to start *alllll* over."

She moved her hands back to Kat's shoulders and arms, stroking lightly again. It was harder to stay still this time. Kat wanted Jude to touch her harder, faster, deeper, but Jude's hands moved at a maddeningly slow pace, teasing until she wasn't sure she could take it anymore. It took everything she had to keep from thrusting forward into Jude's touch.

Then Jude leaned down and added her tongue to the mix, flicking Kat's nipples until she had to hold her breath to keep from screaming.

Jude's tongue moved lower, then lower still. Kat gasped, every one of her muscles tensed and strained with the effort of not moving. Jude ran her tongue between Kat's legs, taking her time, letting her tongue explore every fold and crevice.

Kat's exhales became whimpers, keening from her throat in quick succession, her chest heaving with exertion. When Jude's tongue touched her clit, she couldn't take it anymore. She let out a soft scream, her hands rising to tangle in Jude's hair, her thighs clenching down on Jude's cheeks. Jude tried to pull away.

"You moved," she said. "That means that I—"

"Absolutely not," Kat growled. She turned, catching Jude by surprise and flipping them both over until Jude's back was pressed to the bed and Kat was on top of her. "If you don't touch me right now, I'm going to lose my entire mind."

"Oh yeah? What are you going to do about it?"

This time, Kat pinned Jude's wrists to the bed.

"So feisty," Jude mocked. "But how am I supposed to touch you with my wrists pinned?"

"How do you think?"

Kat climbed forward until she was kneeling over Jude's face. Then she lowered herself onto Jude's mouth.

Jude hummed in pleasure, her tongue darting out to lap up every drop of Kat's wetness. Kat moaned. She dropped Jude's wrists and Jude took her hips in her hands, pressing Kat closer.

Kat tilted her head back, groaning as the pressure hit exactly the right spot. Jude let go of her hips with one hand and reached down. Kat heard unzipping, then felt Jude's arm start to work, touching herself while Kat rode her mouth. The thought made Kat's entire body shudder.

"Don't you dare come," Jude said, her voice thick with Kat's wetness. "Not until I say so."

"I don't know," Kat panted, "if I can wait."

"You'd better wait," Jude said. Her tongue resumed its relentless rhythm, driving Kat closer to the edge, making her thighs tremble. "You'd better wait for me."

"Hurry. Please."

Jude's arm worked faster, and she let out a groan. Kat braced her arms against Jude's headboard, holding on to keep her balance, her entire body clenched as she tried to keep from coming.

"Not yet," Jude said against her clit. Kat couldn't speak anymore. She could only groan and moan and make loud, desperate sounds. Jude's body started to tense underneath Kat's, her muscles tightening. "Almost there."

She sped up the rhythm of both her arm and tongue, until Kat thought she might pass out, the pleasure so intense it almost hurt. The headboard rattled under her shaking hands.

"Now," Jude said, and Kat released the tension, letting it flow through her, her hips thrusting forward against Jude's mouth as she came in waves and waves and waves. Underneath her, Jude shuddered as she came, too, and she let out a cry that got muffled in Kat's wetness. Her tongue kept working, drawing out Kat's orgasm, keeping her coming until she wasn't sure she could take any more, and then she crested into a pleasure so intense that her thighs gave out, sending her tumbling onto Jude.

They lay there, panting and sweaty, pressed tight together. Kat's clit throbbed with aftershocks of pleasure. She buried her face in Jude's chest, clutching Jude around the waist, Jude's arms circled protectively around her back. She took deep breaths. And then, to her embarrassment, Kat started to cry.

"Hey. Hey, sweetheart," Jude said softly, stroking her hair. "It's okay. I got you. You're okay."

Kat shook her head, trying to convey that she wasn't upset. "It's just—" she tried, but got stopped by a sob hitching in her throat. "That just felt . . . so good."

"I know," Jude said. "It's okay to cry. Let it out."

Kat let the tears flow. It felt good to sob, another form of release, another kind of tension leaving her body. She pressed herself closer to Jude, trying to eliminate any space between them. She couldn't get close enough. She wanted to fuse their bodies together, to melt into one being with this incredible person beside her.

Jude seemed to feel the same way, because she pulled Kat as tightly against her as she could, kissing the top of her hair. Gradually, their breathing slowed and evened out, then their grip softened, until they relaxed into each other. Kat felt like she was floating on an ocean of calm, utterly spent.

"How are you feeling?" Jude said softly.

Like I love you.

The words sprang into her head, but Kat swallowed them down. She couldn't say that. They'd been dating for two months. It was way too soon. What was she even thinking?

Instead, she reached up and kissed Jude as deeply as she could, hoping that would be enough.

CHAPTER 35

JUDE

Jude tugged at the collar of her shirt, moving it away from her throat. She'd decided to wear a tie. It was a queer literary organization, so why not look as gay as she wanted? Now that she was sitting in the waiting room, though, the knot seemed to be digging farther and farther into her windpipe, making it hard to breathe. She smoothed out her blazer, double-checked that her folder full of résumés was still in her bag, and tried to take deep breaths.

This was her third interview. Clearly she'd done well enough on the first two interviews to make it here, but the thought didn't make her any less nervous. If anything, it made her *more* nervous. After getting so close, failing now would be even more disappointing.

"Miss Thacker?"

Jude looked up, slightly startled, the way she always was when someone called her "Miss." Sure, she used she/her pronouns, but she thought of her gender more as *butch* than *woman*, and it always felt strange when she got a reminder that the world didn't see her that way.

She stood and shook hands with the tall white man in front of her who introduced himself as Jerome Heirigs, a member of the board of directors. He led Jude into a small conference room and sat down on one side of the table next to Nina Maguire, the woman Jude had met at Richard Gottlieb's party.

"Jude!" Nina shook her hand enthusiastically. "It's so good to see you again. How are things at the bookstore?"

"Sales are up fifteen percent this month," Jude said with a smile. She didn't mention why.

"And have you crafted any more wonderful displays?"

Jude launched into a description of the new section she'd built. She'd found a small press online that had been bringing old queer books back into print and struck an agreement to carry part of their selection in-store, to help bring visibility to these underappreciated stories. Jerome and Nina nodded along, looking impressed. As she spoke, Jude started to relax. This didn't feel like an inquisition. It just felt like talking to two people who also loved books.

After running her through her résumé, Jerome leaned across the table and said, "So, Jude, why do you think you would be a good fit for this job?"

Jude tried to sit tall and sound confident. "I know I might not have the exact experience you'd expect for this kind of position. But I know the queer literary world backward and forward. It's how I spend my working time and my personal time. I am passionate about putting queer stories into people's hands and letting queer people see themselves as the heroes of their own stories. For a long time I've been doing that on the bookselling front, but I would be so excited to have a position where I could make even more of an impact and give queer writers their start. I would take that responsibility very, very seriously."

Nina and Jerome exchanged a glance. A *good* glance.

"I know you would," Nina said. "Which is why we're so excited to offer you this position."

It took Jude a few seconds to catch up. "Wait, what?" she said. "Just like that?"

"Just like that." Nina laughed.

Adrenaline rushed through her, making Jude feel dizzy as they gave her an overview of the salary and benefits.

"I— Thank you," Jude said, hoping she was forming real words. "I'm really excited about this. And I don't want to seem not grateful. But can I think about it for a few days?"

"Of course you can," Nina said. "Take until next week. Think it over."

"But we really hope you'll accept," Jerome said. "You'd be a wonderful addition to our company."

Jude shook their hands and thanked them again. She paused on the sidewalk outside the building, tilting her head to feel the sun on her face. She'd done it. They thought she was good enough for this job. Maybe she *was* good enough for it. She could do this. She could ask Kat to help her practice her public speaking, so she wouldn't choke like she had at the store.

At that thought, the rising euphoria in Jude's chest started to deflate. If she left the store, she'd be giving up her chance to ever buy it back.

This job was an incredible opportunity. But was she really ready to leave The Next Chapter behind for good?

CHAPTER 36

KAT

"The emotional motivation isn't actually important in this scene," Richard Gottlieb said. "Because in this scene you're not playing yourself—you're playing the version that he sees, right? So it's okay that the character feels a bit like a caricature. Because in that moment she is. Because we're looking through *his* eyes. Got it?"

The honest answer was no, but the scene had already been stopped for ten minutes while Richard walked Kat through his vision for this particular part of the script. Her castmates were all leaning against pieces of the set, watching with thinly veiled impatience. "Yeah. Got it."

"Okay!" Richard clapped his hands and the other actors stood up. "From the top."

It was their second week of rehearsals, and they were blocking out the big vagina scene today—the one where the professor spoke to every vagina he'd ever been in. The female actors were supposed to circle around him onstage like ghosts, holding their hands in pointy ovals over their heads. Richard hadn't yet decided if he wanted realistic costumes or for the vulvas to be implied. Kat was really hoping he went for the latter—she hated the thought of herself in a vulva costume making the rounds online.

Kat fought the absurd urge to giggle as she held her hands over her head and swooped around. She glanced at the other actors, but they all had very stoic expressions on their faces—clearly, they were having no trouble taking this seriously.

"With scream and shove and squeeze. Cast out into coldness from this life of ease!" The actor playing the professor's mother began to shout in a dramatic thunder. "Once belonging, now alone. Once whole, now on your own. Seek to return forevermore, but you can never reenter this closed door!"

Kat's mouth twitched and she fought to get it back in line. Someone had been reading way too much Freud.

The actor playing the professor's high school sweetheart shouted out her lines in the same dramatic-monologue voice, as if reciting the opening lines of *Macbeth*. Her lines were about the awkward fumblings and ecstasies in the back of a Toyota, then the loss of first love.

Kat prepared herself for her upcoming lines. She didn't want to deliver them in the same recitation tone. She wanted to add some *nuance,* lean into the cold and calculating way the professor saw her character. How she was more dangerous—dynamite that could light up his entire life—but also more seductive than any of the women he'd known before. She thought she could pull it off, but it was hard to sound dangerous in rhyming couplets. *Why* did the vulvas have to rhyme? The rest of the play didn't.

The actor playing the professor's wife finished up her couplets about how the initial passion of their marriage had faded to obligated routine. On her cue, Kat swooped toward the front of the stage and began intoning, "With youth and life's eager flush did I make you stutter and blush. But as the—"

"Stop!" Richard shouted from the front row. He dug the heel of his hand into his forehead. "Kat, what did we *just* talk about?"

Kat could feel the other actors' eyes on her, but she didn't let herself glance back at them. "You said to play the character as the professor sees her. And he sees her as dangerous and seductive, but—"

"Never mind." Richard cut his hand through the air while snapping his fingers shut, like a choir director cutting off a song. "Just say the lines like the others are saying the lines, okay? Match them. Dramatic. Loud."

Kat knew she should just follow his directions, but she was pretty sure she was right about this. "But shouldn't there be some difference between the women in his past and the woman who's looming large in his present, urging him to destroy his entire life? Shouldn't she feel unique somehow?"

"You're overthinking, sweetheart," Richard said, but it came out sounding like *You're an idiot, sweetheart.* Someone snickered behind Kat. She heard one of the other actors whisper something and distinctly made out the word *Hollywood*. "Just say the lines and let me handle the thinking, okay?"

Kat bit down on the inside of her cheek. A tang of blood swirled between her teeth before she could force herself to wrench open her mouth and say, "Right. Okay."

Then she returned to her mark and took it from the top.

CHAPTER 37

JUDE

Jude had worked hundreds of Tuesday afternoon shifts at The Next Chapter. It was a slow time—so slow today that there weren't any customers. Normally, she would be reading a book at the register or staring at her phone, waiting for the hours to tick by until closing. But today, she kept looking around the store. Her eyes lingered on the mural of famous children's book characters her mom had painted by hand. On Talia, who was supposed to be checking for misshelved books but had gotten distracted by a P. G. Wodehouse novel and was leaning against the humor section, reading. On Rhys and L.J., who were dusting down the shelves. This was her family. Her home.

She hadn't told her friends about the job offer yet. Why bother, when she probably wasn't going to take it?

As she watched, Rhys leaned over and whispered a joke to L.J., who gave a tense smile and then moved away to another part of the store, leaving Rhys to stare miserably after them. Guilt twisted around Jude's stomach. She gave Rhys an encouraging nod, urging him to go after L.J. and try again, but he turned away and started dusting the memoir section instead.

The bell over the door chimed and Stephen walked in, followed by a man in a Carhartt jacket.

"Good morning," Jude said loudly, hoping the others would take the cue to look like they were busy working. Talia hurriedly tucked her book back onto the shelf.

"Morning," Stephen grunted. Then he turned to the man with him and said, "These shelves here."

The man took a tape measure out of his pocket and started measuring the distance between the shelves on the queer-books display. Jude and Rhys exchanged a worried glance.

"What are you doing?" Jude said.

Stephen ignored her. "I'm thinking one fewer shelf, but each one will be a little taller. Give the books more space from each other, so customers can see them clearly."

The guy nodded and started writing measurements down in his phone. Jude strode out from behind the register. "What are you doing?" she repeated.

Stephen gave her an annoyed look, but he couldn't exactly chastise her for not being behind the register when there wasn't a single customer in the store. "We're renovating. Nothing big, it will only take a few days."

"Renovating what?"

Stephen rolled his chin side to side, stretching out his neck. "This whole wall here, right when you walk into the store. It's jam-packed with books, which is bad for title discovery. I want to make the shelves a little bigger so we can display fewer books, with their front covers out instead of their spines. That way, our bestsellers catch people's eyes as soon as they come in."

"But this is our queer book display. We have the biggest one in New York state."

"And now we don't." Stephen turned back to the measuring guy. "How soon can you get me an estimate?"

"Should be an easy job. I'll email it over tonight."

Jude stepped forward, back into Stephen's line of sight. "You can't get rid of the queer book display," she said. "That is a *huge* part of why people come to the store. We have a strong queer brand that makes us stand out from other, bigger stores. That's where our Instagram following came from. Eighty percent of our online sales are queer books ordered by people out of state."

"We'll still have a queer shelf," Stephen said, holding up his hands placatingly. "But it doesn't make financial sense to dedicate *this* much real estate to a niche audience."

The guy with the measuring tape looked between the two of them uncomfortably, then glued his eyes to his phone.

"The whole point of the shelf is to show queer people that they're *not* a niche audience. The point is for them to come into the store and realize they're not alone."

"Touching. But this is a business." Stephen turned back to the measuring-tape guy. "Send over that estimate tonight and then we'll schedule a date, okay?"

"Gotcha." The guy hurried out, looking eager to get away.

"You can't do this." Jude tried to stand as tall as possible.

"This is *my* bookstore. I can do whatever I want." Stephen stepped around her to head to the back room, but Jude followed him.

"If you get rid of it, I'll quit."

Stephen snorted. "Sure. Okay."

"I mean it." Jude expected her voice to shake, but it came out strong and certain. Because she did mean it, she realized as she said the words. She loved this store. But it wouldn't be the store she loved for much longer. If she stayed here, she would become more and more miserable, more and more stuck.

Didn't she owe herself more than that?

"Look, we'll make half of those shelves bestsellers and keep half as queer books, okay? We'll just curate the selection a little better and make them easier to find. That's a good thing, right?"

Jude breathed out through her nose, considering. Today it

was half the shelves. But what about next week? What about the week after?

She walked around Stephen toward the back of the store. Behind her, she heard Stephen let out a relieved breath.

"Okay, great. I'm glad you see my side. It really will help with discov—"

He cut off as Jude reached up and lifted the framed photo of her and her mother on opening day off the wall.

"I quit."

All three of her friends gasped. Stephen made a face like he'd just had a lemon shoved up his ass.

She tucked the photo under her arm. She didn't bother listening to Stephen's angry protests. Instead, she took her time looking around the place she had poured so much of her energy into, memorizing it as it was now, so her mental image wouldn't be tainted by what it would become without her.

She turned to face her friends, who were all gathered by the checkout counter. Talia had her hands over her mouth, but Rhys was beaming at her.

"I love you guys," Jude said.

"We love you, too," Rhys said. Talia nodded. L.J. saluted like Jude was going off to war.

Jude turned and pushed open the door. For so long, the cheery bell on top had reminded her of Becca, walking out of the store and away from Jude's life. It had reminded her that this store was no longer hers. It had reminded her of everything she had lost and everything she could still lose.

But today the bell didn't sound like a door closing. It sounded like a door opening, clearing the way for Jude to figure out what came next.

CHAPTER 38

KAT

Kat pushed open the stage door, mentally preparing herself for another grueling rehearsal. It had been harder than usual to leave Jude's apartment this morning. They'd spent the night before celebrating Jude's new job, at one of those fake speakeasy bars hidden behind an unmarked door. They'd brushed knees in the shadowy light while Jude gushed about everything she would get to do at Gala, and Kat had been so happy she hadn't even cared when someone at the next table took their picture.

Ever since Kat had told Jocelyn that she wouldn't break up with Jude, she'd felt oddly free. As if she'd been carrying a heavy weight for years and then suddenly realized that nothing was stopping her from just . . . putting it down.

For so long, Kat had done exactly what she'd been told to do. But she wasn't a little kid anymore. She didn't have to just accept whatever decisions a manager or a director made. She was an adult, and she could make her own choices. She could say no.

Which was a little terrifying. Kat had almost no practice in making her own decisions. She wasn't used to thinking about what she wanted, or what would actually feel good to her. In fact, she'd spent most of her life trying to actively ignore what she wanted. Trying to shove all her feelings down as far as possible because her feelings only got in the way of the job she needed to do. But she wasn't going to do that anymore.

Kat came to an abrupt halt once she entered the theater and found only Richard waiting for her instead of the full cast. "Where is everyone?"

"I asked them to stay home today, so you and I could do a little work one-on-one."

The inside of Kat's cheek shot between her teeth, and she clamped down to keep herself from saying something she'd regret. The Hollywood child star needed extra help. She could imagine the other cast members laughing about it gleefully. Probably at one of their after-rehearsal drinks at Bar Centrale that they never bothered to invite her to.

She pulled out her script and her pencil, then made her way to the stage. "Where do you want to start?"

"With your big monologue in act one."

She dropped the script and strode to her mark, but she'd only made it through two lines before Richard stopped her and told her to start again, but more seductively. She gritted her teeth and tried that, but only made it through half a line. More *evil* this time.

She started, and he stopped her almost immediately.

"No, no, no." Richard ran both his hands through his hair, leaving one half sticking up higher than the other. "You're not getting it."

"Or maybe, as both the writer and director, you're too close to the script and having trouble relinquishing control." Kat could hardly believe her own daring. But it was true. Richard had been nitpicking her performance for weeks, trying to dictate exactly how she said every line.

Richard pursed his lips, then released them with a smack. "Look, honey, you need to stop deluding yourself."

"Excuse me?"

"I didn't hire you because you can act." Richard flicked his wrist, as if the very idea was ridiculous. "Let's be real. You need a laugh track and ten quick cuts added in post to get the simplest idea across. You're here to be a face on the poster so ordinary idiots who don't go to see plays will think, 'Oh, I know her,' and schlep their asses over to Midtown. Your job is to look pretty and sell tickets. So stop being so fucking difficult and start doing what you're told."

Kat gaped at him. She knew that the whole point of casting her was to boost ticket sales. But to have him say it like *that*? To hear that he didn't think she could act at all? That he clearly thought she was damaging the quality of the play? This stupid, shitty, self-indulgent play?

"Now that we have that settled, we can go back to scene three and work on—" Richard started to say, reaching for his script again, but Kat interrupted him.

"You know what?" she said. "I'm good."

"Excuse me?"

"I quit."

Kat tossed her script at Richard's feet. Then she grabbed her bag and walked out.

CHAPTER 39

JUDE

Jude adjusted her blazer and tried to look like she belonged. Kat was meeting her after rehearsal at this party, which was celebrating . . . something theater related. Jude looked around, hoping for clues. An award? An opening night? Some sort of charity? It was impossible to tell. It looked like every other event Jude had been to with Kat—people in business dress holding drinks and picking at a table of appetizers. A Midtown restaurant had been rented out for the occasion and people were crammed in between the tables, filling the room with a nearly unbearable volume of chatter.

Jude sipped slowly at the whiskey she'd gotten from the open bar just to give herself something to do, feeling out of place in this room of fancy arts people. Everyone seemed so official.

But so was she, she reminded herself. She was part of the arts world now. She had a job at Gala Literary. If she went up to anyone and introduced herself, they would accept that she belonged at this party, in this world. She smiled into her glass.

"Hi!" Kat swooped out of the crowd suddenly. "I'm so sorry I'm late! Can I have a sip of that?" She kissed Jude, then took the whiskey glass from her hand, took a big gulp, and made a face.

Jude laughed. "You won't believe the day I've had. Let's get in line for the bar."

"How was rehearsal?" Jude asked as they pushed toward the bar, but Kat shook her head.

"Not here." She tipped her head at the crowd around them. "How was your day?"

"Good." Jude shrugged. "I cleaned the apartment. I went to the gym. I read a book. I kind of don't know what to do with myself until the job starts."

Kat hummed in agreement, but she looked distracted. She ordered two glasses of wine and pulled them over to a high-top table in a corner, where a large potted plant offered a small semblance of privacy. She took a few big sips of wine as she eyed the crowd.

"Richard isn't here," she said, mostly to herself. "Good." She turned to Jude. "Are people looking at me? I feel like they're looking at me."

"People are always looking at you, darling," Jude said, kissing her temple. "And who can blame them?"

Kat gave a small laugh in response, but she still seemed distracted. Her free hand drummed against the table, and she kept glancing around the room. Jude glanced with her. A few people *were* shooting looks their way, but no more than Kat usually got. At events like these, people found it cooler to pretend they didn't care that someone famous was standing in the corner.

Kat turned, giving her head a little shake as if throwing off the glances. "Cheers!" She held up her glass, and they clinked. "I have some exciting news."

Jude grinned at her, feeling a little jolt in her stomach as their eyes connected. "What is it?"

"I think you're going to be proud of me." Kat leaned forward on her stool and Jude mirrored her, her body responding to Kat's automatically, moving forward to get as close to her as possible. "I quit the play."

"You what?" Jude leaned a little too far forward and almost fell off her stool. She caught herself quickly and stared at Kat.

"Yup!" Kat took a big sip of her wine and held up her glass as if cheersing herself. "I threw my script on the ground and walked out."

"Wow. That's— Wow." Jude tried to catch up. "That's a really big decision. How do you feel about it?"

"I feel *great* about it. Richard said something awful to me. And I didn't take it. I put my foot down."

"What did he say?" Jude asked. But Kat kept talking as if she hadn't heard.

"I'm not dealing with asshole directors anymore. I'm learning to say no to things. Also, that play is terrible. It's probably going to flop. And now I'm free to do whatever I want." She had finished her wine and she picked up Jude's off the table, seemingly not noticing that she was switching glasses. "I can do that indie movie! I can do something that I actually *enjoy.* So this is great. It's a good thing. It's not a big deal to quit."

"Okay," Jude said, even though she could feel uneasiness climbing up her throat. "Yeah. Maybe this is good."

"It's *totally* good." Kat was speaking loudly. Her leg was jiggling on the footrest of the stool, jumping up and down repeatedly. "I feel great. I have so much energy right now. I mean, I can do *anything.* I could write my own play that's better than his. Or I could go on *Dancing with the Stars.* That's always a good comeback. Might as well put those eight years of dance lessons to good use, right?"

Kat laughed loudly. Jude smiled weakly back. Kat's jitteriness was making her nervous.

"Should we head home?" Jude suggested. "Talk about this in private?"

Kat took another big sip of wine, then put the glass down and grabbed Jude's hand. "I want to say thank you. For so long, I did whatever directors told me to do, even when it was some questionable shit. But when I'm with you, I feel like my feelings actually matter."

She picked up the wineglass again. "Maybe that's enough," Jude started to say.

"Oh my God." Kat's attention slid off of Jude, her eyes shifting toward the door as she interrupted. "It's Madelyn."

Jude glanced over her shoulder. Madelyn was coming through the front of the restaurant in a black jumpsuit and tall heels that made her tower over the crowd, her undercut freshly shaven and her long hair falling in glamorous waves down her shoulder.

"Why does she have to show up everywhere? She's like herpes or something. I can't get rid of her."

Jude took advantage of Kat's distraction to ease the wineglass from her hand and move it away. "Let's go home."

"It just kills me, you know?" Kat continued. "She totally destroyed my career and she just gets to go on living her life, more popular than ever."

"I know it's—" Jude said, but Kat kept speaking over her. Jude swallowed the rest of her sentence, trying not to let her annoyance show.

"And she doesn't even have the decency to ignore me, you know? Every time we're at a party together, she has to come over and pretend to be nice and rub it in my fucking face that she's successful and I'm pathetic."

"You're not pathetic," Jude protested.

"She took my spot," Kat practically spat. "I was supposed to be the one who made it after the show. But she stole it from me."

Kat stared at Madelyn, her eyes narrowed, her cheeks sucked between her teeth. "You know what? I'm going to go tell her that."

Jude stood up. "That's really not a good idea."

"This is the new Katrina Kelly," Kat said, sliding off her stool. "I'm in touch with my emotions now. And I'm not going to play nice with the woman who ruined my life. I'm not going to kiss her on the cheek and pretend that it's okay that she stabbed me in the back. I'm going to tell her how I honestly feel."

Jude put her hands on Kat's arms, trying to soothe her and block her from leaving at the same time. "This isn't the right time. You've been drinking and you're in public and it's been a hard day. Let's just go home."

"I'm done waiting," Kat said. "I'm done being nice and quiet and taking everyone's shit. People think I can't act? Well, I've been acting my entire life. Acting like the good little girl everyone wants me to be. And I'm done with it. I'm done!"

She sidestepped Jude and pushed through the crowd toward Madelyn, her footing slightly unsteady. Jude hurried after her.

"Madelyn!" Kat called, her voice a little too loud. Madelyn jerked around, startled, cringing away for a second before she saw who it was.

"Oh! Hi." She laughed nervously, brushing her fingertips against the short hairs of her undercut. "You scared me for a second. I thought you were a crazy fan or something. How are you?"

"I have to talk to you," Kat said.

"Okay. What's up?"

"You ruined my life, that's what's up."

Madelyn sighed. "Look. Kat. Let's not do this here, okay?"

"No." Kat's voice came out strong and clear. "We're going to do this now. I'm done pretending like everything is fine."

"This really isn't the place," Madelyn said, but Kat kept barreling forward.

"You were supposed to be my friend." Kat was talking loudly, and Jude saw several people in the crowd turn to look. Madelyn's eyes darted around, as if looking for an escape route. "And then you ruined my life with that interview."

"I did not *ruin* your life," Madelyn said. "Don't be so dramatic." She stepped forward, leaning in to speak in an undertone so the rest of the crowd couldn't hear. "Everyone knew, Kat.

You thought it was such a big secret, but do you think those guys at the network kept anything to themselves? Word got around. It was a TV set. If it wasn't me, someone else would have done it."

"But you were my friend!" Kat's voice broke, and Jude saw tears start to gather in her eyes. "How could you do that to me?"

Jude grabbed Kat's arm and tried to tug her away, but Kat resisted.

"Oh, please," Madelyn said scornfully. "Like you're a saint. Does your little girlfriend know why you're dating her? Should I tell her about the proposition Jocelyn made to my agent?"

Jude dropped Kat's arm, looking at her uncertainly.

Kat's face went white. "You are such a *bitch*!"

Someone nearby gasped. The restaurant fell quiet around them.

"If I'm a bitch, so are you," Madelyn said fiercely. "You can blame all your failures on me, but you wouldn't have made it anyway. I'm sure you're going to blame me for *this*, too, but you did this to yourself. Just like before."

She jutted her chin over Kat's left shoulder and Kat spun. Jude's heart dropped as she saw what Madelyn had gestured to: a twentysomething man in a suit, holding up his phone. Recording the whole conversation.

Kat looked like she'd been slapped. Jude had never seen her look so scared, not even in the mob at that Old Navy. She was frozen, gaping at the camera. The man flushed red but kept his phone up, still recording.

Jude stepped forward, between the camera and Kat.

"Excuse me, sir," she said in her politest voice. "Could I please ask you to delete that video?"

The man kept recording but lowered his phone. "I don't have to do anything."

Jude wanted to punch him, but she forced herself to smile instead. "We all have bad days sometimes, right? How would you like someone to take a video of you on a bad day?"

"I'm not a celebrity," the man said stubbornly. "She is."

"Look, buddy." Jude tried to keep from cursing, but it was hard. "You have a chance to do a kind thing here. To be a good guy. Don't you want to be a good guy?"

The man turned and started to walk away. Jude grabbed his arm.

"Let go of me," he said loudly.

"Just delete the video," Jude said. "Don't be an asshole."

"You can't tell me what to do. Get off." The man yanked his arm away. Jude released him, and he stumbled backward, dropping his phone.

The man lunged forward, and without thinking, Jude lifted her foot and smashed it down.

The man let out a yell, diving after his crushed phone. Jude watched him, breathing hard. That had been dumb. But at least the phone was destroyed. The video was in progress, so it wouldn't have saved. There was no way he'd be able to recover the file.

Jude heard a small, strangled sound. She turned and saw Kat standing behind her, looking horrified.

And that's when she noticed all the other phones in the crowd, pointed toward them, recording the whole thing.

CHAPTER 40

KAT

Jocelyn arrived at six the next morning. She threw open the door to Kat's bedroom, letting it hit the wall with a loud bang that startled Kat awake.

"Get up," she said.

Kat groaned and clutched her head.

"Oh, are you hungover?" Jocelyn said in a sickly-sweet tone. "Have you tried not getting drunk and yelling at your old coworkers in public?"

Kat lowered her hands. Her brain flashed through images from the night before: Calling Madelyn a bitch. Jude smashing her boot down on some guy's phone. The cold eyes of half a dozen phone cameras staring Kat down as she turned and fled the restaurant.

"You have fifteen minutes to shower," Jocelyn said. "Then we're doing damage control.

Kat nodded. Then she stumbled into the bathroom and threw up. Whether it was from alcohol or shame she couldn't tell. Either way, she didn't feel any better afterward.

She got in the shower, closing her eyes as the water drummed down on her. She didn't want to get out. She didn't want to see what people were saying. The night before, she'd run out of the restaurant and taken a cab home, where she'd collapsed into bed and cried until she fell asleep. She'd been too scared to look at her phone, but she could only imagine how bad it must be.

When she left the bathroom, Jocelyn had taken over the dining table. She was typing furiously on a laptop, two cellphones open to different news articles at her side. Kat sat down across from her, and Jocelyn pushed an iced coffee toward her without speaking.

Kat took it but didn't drink. She didn't deserve coffee.

"I am so, so sorry," she said.

Jocelyn made a *hmmph* noise but didn't respond.

"How bad is it?"

Jocelyn slid one of the phones across the table. Kat picked it up.

"Former Child Star Causes Commotion," proclaimed the *New York Host,* with a photo of an adorable eleven-year-old Kat in *Spy Pigs* positioned next to a blurry still of Kat screaming at Madelyn the night before. In the photo Kat's face was red, and her hair was messy. She looked like she was having a full-blown meltdown.

The reporter, Ned Edwards, had included a helpful timeline, with photos of Kat at various stages of her life. The beginning was filled with cute childhood stills, transitioning into polished glamour shots from *P.R.O.M.* The last four years were bleak: Kat's stay at the Serenity Center, the subsequent cancellation of the show, the few direct-to-streaming projects she'd done afterward. A year and a half of not working. Then a sudden flurry of activity. Kat, shopping in a big box store and nearly getting crushed by fans. Kat caught mid-kiss by paparazzi. Kat getting drunk and screaming at an old coworker in a crowded restaurant.

Ned Edwards didn't need to add much embellishment to paint a vivid picture—one of a former child star doing what former child stars do: imploding.

Could Kat even say he was wrong?

She closed her eyes, but she could still see the stark facts on the timeline looming behind her eyelids. The heavy weight of them pressed down against her, pinning her to her chair, making it impossible to move.

How could she have messed everything up so badly?

Kat dug her teeth into her cheek, hard. She deserved the pain. She deserved the light trickle of blood filming over her tongue. *Stupid fucking idiot,* her brain screamed. *You deserve all of this.*

"What do we do?" she asked Jocelyn, her voice shaky.

Jocelyn *tsk*ed. "There's not much we can do," she said. "We let the news die down. We release a joint statement with Madelyn saying things got out of hand. We organize a few interviews with reporters who agree to paint you in a positive light. Get you photographed doing some community service. Mostly, we cross our fingers and fucking hope that Gottlieb doesn't kick you out of the play."

Kat winced. "I quit the play," she said in a very small voice.

"You *what*?"

"Last night. Before the party. That's why I was acting so . . . that's why I was upset."

Jocelyn dug both hands into her hair. "And why, exactly, did you decide to quit the show we spent the last two months getting you into?"

The words got stuck in Kat's throat. It sounded so silly now. "He's been criticizing me constantly in every rehearsal. And then yesterday he said that I . . . that I should stop deluding myself into thinking I can act. That I was just a pretty face there to sell tickets."

Jocelyn's mouth twitched with barely concealed rage. "So you quit."

Kat nodded.

"You quit the show that was supposed to save your career because the director was *mean* to you."

Kat huddled miserably over the iced coffee she hadn't drunk, unable to meet Jocelyn's eyes.

"This is all that girl's fault," Jocelyn said. She pushed her chair back and started pacing. "Ever since you met her, you've been out of control. Questioning all of my decisions. Not wanting to do what fucking needs to be done. But guess what? This is the job. And there are a million other people out there who would happily take your place."

Jocelyn pointed a finger at Kat from the far side of the room. "I told you this would happen," she said. "I told you that playing house with this girl would mess up your career. The rules are different for you, Kat. Normal people don't understand what it takes to make it in this business. So you start running around with this retail worker, and she tells you, 'Oh, listen to your feelings, follow your heart.' Well, guess what? That's not how it works in Hollywood."

Kat thought she might throw up again. She had thought she was *growing*. She'd thought she was *getting in touch with her emotions*. She'd tricked herself into thinking that she was finally taking control of her own life. But in reality, Kat had been spiraling through a months-long breakdown. And now she was exactly where she always feared she'd be.

"I'm so, so sorry," she whispered. "I want to fix this. I'll do anything. Please."

Jocelyn paced back to her side of the table and braced her arms on it, leaning over toward Kat. "Are you going to listen to me this time?" she demanded. "Are you going to stop questioning me and actually do what needs to be done?"

Kat nodded. "I promise."

"Fine," Jocelyn said. "Then you know what you need to do first."

CHAPTER 41

JUDE

Jude lay in bed all morning, trying not to move.

The night before, Kat had run out of the restaurant, leaving Jude behind with an entire party staring at her. Heart racing, mouth dry, and face red, Jude had apologized over and over, first to the man whose phone she had smashed and then to the restaurant's manager. The man had eventually agreed not to get the police involved if Jude venmoed him $800 for a new phone, which she had. Then Jude had walked home, calling Kat over and over, clenching her fists a little tighter every time that Kat didn't pick up.

Yes, Jude shouldn't have stomped on that guy's phone. But had Kat seriously picked a fight with Madelyn and then run away, leaving Jude to deal with the consequences?

And what had Madelyn been talking about? *Does your little girlfriend know why you're dating her?* Jude wanted to dismiss the comment as nothing, but Kat had looked horrified. What did Madelyn know that Jude didn't?

The question had haunted her all night, keeping her from sleeping. Finally, around nine A.M., Jude grabbed her laptop and got back in bed. She googled *Katrina Kelly* and started reading through the news articles about last night's event. They were horrible. And most of them included Jude's full name, along with a shaky video clip of her stomping down on the phone. It made Jude's heart race at a panic-attack pace to watch the videos, but she couldn't help herself. What had she been thinking? She'd never done anything like that. She'd never been impulsive or destructive or violent before. What was wrong with her?

She'd just wanted to protect Kat. She'd been trying to help. But she had made everything so much worse.

What had Kat been thinking, confronting Madelyn in public like that? And then she had totally abandoned Jude and couldn't even be bothered to pick up her phone. Which was seriously messed up.

Jude tried calling her again, but it went straight to voicemail. Looking for something to keep her mind from spiraling, she scrolled deeper into the Google results. Past all the articles about Katrina Kelly coming out and into photos from before. A younger Kat with a younger Madelyn, sticking their tongues out backstage. Teenage Kat posing on a red carpet in a hideous purple leather beret. Tween Kat in a wetsuit, riding a jet ski in some movie still. An even younger Kat, holding a baby pig while on a late-night talk show. Thousands of images of Kat at every stage of her life.

Jude clicked on a video called "P.R.O.M.—Lily Carlson's Greatest Hits." It opened with a clip of a heavily made-up Kat in a cheerleading uniform, shaking two red pom-poms. Then a clip of her putting on lipstick as she ran to fight some monster. "Just because we're saving the world doesn't mean we can't look our best," she quipped, passing the lipstick to Madelyn. Then Kat, standing on a football field with tears in her eyes, reaching for the hands of some boy with long, greasy hair. It was unsettling to see how truly in love with him she looked. "I asked you to stay because I felt like our story wasn't over yet. I could tell that—"

Jude's phone vibrated with an incoming call, and she paused

the video, flailing around her bed until she untangled her phone from the sheets.

"Kat?"

"Hi, Jude. This is Nina Maguire from Gala Literary."

Jude sat up, her heart thumping. *Shit*. She was not ready to talk to her future boss right now. "Hi. How are you doing?"

"You've put us in a really difficult position here, Jude." Nina sounded tense.

Jude's stomach cramped with dread. "What do you mean?"

"I mean that the head of our board checked the news this morning and saw a video of you destroying someone's phone in a restaurant."

Fuck.

"I didn't—" She cut off, then tried again. "You're right. I'm so embarrassed about what happened. It was totally out of character for me. I would normally never do something like that. But you see, my girlfriend is a public figure, and she was having a tough day and this guy started taking a video and—"

"I'm sure that's very hard to deal with," Nina said. "But I'm sure you can also understand why we have to rescind your job offer."

Jude felt a pulling sensation, as if a vacuum had opened up underneath her and was slowly suctioning all of her organs out through the bottoms of her feet.

"What?" she said.

"Our organization relies on donors. Our reputation is everything. We just can't have this kind of scrutiny."

"It won't happen again. I promise. I'll do anything to—"

"I'm sorry, Jude," Nina interrupted. "Good luck."

Jude lowered her phone and looked at the screen. Nina had hung up.

Oh no. Oh no. Oh *fuck*. Was this really happening? Had everything gone wrong in one night? Had she quit the bookstore and left her friends for nothing?

Jude's chest tightened. Her wrists were tingling, and she was having trouble breathing. Desperate for something else to focus on, she pushed play on the video again. Kat stared into the greasy boy's eyes as if she loved him. "I could tell that underneath that bad boy exterior, there was something else, longing to come out. From the moment I saw you, something about your soul just hooked into mine."

Jude sucked in a breath. She moved the video cursor back and replayed the scene. Watched Kat reach for the boy's hand. Heard her say those exact same words.

Something about your soul just hooked into mine.

CHAPTER 42

KAT

A few hours after her meeting with Jocelyn, Kat let herself into Jude's building. She had to stop halfway up the four flights of stairs and lean over the railing for a moment to sob before she could pull herself together.

She pulled her key out in front of Jude's door, then reconsidered and knocked instead. She expected Jude to open it and immediately hold out her arms for Kat to fall into. She longed for the feeling of Jude's steady body against hers, even though she knew that after the conversation they were about to have, she would never feel that embrace again. Did that make her a bad person, that she wanted Jude to comfort her even as she was about to end things between them?

Probably. She *was* a bad person. She'd messed everything up, and all she wanted was to hide in Jude's apartment forever, but she had to start listening to Jocelyn or she would ruin her career for good. If she hadn't already.

But Jude didn't open the door and embrace her. She didn't open the door at all. Instead, Kat heard a tense "Come in" from inside and pushed the door open to find Jude sitting at the table, a laptop in front of her.

"Look who finally showed up," Jude said without looking up.

"What do you mean?" Kat said, lingering uncertainly in the hallway.

"I mean that I've called you thirty times since last night and you never picked up."

"I'm sorry. I just needed a little time to process."

"Of course. And while you were processing, I guess you didn't stop to think, 'Hey, I left Jude alone to deal with that mess.' Or 'Hey, Jude's probably freaking out about what happened right now, maybe we could talk this over together.'"

Kat winced. Jude was right. She *hadn't* thought that. She hadn't thought about Jude at all last night. She'd only focused on the fact that she needed to get out of there as fast as she could.

Gathering her courage, Kat came inside the apartment, shut the door, then sat down on the other side of the table, facing Jude. "I didn't think," she said. "I'm sorry."

"You mean you didn't think about *me*," Jude corrected. "You just thought about yourself and what would make you look good. Like always, right?"

"Hey." Kat's voice broke. "Why are you acting like this?"

In response, Jude shoved her laptop across the table to Kat and then angrily stood up. She strode over to the window as Kat stared at the screen. It was a *P.R.O.M.* fan edit, paused halfway through.

"What is this?"

"Hit Play."

Kat did, grimacing as a younger, overly made-up version of herself put on lipstick. Then the scene switched, and she watched herself reach for Bill Parker's hands. *I asked you to stay because—*

Kat hit Pause, as if keeping Jude from hearing the rest could keep the truth from her. As if she could fix this, when it had clearly already gone so wrong. Her mind raced. Could she pretend she didn't realize she'd been copying the lines? Could she say she'd thought they were really romantic and she had always wanted to say them to someone? Could she—

"Don't bother." Jude had turned around and leaned against the windowsill with her arms crossed, watching Kat stare at the computer. "Whatever excuse you're working on right now, just don't."

"I'm not coming up with excuses," Kat lied. "But this isn't what it looks like, I swear."

"Oh yeah?" Jude said. "And what does it look like?"

Kat stayed silent, not wanting to damn herself any further.

"Last night," Jude said, "Madelyn asked you if I knew why we're dating. And all night, after I got home, I lay there thinking about it."

Fuck. The horror of realizing they were being filmed had driven that moment right out of Kat's head. She'd been too focused on the consequences for herself. Just like Jude had said.

"I didn't want to believe it," Jude said. "But then"—Jude gestured at the computer—"I saw this. And I started thinking. *Hey, remember how weird it was that Kat asked you out again after that first date? Remember how eager Kat was to get your photo taken at that gala?*"

Kat couldn't look at Jude. She stared at her own face, frozen on the screen, halfway through confessing her love.

"At first, I couldn't make any sense of it. What would Katrina Kelly, famous movie star, need from *me*? I'm nobody. But then I put it together. I mean, you *told* me when we went shopping that you were trying to change your style. You've talked about how your manager wanted you in this play to give you a serious reputation. You've been trying to change your image, and being queer is part of that, isn't it?"

Kat didn't answer. Tears dripped down her face, blurring her view of herself on the screen.

Jude strode over and slammed the laptop shut, making her jump. "Isn't it?"

Kat was afraid that if she tried to speak, she'd break down. She nodded.

Jude closed her eyes. "Jesus Christ." Her hands balled into fists at her sides. "Was any of it real?"

Kat forced herself to speak, even though sobs started shaking her voice. "Of course it was real. It was real, Jude. I promise."

"Getting mobbed at the Old Navy? Was that real?"

"*Yes.*" Kat stood up and walked around the table, reaching for Jude. "I would never orchestrate something like that. It was completely accidental."

"What about those paparazzi photos of us kissing?"

Kat froze.

"Of fucking course." Jude pushed Kat's arms away. "I was falling in love with you, and you were lying to me the entire time." She sat down on the couch and put her head in her hands.

Kat's gut twisted with shame. She'd thought this morning with Jocelyn was the worst she could ever feel, but she'd been wrong. This was.

She sat down next to Jude. "It wasn't all a lie," she said. "My feelings are real, Jude. I've loved every minute I've spent with you. I've never felt this way before."

Jude lifted her head out of her hands, her cheeks wet. "Why did you come over here today?"

"What?"

"Why did you come over? What was your plan? To apologize for not answering me last night? To tell me the truth? So we could figure out how we're going to deal with this situation together, as a couple, since this affects both of us?"

Kat had been wrong again. She *could* feel worse. Every minute, she felt like she couldn't possibly feel more small, more shameful, more selfish, but then the next minute came crashing down, a relentless wave of truth.

She couldn't think of a lie. And she didn't want to lie, either. Jude deserved better than that. Her shoulders shook as she tried to hold in her tears. "Jocelyn told me to . . . she thinks . . . she's worried this relationship is distracting me."

Jude laughed. A cold, bitter laugh. "Right. Jocelyn wants you to break up with me. So here you are."

"I don't want to end things," Kat said. A sob hiccupped out of her throat. "I really like you, Jude. I've been so happy with you these past two months. But she's been my manager for thirteen years. And she's right. I've been distracted lately. I've been letting my feelings get in the way of my career. I haven't been in the right headspace and I've been making all these mistakes and—"

"Do you even hear yourself right now?" Jude said, incredulously. "Are you actually this selfish?"

"I'm not trying to be selfish. My feelings for you are real, but—"

"Please. The only thing you feel is ambition."

Kat scoffed, some of her shame melting away to anger.

"You think I don't *feel* things?" she said. "Do you know why Jocelyn wants me to end things between us? Before I met you, I had a plan. I was going to fix my career. And then you showed up and started asking me all these questions. Encouraging me to *trust my gut* and *think about what I really want* and all of this touchy-feely bullshit. And suddenly I can't do anything I used to be able to do! Suddenly, I feel things *all the fucking time*. I overthink my answers in interviews. I feel guilty every time I write a fake caption on Instagram. I can't put up with asshole directors anymore. I'm anxious or upset or mad constantly, and it's destroying everything."

"Are you kidding me?" Jude said. "You're trying to blame me for that? Instead of blaming your fucked-up childhood that encouraged you to suppress everything so you could be a perfect movie star robot?"

"I was *fine* until you came along!"

Jude's mouth had become a twisted, cruel shape. "You were miserable. You had no idea who you were and literally no one to talk to. You have no friends. You don't talk to your family. Have you ever realized how empty your life is? Maybe you care so much about your career because you have nothing else."

An ice pick to the chest might have hurt less. Kat's mouth fell open. A look of shame crossed Jude's face for a moment, but then she shoved it away, her expression frosting back over.

"Fine," Kat spat. "If I'm just a selfish movie star robot, then I guess you don't need me in your life."

Jude's mouth spasmed, but she pressed it back into a tight line. "You're right," she said. "I don't." Her voice was cold. "Enjoy the rest of your life, Kat. I'm sure you'll be very famous."

Kat stared at her cracked expression, desperate to see some glimmer of the real Jude there. But Jude turned away.

Kat waited a few more seconds. Then she turned around and fled.

CHAPTER 43

JUDE

Jude's dreams were interrupted by a strange, repetitive pounding sound. Like a judge's gavel, banging down again and again to cast judgment on her life. She turned over in her already twisted blankets, trying to escape the incessant, annoying sound.

"Jude!" A voice called from the hallway. It sounded like Talia. "Let us in."

Jude cracked one eye open. She was on the couch, where she'd been ever since her fight with Kat. Her eyes were scratchy from crying, and her head pounded with dehydration, making her feel hungover. She'd spent the past three days ordering takeout she couldn't afford and playing reality TV shows on an endless loop, not bothering to follow the plots. She needed the constant noise to keep her from thinking. Because once she started thinking, she would realize how completely fucked she was.

"We know you're in there!" Another voice called from the hallway. L.J. this time.

Jude covered her head with her pillow. She didn't want to talk to anyone. Maybe she would never talk to anyone again. She'd stay here, fused to this couch, for the rest of her life. Her friends would miss her at first, but they'd be better off without her in the long run. They would move on. Like Becca had. Like Kat would.

The pillow muffled the knocking, and she drifted back into a half sleep, not fully gone but not present, either.

Until someone grabbed the pillow off her head and yanked it away.

"Hey!" Jude twisted around, startled, and fell off the couch and onto the floor. L.J., Talia, and Rhys stood above her, their arms crossed. "How did you get in here?"

"I convinced George to give me his key," Rhys said. "We told him it was an emergency."

"I'm fine." Jude tried to get up, but her legs were hopelessly tangled in the blanket. "You can go now."

"You're not fine," Talia said. "You haven't answered a single text or call for three days."

"Also, look at this place." L.J. examined the apartment with a wrinkled nose. "This is not the apartment of someone who's fine."

"Just leave me alone." Jude finally succeeded in pulling her legs free, and she got off the floor and back onto the couch, glaring at them.

Rhys sat down beside her. He put a tentative hand on her shoulder. "Jude. Buddy," he said. "We saw the video of you destroying that guy's phone. What happened?"

Tears pooled in Jude's eyes. A wave of exhausted sadness washed away her resolve.

"I fucked up," she said, her voice cracking. "I lost control, and then Gala rescinded my job offer. Which means I left the bookstore for nothing. And I'm going to lose this apartment. And Kat—Kat never actually cared about me. She was lying the whole time. She just needed a girlfriend for publicity." Jude started to cry for real, and she covered her face so her friends couldn't see. "I have no job and nowhere to live and no girlfriend and no family and I'm losing *everything*. I always lose everything.

I try so hard to hold on to things, but I'm always getting left behind."

"Oh, Jude." Rhys put his arm around her. Jude started to cry and the other two piled on, forming one big, unstable hug. "We've got you. We're here. We're here."

CHAPTER 44

KAT

The gym in Kat's apartment building had large windows overlooking the Hudson River. The view was supposed to be a perk, but in the late afternoons, the sun was blinding. It dug directly into Kat's eyes while she ran on the treadmill, sharp and glaring, giving her a headache even worse than the one she already had. Every minute of sunlight filled her with a compounding fury, and she raged in her head against the architect, the building management company, the real estate agent who'd found this apartment for her. She let the rage spur her on, pressing the button to go faster and faster with every mile. It was easier to feel angry about the poor design choice than to think about the fight or the three endless, miserable days since.

She'd been running for nearly an hour. Plus, she'd lifted weights that morning and done a spin class. She shouldn't be on the treadmill right now. But she couldn't stop.

Have you ever realized how empty your life is?

Every time she tried to stop running, she heard Jude's words in her head again. They turned her organs into worms, squirming around inside her, and that uncomfortable panic drove her right back onto the treadmill, punching the speed higher in an attempt to push her thoughts out of her head.

Because wasn't Jude right?

She jabbed the control panel again, hard enough to hurt her finger, speeding up until she was practically at a sprint. It wasn't enough—Jude's words still rang through her mind. *Enjoy the rest of your life. I'm sure you'll be very famous.*

A sudden sob stole her breath, and she stumbled. She fell, grabbing wildly for the emergency stop cord, and managed to pull it as she landed on the belt, smashing her elbow into the machine's side and twisting awkwardly over her ankle.

"Fuck!" Kat screamed. Gingerly, she lifted her body into a normal position. Her ankle throbbed underneath her. Still sitting on the belt, she buried her face in her hands.

She let herself cry for a few minutes. Then, she reached up and took her phone out of the cup holder. She found the number she needed and pressed Call.

"Hi," Kat said when the other person picked up, her voice wavering. "Can we talk?"

■ ■ ■

Madelyn lived in a converted loft in Brooklyn Heights, full of high ceilings, exposed brick, and enormous windows that let sunlight stream in. The entire place was too color coordinated to be anything but the work of a decorator, but Madelyn had clearly been very involved in the direction. The whole place echoed her personality, from the framed Kinks and Ramones posters on the walls to the California flag throw pillows. It felt cool and stylish, but also personalized. A far cry from Kat's sterile Chelsea box.

"Nice place," Kat said, trailing her hand along a shelf full of records.

"Thanks." Madelyn came out of the kitchen holding two

glasses and a bottle. "Sparkling cider?" she offered. "I don't drink anymore, so it's all I've got."

"Sure. Thanks." Kat perched awkwardly on the other end of the couch while Madelyn poured for them both. Now that she was here, she didn't know what to say. She opened her mouth, then closed it again. There had been too many years of hurt to know where to begin.

Madelyn watched Kat over the rim of her glass. Then she said, in a soft voice, "Do you ever think about how young we were when *P.R.O.M.* started?"

"What do you mean?"

"I was fifteen." Madelyn leaned back against the arm of the couch, half turned so she could look at Kat. "My youngest cousin is fifteen now, and all she thinks about are TikTok dances and volleyball tournaments."

Kat picked up her glass but didn't drink. "I mean, I started working full time at eleven."

"I started doing commercials when I was five," Madelyn said. "By the time we were teenagers, we had adult schedules and responsibilities, with hundreds of people relying on us to show up, work hard, and make them money. We had all these fans and journalists watching our every move, calling out every mistake. We never got a chance to actually be kids. I mean, no wonder we're both messed up."

"Are you?" Kat turned to her in surprise. "Messed up?"

"Oh yeah," Madelyn said casually. "My therapist thinks I have PTSD. Which is part of why I panic whenever I feel like I'm being less than completely perfect all the time."

"I didn't know that," Kat said. "From the outside, you seem so sure of who you are. Coming out, getting on *The Qties*. Your life looks so put together."

"From the outside, sure," Madelyn said, rolling her eyes. "But you know better than to believe what it looks like from the outside."

Kat watched the bubbles fizz in her apple cider. She should have known better. But she'd spent the past few years convinced that Madelyn's life was as perfect as she made it seem on Instagram.

"Coming out was actually really hard," Madelyn said. "I've known I'm into girls forever. But I was so worried about what people would say. So worried that suddenly I'd be this completely different person in so many people's eyes. But it was killing me to hide it. I was second-guessing everything I said or did, afraid I'd give myself away somehow. Eventually, I decided it would be easier to stop hiding and deal with the consequences. But I didn't come out until the pain was unbearable."

"You still figured it out years earlier than me," Kat said.

Madelyn shrugged. "We're all on our own timelines."

Kat took a sip of the cider. She was surprised to find that it was delicious. She hadn't had a drink this sugary in more than a decade, probably. Too many empty calories. The thought made her sad, suddenly. What would it be like to live without that constant calorie math in her head?

"I have some issues, too," Kat said. "Although I guess you already know that, since I called you a bitch in public last week."

"Well, I was kind of acting like a bitch." Madelyn half smiled at her, and Kat tentatively half smiled back.

"We were the *lucky* ones, too," Kat said. "We didn't get sexually or emotionally abused, like the horror stories you hear from other shows."

"I mean, there was some questionable stuff. Joel would get really mean if you weren't doing a scene exactly the way he wanted."

"True." Kat crossed her free arm around her body, hugging herself. "He yelled at me in front of everyone for not wanting to do that skinny-dipping scene."

"I remember that," Madelyn said. "That was fucked up. It was, like, forty degrees. The crew were in parkas, and we were all in bikinis with our lips turning blue, then he wanted you to actually go in the water."

Kat swallowed. She could still feel that unique mix of shame and helplessness and panic, so familiar from her days on set, rising up in her. That *I really don't want to do this* alarm bell, mixed with the constant parade of *I'm messing up the scene. I could delay the whole shoot. What if they replace me? I'm lucky to be here* that reminded her she would have to do whatever they asked.

"We should have done something about that," Madelyn said. "All refused to do it or something. But we were too scared." She shook her head slightly. "It kind of blows my mind that none of the crew stepped in."

"It's nice to talk with someone who gets it. Who was there," Kat said. "I've been feeling . . . really alone lately in my experiences."

"This industry turns everyone who should be your friend into competition. It makes you paranoid."

There was a beat of silence. Kat felt an urge to jump in and change the subject to something lighter. Smooth things over. But instead she took a deep breath and forced herself to say what she'd come to say.

"You were my best friend," Kat said. "Why did you leak the news about my stay at the Serenity Center?"

Madelyn shifted in her seat, tucking her legs underneath her. "Isn't it obvious?" she said. "I was in love with you."

"*What?*" Kat said.

Madelyn cocked her head. "You had to know, Kat. We spent all our time together. We told each other everything. You were always touching me. But then I kissed you and you freaked."

Kat put her glass down. She didn't like thinking about that day. They'd been in Kat's trailer, stretched out on the bed the way they usually were during breaks, their toes tangled together. She remembered the way they kept finding excuses to get closer together. The held-breath feeling of expectation. The eye contact that stretched out unbearably long. The inevitability of it all, when Madelyn had leaned in and closed the space between them.

"You said you didn't feel the same way about me," Madelyn said. "Then you stopped talking to me, practically overnight. You cut me out. And then you started dating Frasier."

Kat *had* stopped talking to Madelyn. She'd been so nervous that someone would guess what had happened between them. If rumors got out, the network could probably have sued them—they'd both signed contracts saying they wouldn't do anything to materially change their public perception while on the show. Every time they'd been close to each other, Kat had been filled with a panic so loud she could barely think. Wasn't that why she'd finally agreed to go out with Frasier? Not because other people were asking questions, but because Kat herself was?

"I was so hurt. And I'm not proud of this, but I wanted to hurt you, too." Madelyn looked up, holding Kat's gaze, and Kat's chest lurched in uncomfortable recognition. "I know it was wrong. I'm sorry. I can't tell you how much I've regretted it since."

Kat let out a long, slow breath. She'd been waiting for that apology for four years. Two months ago, she might not have accepted it. But now Kat knew what it was like to hurt someone you loved.

"Is it true what you said the other night?" she asked. "That everyone on set knew?"

Madelyn winced but nodded. "Word had started getting around."

Kat closed her eyes. For so long, she'd blamed Madelyn for damaging her reputation with directors. But if this was true, Madelyn had just hastened the inevitable. The press would have found out eventually, with or without her.

If Kat was really being honest with herself, how much had that interview actually affected her chances of making it as an adult actor? An eating disorder was a minor scandal in Hollywood. The much bigger problem was that directors didn't believe audiences could see her as anyone but Lily Carlson.

Had Madelyn's interview really ruined her career? Or had Kat just wanted someone she could blame?

She opened her eyes. "I'm sorry, too," she said. "I shouldn't have cut you out like that. I was scared. Of the network and our fans and my career and—all of it."

"I know," Madelyn said. "Trust me, I know."

They sat in silence for a few seconds, Kat's head spinning with her new revelation.

"Do you want to talk about whatever's going on with you?" Madelyn asked. "Since clearly you're in the middle of something?"

Kat considered the question. Jocelyn had always told her not to tell people the full story, just in case they did exactly what Madelyn had done so many years ago. The more people knew about you, the more you left yourself open to scandal and hurt. But she was tired of holding things in all the time. She was tired of not trusting people. And if anyone could understand why she'd done the things she'd done, it might be Madelyn.

So Kat told her everything.

"I really fucked up," she said when she'd finished.

"I don't think you fucked up," Madelyn said. "Or, well, you did fuck up. But I don't think you fucked up in the way you think you did."

"What does that mean?"

"It means, are you actually mad at yourself for quitting that play? No offense, but it sounds like pretentious bull crap. And that director was a dick. Did you really want to spend the next four months pretending to be a vagina onstage?"

"No, but it would have helped transition my image, so my career—"

Madelyn waved a hand, cutting her off. "There's no one way

to save a career," she said. "When my agent got me the *Qties* audition, my manager told me not to take it. She thought the show would flop. But it was the first time I found myself actually excited about a script. The first time I wanted to do a project not because of how it would help my career but because I liked it. So I did it anyway. And guess what? The show was a hit. We're three seasons in with no sign of stopping."

"Yeah, but that doesn't always happen," Kat argued.

"Exactly," Madelyn said, leaning forward. "Because this industry is unpredictable. You can have the biggest names and the biggest budget for a movie and it can *still* flop. So why not do something you actually enjoy?"

Kat shrugged uncomfortably.

"I also don't think you fucked up by screaming at me in that restaurant," Madelyn said.

Kat laughed. She couldn't help it.

"I mean, it wasn't the *best*," Madelyn said, chuckling, too. "Obviously it wasn't the ideal location for that conversation. But how long have you wanted to call me a bitch? You've been holding on to this anger for four years, and you've never once done *anything* about it. Didn't that feel good?"

"I don't know, I was a little distracted by the fact that every news outlet in the country was writing about my public breakdown."

Madelyn's face turned serious. "I know that's really hard. But also . . . the press is going to write shitty things no matter what. You can't let it get to you too much."

"Sure." Kat rolled her eyes. "Okay, so, if ruining my career and reputation wasn't how I fucked up, what was?"

"You didn't stick to your guns!" Madelyn said, banging her fist down on the couch cushions beside her. "You've done all this great work lately to figure out who you actually are and what you actually want, but when things got bad, you reverted right back to being the obedient child star again. Like, sure, things got a little messy. But being a human is messy! You've literally never let yourself be messy in your life, so you freaked when you started to see the consequences. But if you're done shoving down your feelings, you have to deal with some hard shit."

"You can't be serious," Kat said. "You think the mistake I made was . . ."

"Breaking up with someone you're clearly in love with," Madelyn said.

Kat put her glass down on the coffee table. She felt a little sick. "Technically, she broke up with me."

"Yeah, but did you fight for her?"

Kat didn't answer. Of course she hadn't. Because Jocelyn had told her not to.

"If I dated Jude and only took the roles I wanted," Kat said, tentatively, trying to figure out how to phrase what she wanted to say. "If I started choosing my happiness over the biggest paycheck or the biggest role . . . a lot of people would say I was failing. Even if I was making the choices I wanted to make. They'd look at me and see a child star who didn't make it."

"Yeah." Madelyn held out one palm in front of her. "They would. Industry people would whisper behind your back. Magazines would make jokes about it. People would leave snide comments on your social media. But"—she held out the other palm, then moved her hands up and down like she was comparing their weight—"you'd be happy."

Kat felt a crack through her heart. She lowered her head.

"Hey, hey. Come here." Madelyn held out her arm and Kat leaned against her friend's shoulder for the first time in four years.

"It's just— If you're right, if this is all industry bullshit," Kat said through tears, "then I broke up with Jude for nothing. I hurt her so, so badly, for nothing."

"Maybe you can fix it."

Kat shook her head against Madelyn's shoulder. "She hates me."

Madelyn chuckled. "It is really hard to hate you, Kat. Also, people forgive each other. Just look at us."

Kat sat up. She grabbed a rainbow flag cocktail napkin off the table and blew her nose into it.

"You love her, right?" Madelyn asked. Kat hesitated, the napkin still held to her nose. Then she nodded. "Well, then you have to at least try, don't you?"

Kat wadded up the soggy napkin in her hand and stared at it. How could a relationship ever come back from the things they'd said to each other? The things Kat had done?

But Madelyn was right. Kat did love Jude.

So, didn't that mean she had to try?

CHAPTER 45

JUDE

Jude spent the rest of the week wallowing. She stayed on the couch with the blinds drawn, watching TV and not moving. But she wasn't alone anymore.

That first day, Jude's friends had stayed late into the night, cleaning Jude's apartment and then watching movie after movie with her. As they started *Sleepless in Seattle,* L.J. and Rhys had been pointedly ignoring each other. But by the time they'd finished *Four Weddings and a Funeral,* they had both relaxed, cracking jokes back and forth like they usually did, while Talia shot amused smiles their way.

After that night, the three of them came over in shifts, making sure Jude got some human contact every day. They didn't shame her or try to pep-talk her or suggest that she get off the couch. Instead, they just sat beside her and kept her company.

It felt good to just sit there and fall apart. But Jude could only sit still for so long. After a week, she asked Rhys to meet her for lunch in the triangle-shaped park across from Joe's Pizza.

"Hey." Rhys reached down to hug Jude, then sat on the wooden bench next to her. The fountain in front of them burbled soothingly over the usual West Village hum of car horns and shouting. "It's good to see you in clothes without an elastic waistband."

"Ha, ha," Jude said dryly. She pulled two enormous Alidoro sandwiches out of a paper bag and handed him one. "How was your day?"

"Fine," Rhys said, shooting her an assessing glance as he unwrapped the foil.

"You can talk about the bookstore," Jude said. "I can handle it."

"Okay, things have been kind of shitty since you left," Rhys said. "Stephen's been in every day, acting as interim manager, and talking about changing literally everything."

"I'm sorry." Jude twisted the foil on the end of her sandwich. She'd known that would happen. But she'd abandoned her friends anyway.

"It's not your fault," Rhys said. "He's just a dick. The good news is that it spurred me to finally apply to grad school."

"Hey! That's amazing." Jude knocked him in the shoulder with a fist, and he smiled. "In two years you could be starting your glamorous library career!"

"Oh yeah," Rhys said. "*So* glamorous. I definitely won't be underpaid and overworked at an insufficiently funded institution."

"I mean, why else do people become librarians but to make the big bucks?"

Rhys grinned. He took a bite of his sandwich, nearly dropping a giant piece of balsamic-soaked mozzarella. He caught it just before it fell onto his lap and popped it into his mouth. "How are you doing?"

"I mean, bad," Jude said. "But I'm outside, at least."

"You've been through hard things before," Rhys said. "I know that doesn't make it easier, but at least you know you can get through it."

"I guess," Jude said. "It's a little embarrassing, though. I mean, having a total breakdown and refusing to get off my couch for a week? Needing you guys to come rescue me? How pathetic can I get?"

"That's what friends are for," Rhys said. His hands and face were thoroughly coated in balsamic now. "Also, sometimes you just need to fall apart for a little bit. It's part of the healing process."

Jude handed him a napkin. "I've never fallen apart like that before, though. Not even when my mom died."

"Maybe you should have," Rhys said, scrubbing his face with the napkin. "Maybe it would have helped."

When Jude looked back on those years—the surgery, the radiation, the endless hospital visits, finding cars to borrow to get her mom to the hospital, cooking any meal she thought her mom would eat more than a few bites of, studying for tests in cancer center waiting rooms—what she mostly felt was weariness. She had been bone-tired for two years. Fear and panic had run through her so many times, an endless wash cycle, and by the time grief hit, she'd felt faded. Jeans gone threadbare, a shirt washed down almost to white. She'd wanted to sleep constantly, but there had been an endless parade of tasks: wills and calls to insurance companies and canceling credit cards and moving utilities into her name. When she looked back on that year after her mom's death, all she remembered was a never-ending shift at the register before coming home to a never-ending to-do list and tumbling into bed too tired to enjoy finally falling asleep.

"Maybe you're right," Jude said. "I didn't feel like I could fall apart, though. There was so much to handle. I felt like I had to keep moving, and if I stopped or thought about things at all, I'd never start back up again."

Rhys let out a thoughtful *hmm* as he chewed. Once he'd swallowed, he said, "You were in survival mode."

"Yeah." Jude unwrapped one end of her sandwich but didn't eat it. "I feel like maybe I've been in survival mode ever since. And I've only recently started to lift my head and look around and think about what I actually want beyond just getting by."

Rhys went to touch her knee, then stopped himself, seeming to remember how sticky his hands were. "That's not easy to do."

"But other people lose parents and they don't fall apart." Jude's voice wavered. She'd been doing so much crying lately. Someone was going to come confiscate her tough-butch card any day now.

"How do you know?" Rhys said. "Maybe a lot of people are falling apart and they're just hiding it, the same way you were."

"Maybe. Although I wasn't hiding it very well, apparently."

"I know you too well, dude. You can't hide anything from me."

Jude let the corner of her mouth flicker upward. Rhys was an incredible friend. Which was why it was time for her to repay the favor.

"I have to tell you something," she said. "The reason I told you not to date L.J. isn't because I thought they weren't serious about you. It's because I was afraid you guys would start dating and wouldn't need me anymore. Which I know was really, really shitty of me."

Rhys chewed his next bite very slowly, clearly buying himself some time to think. "That is pretty shitty," he said finally.

"I know. Especially because you've supported me so much these past few years," Jude said. "I'm sorry. I'm sorry I made you doubt yourself. L.J. clearly likes you a lot. I mean, how could they not? You're hilarious and caring, and you're also jacked as hell now that you're juicing."

Rhys snorted. He didn't smile, but he did flex his biceps in Jude's direction.

"See? Look at that. You're a fucking meathead now."

Rhys rolled his eyes, but the corners of his mouth twitched.

"I got you something." Jude pulled an envelope out of her

pocket and handed it over to him. He pried it open delicately, trying not to get it too sticky.

"Tickets?" he asked.

"Yup. To see *The Empire Strikes Back* with a live orchestra playing the score."

Rhys started to grin. "That's L.J.'s favorite movie."

"Imagine that," Jude said. "It's in three weeks, and you know they're going to want that whole time to make your costumes, so you'd better text them now."

Rhys groaned. "They're going to make me dress up, too, aren't they?"

"Yup. That's what you get for crushing on a major dork."

"I don't care how cute they are. I am *not* being Chewbacca," Rhys said, but he took out his phone and started typing. After he pressed Send, he stared nervously at his phone, his leg bouncing. A few seconds later, his face broke into a smile.

"They said yes."

"Of course they did," Jude said. "I hope you have an amazing time."

Rhys put his phone back in his pocket, but he couldn't stop grinning. "What about you? What are you going to do next?"

"Start applying to jobs," Jude said. "I have enough saved to pay rent for a little while. So I can afford to look for something that I'm really excited about. I'd like to stay in the literary world if I can. That Gala job made me realize how much I'd like to be a part of getting queer stories out into the world."

"That's really exciting." Rhys balled up his empty sandwich foil in his fist. "What about Kat? Do you think you'll ever see her again?"

Jude stared at the tumbling fountain. She was furious with Kat, but she also really fucking missed her. The pain was like a toothache—she could distract herself, but she could never fully ignore the sharp ache of walking through each day without this person she loved.

But it had all been a lie. Kat had been pretending that entire time. Nothing that had happened between them was actually real.

"No," she told Rhys. "It's over. The sooner I forget about Kat and move on, the better."

CHAPTER 46

KAT

Kat rang Jude's buzzer a second time, shifting the package she was holding to her other arm. She still had her key, but it felt wrong to use it. She was starting to worry that Jude wasn't home when the door finally buzzed and unlocked.

Kat climbed the four flights of stairs, her heart hammering with nerves. Jude hadn't even called down to check who it was, and Kat wasn't sure her appearance after two weeks of not talking would be a welcome surprise.

She knocked on Jude's door and heard Jude call, "It's open." Taking a deep breath, she stepped inside. It took some maneuvering to close the door behind her without dropping the big paper-wrapped package she was carrying.

Jude was lying on the couch in the living room with a book but sat up, clearly startled, when she saw Kat. They stared at each other for a few beats. She was wearing jeans and an old softball T-shirt, a soft one that Kat knew intimately from burrowing into the crook of Jude's arm.

"I thought you were Rhys," Jude said. "What are you doing here?"

Kat set the package on the ground and leaned it carefully

against the wall. Then she walked over to stand in front of Jude. "I came to say that I'm sorry. I've been cruel to you, and I owe you an explanation."

Jude didn't say anything, but she also didn't yell at Kat to get out, so Kat went on.

"Three months ago, Jocelyn told me that I needed to be seen with someone in public as a way of coming out without actually coming out. And then you sent me that DM, or Rhys did, and it seemed perfect. Because I really, really liked you when I first met you in the bookstore and I wanted an excuse to see you again.

"Ever since I was eleven, everything I've done has been for my career. I never paid any attention to who I was or what I wanted. Thinking about those things felt selfish when so many people were counting on me—my fans, my parents, the network, my costars. I became an expert at shoving down my real feelings so I could be perfect for everyone else. Whenever it felt unbearable, I reminded myself how *lucky* I was, and not to be ungrateful for everything I had."

Jude picked up a pillow and put it in her lap, crossing her arms over it, hugging it close to her chest. Kat couldn't read her expression.

"I told myself that I was dating you to advance my career, but the truth is you always meant more to me. I fell for you at the very beginning, in the bookstore. You were so kind to me, and you talked to me in this open way that made me feel like it was okay to not fully know who I am. You made me feel safe. I wanted more of that feeling. And the more I got to know you, the more I wanted you in my life.

"These past months, you've made me realize that it's not selfish to be myself. You got past all the defenses I'd been clinging to and made me feel like I could trust someone else for the first time in a long time. That I could trust myself."

Kat's voice shook.

"I fired Jocelyn. I realized that I don't want a manager who urges me to act like that anymore. And I can't blame her for what I did, because I'm the one who made those choices, but I promise you I'm going to make better ones in the future. I should have told you the truth right away, but I was too scared of losing you. I was so wrong, and I'm here to ask for your forgiveness." A few tears escaped down her cheek as she continued. "I should never have lied to you. I should never have left you alone in that restaurant. But most of all, I should have fought for you, Jude. I should have told you how real my feelings are. I should have told you that sometimes when you kiss me, I feel so happy I can't breathe. I should have told you that sometimes when we spend the night together, I don't fall asleep for hours because I don't want to miss a single second of how good it feels to be in your arms."

Kat stepped forward, slowly, waiting to see if Jude would pull back. When she didn't, Kat reached out a hand and pushed it gently through Jude's hair, savoring the softness between her fingers. "I should have told you that I love you, Jude."

Jude let out a small breath at those last words. Her eyes were shining, and for a glorious moment, Kat was sure that she was going to stand up and close the space between them.

But instead Jude leaned back.

Kat's stomach dropped. She stood there with her arms still outstretched for a few seconds before she recovered enough to lower them. Dread pooled in her throat, making her tongue taste bitter.

Jude rubbed her hands together, the thumb of one hand pressing into the palm of the other, then switching. Finally, she said, in a slightly unsteady voice, "Thank you. I really appreciate you coming here and saying all of that. But I can't do this."

Once, when she was a kid, Kat had jumped off the swings on the playground, expecting her dad to catch her. She'd realized too late that he wasn't paying attention. That was what this moment felt like: hoping for a soft landing, then smashing into the wood chips instead.

"I don't think a relationship can recover from a lie like that," Jude said. "How am I supposed to know you won't do something like this again? That you won't suddenly leave, the way Becca did?" She shook her head. "How am I supposed to trust you?"

Kat's throat was closing up. She could barely breathe. She wanted to beg, to plead, to keep making her case. But part of making amends was accepting the other person's response, even if it wasn't the one you'd hoped for.

It took everything she had to say, "I understand. Thank you for listening."

"I'm sorry," Jude whispered. Kat walked to the door, then turned back to let herself take one last tear-blurred look at the person she'd thought she could have a future with.

"Goodbye, Jude," she said.

Jude stared at her as if she, too, was memorizing Kat's face, trying to hold on to every small detail of the last time they'd see each other.

"Goodbye, Kat," she said.

CHAPTER 47

JUDE

Jude had never seen so much food in her life, let alone in her apartment.

Earlier that day, she'd gone back to The Next Chapter to clean out all her remaining stuff, so the bookstore crew was throwing her an official goodbye party. They'd decided to make it West Village–themed, so they'd gone out and collected as many neighborhood delicacies as they could possibly find.

They had three kinds of pizza: slices from Joe's and Bleecker Street, plus a thick rectangular pie from Emily. They had samosas and popadams from Taco Mahal, hummus and pita from 12 Chairs, and an enormous meatball sub from Faicco's. Talia had gotten a selection of fancy meats and cheeses from Murray's to make a beautiful charcuterie board. L.J., who was a foodie, had somehow managed to get takeout arancini and salad from Via Carota and a spread of mouthwatering vegetable dishes from Buvette. For dessert, they had a box of Molly's cupcakes, a dozen donuts from The Donut Pub, cookies from Rocco's, fluffy banana pudding from Magnolia Bakery, and cronuts from Dominique Ansel, which prompted a brief argument between Talia and L.J. about whether the cronuts belonged in their West Village party, since Dominique Ansel was actually in SoHo. Jude's apartment was filled with a confusing mix of smells, and the four of them were crammed together on the couch—coated in a light sheen of sweat, since it was an unusually hot day and Jude hadn't bothered to install her AC unit. Rhys and L.J. sat next to each other, blushing whenever their knees brushed. Their *Star Wars* date wasn't until next week, but L.J. had already finished Rhys's Chewbacca costume.

Jude stood up and took one of her mom's records out of the crate by the wall. She almost never played the Beatles records. It usually hurt too much. But today, she picked up *Sgt. Pepper's Lonely Hearts Club Band* and dropped the needle in a bit so "With a Little Help from My Friends" started to play. She switched off the playlist and Rhys stood up, taking Jude's hands and twirling her around the room. As the song faded into "Lucy in the Sky with Diamonds," they swayed together, arms around each other.

"I love you," Rhys said, and Jude turned their sway into a squeeze.

"I love you too, buddy," she said. "Always."

"Hey, what's this?" L.J. called as they came back from the bathroom.

Jude picked up her slice of pizza. "What's what?"

"This big wrapped package."

"Oh, that." Jude tried to sound casual. "Um, Kat gave it to me."

"*What?*" Rhys shoved her in the side. "Kat came over? When?"

"Like two weeks ago?"

"And you didn't tell us?" Talia shrieked.

Jude shook her head. It had hurt too much to think about, let alone talk about.

"*Dude.*" L.J. shook their head at her and collapsed into an armchair. Rhys went over and sat on the ground in front of them.

He casually leaned back against L.J.'s knees, and Jude saw L.J. try and fail to suppress a smile.

"There's nothing to tell."

"What did she want?"

Jude put down her pizza and slowly wiped her hands. "She wanted to get back together."

"After admitting that she lied to you about your entire relationship?" Rhys sounded outraged.

"Yeah," Jude said. "She apologized for everything."

"What did she say?" L.J. asked, leaning forward.

Talia patted the couch next to her. "Don't leave out a single detail."

Resignedly, Jude took her seat. Then she told them everything. How Kat had taken responsibility for her actions without providing excuses. How she'd insisted that the feelings between them were real so sincerely that Jude couldn't help believing her. How she'd told Jude that she should have fought for her. As she spoke, she found herself swallowing down tears.

Jude looked around the circle. Her friends all had rapt, dreamy expressions on their faces. "And then she said she was in love with me," Jude added.

"Wow," L.J. whispered, then immediately blushed as if they hadn't meant to say it out loud.

"That's . . . a very good apology," Talia said, delicately.

"Extremely romantic," Rhys added.

"Like something out of an Eileen Styles book," Talia chimed in.

"I know," Jude said, burying her face in her hands. "But she lied to me for so long. How can I trust her after that? I can't, right?"

There was a very long pause, long enough for Jude to look up and catch her friends glancing around the circle at one another.

"Right," L.J. said doubtfully.

"Absolutely. We support you in all of your decisions?" Rhys said. It sounded like a question.

Talia sighed dramatically. Jude ignored her.

"Wait, so, what's the present?" L.J. asked.

Jude shrugged. "I don't know."

"You haven't *opened it*?" Talia looked scandalized.

"What if it's a giant 'welcome home' sign because she bought you an apartment?" L.J. said.

"Or a collage of all things French because she got you plane tickets to Paris and wants to meet you on top of the Eiffel Tower?" said Talia.

"I highly doubt both of those things," Jude said, but her words were drowned out by Talia chanting "Op-en it! Op-en it!" and the others joining in.

"I regret ever becoming friends with any of you!" Jude shouted over them. When she stood up and headed toward the gift, they all burst into cheers.

Lifting the large, flat rectangular package, Jude found it was heavier than she expected, and couldn't help thinking of Kat struggling up four flights of stairs to bring it to her. She carried it into the living room and set it down on the floor.

Jude swallowed. She still wasn't sure she wanted to open it. She didn't need any more reasons to miss Kat. But Talia looked ready to rip the package open herself if she didn't, so Jude reluctantly let her fingers find the piece of tape at the back and start to tear it open. Her heart was in her throat, even though she kept reminding herself that it didn't matter what was inside, because she'd already made her decision. Finally, the paper fell to the ground.

It was a painting of her apartment. Her and her mom's apartment. Captured during the afternoon, when sunlight streamed through the windows, alternating golden and green as it filtered through the long leaves of the potted plants, illuminating the worn couch and the framed Beatles posters and the crates of records. It had clearly been painted off a recent photograph

(Jude could see the water stain on one wall that had appeared over the most recent winter), but it looked so bright and cozy that it made Jude feel like her mom could at any moment throw open the door and stroll through the frame. The colors were soft, realistic but gentle, with a swirling style of paint that looked very familiar.

"Is that—" Rhys started to say.

"It *is*," Talia shrieked. "Look at the signature! Fatima Halabi. No *way*."

Jude reached out and touched the painting, trying to convince herself it was real. Had Kat really done this for her?

"There's a note." L.J. picked up a white card that had fallen out of the paper and handed it up to Jude.

It was thick cardstock, with a plain border around the edge. In Kat's scratchy handwriting, it said:

We carry the people and places that we love with us, even when we have to leave them behind. No matter what, I'll carry you with me. For the rest of my life.

Jude held the card out to Talia, registering with vague surprise that her hand was shaking. Slowly, her friends passed the card around the circle. When they had all read it, they stared at her in silence, their faces solemn.

"Kat's right," Jude said sadly. "At least I'll be able to carry the memory of her, of us, around with me, for the rest of my—"

"Oh my God," L.J. interrupted. "Jude, you dumbass!"

"Excuse me?" Jude said.

"Kat came to your apartment and begged for you back. She got you a present that shows she knows you *perfectly*. Not to mention, we all saw the way she looked at you at the fake bar night. And you're just going to *walk away*? Do you know what I would do to have the person I like do something like this for me?" They glanced at Rhys. "For once in your life, stop thinking and just go for it, man."

"They're right," Talia said. "This is literally the most romantic thing I've ever heard of, and if you don't try to win her back with some enormous gesture, I will disown you as a friend."

Jude shook her head, overwhelmed. "But she *lied* to me. How can I trust her?"

"People make mistakes," Rhys said. "In fact, didn't you make a mistake with someone recently? And that person forgave you, didn't they?"

He raised his eyebrows, and Jude flushed. L.J. and Talia peered between them curiously.

"I guess," Jude said. "But if it doesn't work out . . . I don't know if I can handle getting hurt again."

Rhys put his hand on her shoulder. "We don't get to choose whether we get hurt or not, bud. We only get to choose who hurts us."

Jude scrubbed her face with her hands, trying to think. Trying to make a quick mental pro/con list, trying to weigh the risks and benefits, trying to—

She cut herself off.

Forget the pro/con list, she told herself. *What do you want?*

She looked up at Rhys, L.J., and Talia. They were her family. They were her home. And they would have her back if she got hurt again.

"You're fucking right," she said. "I want her back."

They cheered and surged forward, collapsing in a giant group hug.

"Call her!" Rhys yelled, his voice muffled in L.J.'s hair. "Call her right now!"

"No, no!" Talia swatted his arm. "She can't just *call*. This painting is an incredible gesture. Jude needs to do something big back."

"But what?" Rhys said, and they all lapsed into silence, thinking.

"I'm going to check her Instagram," Talia said.

"I'm googling 'big romantic gestures,'" L.J. said. They pulled out their phone and frowned at it. "Is she going to be in an airport anytime soon? Do you know of any cheaply priced string quartets?"

"Oh my God!" Talia shouted. "Wait, wait, wait. Look at this."

She shoved her phone in Jude's face, but her hand was moving too much for Jude to read it. "She's making a new movie, and there's a press conference coming up."

"Really? What movie?"

"Something called *Rom-Con*."

Jude felt a burst of pride. Kat had taken the role in the movie she loved, even though it wasn't attached to a big studio. She really was making a change.

"When is it?" Jude said.

"Um." Talia peered at her phone. "In fifteen minutes."

Jude swore. "Where?"

"The Luxembourg Hotel. On Sixty-third and Park," Talia read off her phone.

"Shit!" Jude said. "That's more than sixty blocks from here *and* on the East Side. We'll never make it in time."

"Car!" L.J. shouted. "I have my car! So I could pick up the food!"

They looked around at one another. Then they all hustled for the door and down the stairs to L.J.'s beat-up old teal sedan.

"Are you sure taking the subway wouldn't be faster?" Jude asked as L.J. navigated them through the narrow streets to Sixth Avenue.

"Erm." L.J. swerved to go around a double-parked Amazon truck and narrowly avoided hitting someone on an e-bike. "No."

"Google Maps says they're about the same, and we're already in the car," Rhys said, staring at his phone. "Plus, you'd have to transfer to the Q, and who knows how long you'd have to wait for a train."

"Okay, okay." Jude clenched the handle over the door and

tried not to curse every time L.J. stopped obediently at a yellow light—driving in Manhattan made them nervous.

They made it up to Twentieth Street at a relatively normal pace, then found their way blocked. Police officers in neon vests were directing cars off of Sixth Avenue, causing a confused snarl of traffic.

Rhys rolled down his window. "What's going on?" he asked.

"Vegan food festival pop-up," the traffic conductor explained. "Blocking the whole street."

Everyone cursed.

They had to divert down a side street. Several lanes of traffic were all trying to merge into one, and L.J. wasn't aggressive enough to cement their place. It took them several minutes before they managed to merge, and then traffic crawled forward. Jude drummed her hands nervously on the dashboard.

"Fuck it," L.J. said suddenly. They swung the car into a not-quite-legal spot on the side of the road. "The F is three blocks uptown. We can take it to the Q. Go, go, go!"

They opened their door and started jogging away. Jude jumped out to follow them and heard the others do the same. Once they passed the traffic barricades, however, running became impossible—the road was completely clogged with the lines for various vegan food stands. They had to weave and dodge their way through the crowd, gaining dirty looks from people who thought they were trying to cut in line for fried chickpea sandwiches.

They finally pushed their way through the last foodies and into the Twenty-third Street F station. Luckily, a train was just pulling up, so Jude ran ahead and held the doors until the others caught up, gaining her some very dirty looks from the other passengers. Rhys limped in last, wincing and rubbing his knee.

They all wheezed heavily by the doors until the train stopped at the next station, and then they walked at a slow pace over to the Q platform after Rhys verified on his phone that the next train was still seven minutes away. Jude bounced in place on the platform until the train came.

The others gratefully threw themselves into seats, but Jude stood by the door, staring at her reflection and the tunnel flashing by. If she sat down, she would start thinking. And if she started thinking, she was afraid doubt would creep in and she wouldn't be able to do this.

What if she was too late? What if Kat had already moved on?

Now that she was faced with the possibility that she might be able to get Kat back, the idea of not getting her was devastating.

"This is Lexington Avenue–Sixty-third Street," the automated voice said, and Jude's friends let out a cheer. Once they reached the top of the escalator and started down the street, though, Rhys stopped, wincing.

"Go ahead without me," he said. "I'll catch up. My body can't take any more."

"Don't be ridiculous," Jude said. "We're not doing this without you."

"What if I piggyback you?" L.J. said suddenly.

"Are you serious?" Rhys said. "It's two blocks. I don't think you can lift me."

"I walked around wearing forty pounds of metal for sixteen hours when I dressed as Alphonse Elric for Comic Con. Try me." They crouched down in front of Rhys. Looking flustered, he tentatively put his hands on L.J.'s shoulders, then jumped up. L.J. adjusted him confidently on their back, then set out at a steady trot. Everyone cheered, and Rhys blushed furiously as he tightened his grip around L.J.'s neck.

They all kept pace with L.J., jogging along, until they saw a pink-and-gold awning ahead that said "The Luxembourg Hotel." They sprinted past a surprised doorman and swung through the revolving door into a marble lobby with elaborate crystal chandeliers and velvet couches.

L.J. crouched to gently lower Rhys onto one of the couches so he didn't have to jump down on his knee, then they collapsed on the couch next to him, breathing heavily.

"That was . . ." Rhys started to say, an awed look on his face. Then he shook his head. "Fuck it." He grabbed L.J.'s cheeks and kissed them.

L.J. kissed him back, their hands rising to wrap around Rhys's shoulders.

"Finally!" Talia cheered. Jude just smiled.

"Right." Rhys broke away from L.J. "That's— Thank you." He seemed to remember himself and stood up, but he was grinning uncontrollably, and so was L.J. "Okay, where do we go?"

They all looked around the lobby. They didn't see any sign indicating that a press conference was happening. Had they missed it?

Rhys strode over to the front desk and asked which room the press conference was in. The front desk clerk eyed their sweaty, casual clothes.

"Are you a member of the press?"

"Yes," Rhys said confidently. "I'm a reporter for *Autostraddle*."

The man smirked. "Let me see your press pass."

"Excuse me?" Rhys's voice started to rise. "*Autostraddle* is one of the top queer media outlets in the United States, and when the movie directors hear that you kept *queer reporters* out of the press conference for this *queer movie,* I don't think—"

"All right, all right!" The man glanced anxiously around the lobby, seeming desperate to stop Rhys from shouting the word *queer* again. "It's in the Rose Room on the third floor."

L.J. piggybacked Rhys again, and they all took off running. In the wrong direction, at first, but eventually they found an elevator. When it finally reached the third floor, they rushed out at a sprint, only to realize that the door to the Rose Room was directly in front of them.

Jude bent over and panted for a few seconds, then straightened up and approached the door. She could hear voices from inside. She wasn't too late.

Was she really going to do this? Go in there and make some sort of unplanned declaration in front of a lot of people, without fully thinking this through?

She thought about Kat sleeping on her shoulder while they watched TV. Taking Jude to a museum after hours. Tilting her head back with laughter while they danced to "Fast Car." Coming to Jude's apartment to tell Jude she loved her and beg for a second chance.

Kat had come back to fight for her. Now it was Jude's turn.

And besides, no matter what happened, she wouldn't be alone.

Jude smiled around at her sweaty, disheveled friends. "I love you guys," she said.

Then she took a deep breath, squared her shoulders, and pushed open the door.

CHAPTER 48

KAT

"Ms. Kelly! How does Frasier Pierce feel about you coming out?"

Kat put on a polite smile. "I'm not sure," she said into the microphone in front of her. "You'd have to ask him."

"So, you and Frasier don't keep in touch?" The journalist followed up eagerly.

The conference room was crowded. Kat and her costars were sitting behind a long table on a small stage at the front of the room, facing rows of folding chairs, but the reporters had quickly abandoned their seats in favor of crowding up toward the table. The crush of people made Kat feel claustrophobic.

"Only one question at a time please," Anya Oliviera, the director of *Rom-Con*, said, smoothly sweeping in. Kat sent her a grateful glance. The press conference was supposed to be about the movie, but so far nearly every question had been for Kat.

"Another question for Ms. Kelly," the next reporter said. "What made you decide to go from big-budget films to independent?"

Kat sat up straight. "This movie is special. I loved it from the moment I read the script. As I move into the next phase of my career, I'm looking for projects that I feel passionate about. To me, it's not about the paycheck or the names attached but the quality. That's how I intend to determine which projects I take, going forward."

The man nodded, lowering his notebook, and Kat's shoulders relaxed. She'd been dreading that question, but answering it made it feel like not that big a deal. And her answer had actually been *true*, too. After talking to Madelyn, she had realized how much she wanted to be part of a project she genuinely believed in.

So she'd taken the role. Without calculating what it would do for her career or thinking about how it fit into her ten-year plan. Instead, she'd focused on what was right in front of her.

The door to the conference room opened, and Kat heard whispered commotion as a latecomer tried to push their way to the front and was rebuffed. She couldn't see them over the crowd, but she could see the turned heads and disapproving frowns of the reporters closer to the door.

Anya called on the next journalist, and Kat forced herself to pay attention again.

"Ned Edwards from the *New York Host*," the man said pompously. He was wearing a tie with little golf balls and clubs on it. "Ms. Kelly, are you still involved with the individual that you were seen kissing in the street several weeks ago?"

Kat thanked fifteen years of acting for keeping her from immediately bursting into tears. She wanted to snap at Ned Edwards that he'd ruined her life enough for one year. But the movie deserved better than that.

And what was the point of hiding the truth? Jude had made it very clear that she would never forgive Kat for what she'd done, and Kat couldn't blame her.

"No, I'm not," Kat said.

Another reported eagerly waved his notebook, and Anya reluctantly pointed to him. "What happened between you two?"

he asked breathlessly. Anya sent her a glance, making it clear that she didn't have to answer. But hadn't Kat wanted the chance to be more authentic with her fans?

"Dating while being in the public eye has unique challenges," she said. "Challenges that my partners might not be ready to face, but in this case, challenges that *I* wasn't ready to face. Growing up as a professional actor, I've struggled to get to know who I really am when I'm not in the spotlight. It's so easy to fall into people-pleasing and thinking about what you *should* do instead of what you really want. I'm trying to get better at paying attention to who I am when I let go of others' expectations."

Kat felt a little rush of adrenaline. She'd never spoken that honestly at a press conference before. She'd never given a messy answer that implied she wasn't 100 percent put-together and perfect all the time. It felt *good* to not just recite a memorized answer.

There was a disturbance at the back of the crowd. Heads turned to glare, and Kat saw a few people stumble as if they were being pushed. Anya was in the process of pointing to the next reporter when a head popped up above the crowd and shouted, "I have a question!"

Kat's breath caught in her throat. Was she so sad from her breakup that she was hallucinating? Or was that actually Jude, standing precariously on a folding chair so she could be seen above the rest of the crowd?

Jude caught her balance. "My question is: that individual you were seen kissing a few weeks ago. If she fought for you the way she should have and begged to have you back, would you take her?"

The reporters all leaned their heads together, asking one another what the hell was going on. But Kat could no longer hear them. All she could focus on was the hopeful face of the woman she thought she'd never see again. The woman she loved.

Kat didn't understand. Jude had been so insistent that she could never trust Kat again. Where had those concerns gone? Did she actually think they could make a relationship work? Or would she change her mind and shatter Kat's heart yet again?

It didn't matter, Kat realized. She would have to take that risk. There was only one answer she could possibly give.

She leaned forward into the microphone. "Absolutely, I would."

The room erupted. Reporters waved their hands desperately. Ned Edwards actually shoved the person next to him to make his way toward Jude.

Jude jumped down off her chair. Journalists swarmed her, asking for comments, but she pushed her way resolutely through the crowd until she reached the front.

Kat went to the edge of the stage and held out her hand. Jude took it and clambered up. Several cameras flashed, but Kat didn't stop to pose. This moment was just for her.

She pulled Jude back behind the step-and-repeat, down the stairs at the back of the stage, and through the door to the empty greenroom. Behind her, she could hear Anya telling the reporters to settle down. She kept going, tugging Jude out another door into an empty carpeted hallway.

Once the door closed behind them, Kat stopped. She looked at Jude, trying to drink her in, trying to savor every detail of this person she'd been missing. The person she had wanted to call every single day for the last two weeks. The person who, between calls for *Rom-Con* and appointments with her new therapist, had left Kat gasping with sobs at unexpected moments. Jude's blond hair was disheveled and her cheeks were red and her gray-green eyes searched Kat's face insistently. As if she, too, needed to catalog every last detail of the woman in front of her in order to believe that this was really happening.

"I thought you could never trust me again." Kat's voice came out as a whisper.

Jude took one of Kat's hands. She lifted it to her mouth and pressed her lips against it, then held on to it while she spoke.

"Three years ago, my entire world fell apart. And ever since, I've been waiting for that to happen again. Anytime something good happened, I kept expecting something to come and take it away. I didn't trust the world not to keep hurting me.

"When I found out that our relationship started as a lie, I thought, Of course. Here it is, that bad thing you always expected would happen," Jude continued.

Kat looked away. She hated that she'd made Jude feel that way. She'd been so selfish.

Jude reached up and tilted Kat's gaze back toward her. "I don't want to live that way anymore, Kat. Always waiting for something bad to happen. Not trusting anyone, because then they can't let me down. Not letting myself be fully happy, just in case things go wrong, so at least the world doesn't get to tell me, 'I told you so.'"

Tears started to build in Kat's eyes. One spilled out, and Jude smiled softly as she wiped it away with a gentle thumb.

"I can't control the world. I can't control whether good things happen. I can't control whether we stay together for the rest of our lives, or even how long we live," Jude said. "But trust isn't something you do or don't have. It's a choice. A choice I want to start making."

Kat's heart fluttered with hope.

"I'm choosing to trust that I know who you really are, underneath all the lies. I'm choosing to trust how you make me feel. I'm choosing to trust you, and believe that everyone makes mistakes, but that doesn't mean we can't get better."

Jude's eyes started to shine now, too. "Most of all, I'm choosing to trust myself. I trust that if something bad happens, I'll survive it, the way I always have. Because loving you is worth the risk."

Kat inhaled sharply. Jude cupped Kat's cheeks with both of her hands and nodded.

"I love you, Kat Kelly," she said. "And I want to keep loving you, for as long as you'll let me. Until you love yourself just as much as I love you and I love myself just as much as you love me."

"Jude," Kat whispered. It was all she could manage.

Jude pressed her forehead against Kat's. "Do you love me, too?"

"I love you," Kat said.

"Say it again."

"I love you, Jude."

Jude kissed her, all the longing and pain and happiness that Kat felt in herself reflected in the pressure of her lips, the grasping of her hands. Kat kissed back, breathless with disbelief that she got to kiss this beautiful person when she'd thought she would never kiss Jude again.

"I never want to let you go," Jude whispered in her ear when they finally broke apart.

Kat closed her eyes. She wrapped her arms around Jude and pulled her in as tightly as she could.

"You never have to," she said back.

EPILOGUE

KAT AND JUDE

Six Weeks Later

"Why do you have *three* power drills? What kind of non-professional-builder could possibly need *three* different power drills?"

Jude put her arms around Kat's waist from behind and swung her away from the cardboard box she'd been peering into. "I already told you," she said into Kat's ear. "One's cordless and one has a cord."

"And the other one?"

"The other one . . ." Jude kissed the back of Kat's neck as she struggled to come up with a response. "The other one just feels different, okay? I use it for bigger projects."

Kat tilted her head back, urging Jude to keep going. "You just have three drills because you want people to think you're a big, tough butch."

Jude used one hand to lift the back of Kat's hair and swipe her tongue across the sensitive skin there, making Kat moan. "I *am* a big, tough butch."

"I literally saw you crying during a Budweiser commercial last night."

"It was one of the ones where a horse and a puppy are friends!"

Jude protested. "Anyone would cry! Also, big, tough butches get to cry, too."

"They certainly do." Kat turned around and kissed Jude, letting herself lean into the kiss until desire ran through her, hot and energizing like coffee. It had been almost two months since the press conference and she still couldn't believe that she got to kiss Jude whenever she wanted. A little hot spring of happiness welled up inside her every single time she ran her fingers lazily through Jude's hair on the couch, or fell asleep with Jude's arm around her, or sank to her knees to bury her face between Jude's legs.

Jude kept kissing her, teasing her lower lip with her teeth. She moved them forward until Kat was pressed against the wall, and then she let her mouth roam, nipping along Kat's neck as her hands slid into the waistband of Kat's shorts.

Kat tilted her head back, losing herself in the sensation of Jude's soft, dancing touch, feeling herself slicken under Jude's fingers. But then, suddenly, she came back to her senses and swatted Jude's shoulder.

"Rhys and L.J. are waiting in the U-Haul outside!"

"They'll be fine," Jude said, kissing her neck again. But Kat slipped out of her grasp.

"They're double-parked," she said. "Some guy from New Jersey is going to scream at them at any moment."

"I'm sure they're doing the exact same thing down there that we are."

Kat laughed. Rhys and L.J. had been dating since the press conference, and they couldn't seem to keep their hands off each other.

"Come on, tiger. We're almost done." Jude tossed her head back in dramatic protest. Kat stepped forward and let her breath tickle Jude's ear. "What if I promise that as soon as we get home, I'll make it up to you?"

"You'd better." Jude kissed her again, but she broke off after a few seconds. Jude smiled down at Kat, her face suddenly radiant. "When we get home. I like that."

Kat beamed back. "It sounds good, doesn't it? Our home?"

Jude lifted Kat's hand and kissed her palm softly. "I am so excited to live with you, Kat Kelly."

"I'm so excited to live with *you*, Jude Thacker," Kat said. "But in order for that to happen, you have to actually move your stuff out of this apartment."

Jude groaned theatrically but let go of Kat's hand and grabbed the box of power drills.

"Good girl," Kat called as Jude started lugging the box toward the stairs. She grabbed a box of books and followed. They were moving into an apartment in Williamsburg together, a one-bedroom with big windows and a sunny kitchen. They knew they were being a stereotype by moving in together so quickly, but they didn't care. They had both decided that they didn't want to play it safe anymore. They were ready to take risks for the important things.

An hour later they finished packing the U-Haul, and Kat was feeling distinctly grateful that after today, she'd never have to climb up and down these four flights of stairs again. Particularly since, at the recommendation of her new therapist, she'd been taking an actual break from exercise for the first time since she was twelve. She had felt restless and anxious and guilty at first, but it was getting easier over time. Eventually, she would work on adding it back in to her life in healthy ways. She wanted to learn how to process her emotions without taking them out on her body. It was really hard, but she was working on it.

They'd already done one U-Haul run this morning to get the bigger furniture. Talia was currently at the new apartment, reassembling their bed frame.

After they put the last boxes into the truck, Rhys squeezed Jude's shoulder. "We'll meet you there, okay?" he said. "Take your time."

Jude nodded, chewing her lip. Then she wrapped her arms around Rhys. "Love you, buddy."

"Love you, too."

Rhys got into the truck. L.J. waved from the driver's seat and started carefully maneuvering the truck down the street.

"Do you want to be alone?" Kat asked, but Jude shook her head.

"No," she said, reaching for Kat's hand and twining their fingers together. "I want you with me."

They kept holding hands as they went up the four flights of stairs for the final time. Jude was silent as they climbed. On every landing, she thought to herself, *Today is the last time I'll see that dent in the wall. The last time I'll see that big water stain on the ceiling.*

When she opened the door to the apartment, she stood in the doorway for a long time. The rooms looked smaller without furniture in them. Light came in through the curtainless windows, highlighting the dirty floors and the dust drifting through the air. It felt empty without the framed posters and the plants, the records and the throw pillows. But in a lot of ways, it had felt empty for a long time.

Jude dropped Kat's hand and wandered aimlessly inside, running her fingers over the countertops, skimming her hand along the walls. She wanted to remember every inch of this place. Kat drifted along behind her, not saying anything, letting her have this moment.

Jude went into each room, taking a moment to breathe the space in. She saved her mom's room for last. Kat leaned against the doorway as Jude shuffled her feet through the dust balls left behind where the bed had been.

With all the art taken down and the furniture moved, there were no signs left that Jude's mom had lived here. No signs that Susanna Thacker had spent nine years getting dressed here every morning and dreaming here every night. No evidence left of the woman who had filled this home with so much laughter and love.

Well, almost no signs.

Jude found a tiny red mark on the white paint of the wall, near where her mom's dresser had been. She remembered that mark. She and her mom had been dancing around the room while they got ready for . . . something. Jude couldn't remember what. Her mom had been singing along to Carly Simon, spinning and dipping Jude to "You're So Vain." They'd both been laughing hysterically until Jude spun a little too enthusiastically and knocked her mom's open lipstick off the dresser. They'd been able to scrape the red off the floor, but even with scrubbing, the red mark had never fully come out of the wall.

Jude crouched down next to the mark. It had been three years, but she still missed her mom so much it ached. There was just so much she wished she could tell her. Her mom would have loved hearing stories about Jude's new job at a literary agency. She would have loved hearing about how things were going with Kat. How Jude fell asleep smiling every night, her face in Kat's hair and her heart so content it seemed impossible.

All her mom had ever wanted was for Jude to be happy. And Jude was finally making that happen.

Jude kissed her fingers, then pressed them to the mark. "I love you, Mom," she whispered.

Jude stood up and turned back to Kat, who put her arms around her and pulled her in tight. She let herself soften into Kat's hug. It was okay to be sad. But she wasn't just sad. She was also excited, for this new life they were building together. For all the chances Jude would take going forward, and all the new things she would experience.

"Do you need more time?" Kat said. "You can take as long as you need."

Jude shook her head. Then she walked through the hall for

the very last time, only pausing to lay her key down on the kitchen counter.

They stopped in the doorway again and looked back.

"Are you ready?" Kat asked.

"You know what?" Jude said. "I actually am."

She closed the door gently behind them. Then she took her girlfriend's hand and kissed it. She intertwined their fingers and they walked down the stairs together, hand in hand, into their new life.

RESOURCES

National Alliance for Eating Disorders

This national nonprofit organization provides referrals, education, and support for individuals experiencing eating disorders and their loved ones.

allianceforeatingdisorders.com
Call 1-866-662-1235

SAMHSA's National Helpline

The Substance Abuse and Mental Health Services Administration's National Helpline is a confidential, free 24/7 information service, in English and Spanish, for individuals and family members facing mental health and/or substance use disorders. This group provides referrals to local treatment facilities, support groups, and community-based organizations.

samhsa.gov
Call 1-800-662-4357

The Trevor Project

The Trevor Project provides free, confidential counseling to LGBTQIA+ people ages thirteen to twenty-four. All ages can visit their website for helpful resources on LGBTQIA+ topics and issues.

thetrevorproject.org
thetrevorproject.org/resources/guide/the-coming-out-handbook
Text START to 678-678 or call 1-866-488-7386

ACKNOWLEDGMENTS

Before I start thanking the many, many people who made this book possible, I want to call attention to an issue that came up again and again as I did the research for this book: the vulnerability of child actors and performers. Child acting is an extremely unregulated industry that leaves many young performers with severe self-esteem and mental health issues, and leaves them vulnerable to exploitation, abuse, and more. I highly recommend checking out Alyson Stoner's podcast *Dear Hollywood* to learn more about this issue and what we can do to advocate for better regulation for all types of young performers.

This book exists thanks to the hard work and belief of so many people. First of all, Katy Nishimoto, my insightful, patient, passionate, and wise editor. Thank you for all of your brilliant editorial notes and enthusiasm.

Thank you to Jessica Alvarez, my steadfast and wonderful agent, for believing in me and always having my back. Thank you to the rest of the BookEnds team for your kindness and support.

Thank you to the entire team at The Dial Press. I'm so grateful that my books found such a wonderful home. Thank you especially to Whitney Frick, Debbie Aroff, Jordan Hill Forney, JP Woodham, Cara DuBois, Hope Hathcock, Rebecca Berlant, Alexis Flynn, Ali Wagner, and Donna Cheng. A huge thank-you to the extremely talented Sandra Chiu for this beautiful cover.

I've made so many wonderful author friends during my publishing journey, and I'm so grateful for every one of you. I particularly want to thank Laura Piper Lee, whose early love for Jude kept me going through multiple drafts, and Yume Kitasei, who repeatedly reassured me that this book isn't terrible. Thank you both for all of the support.

A huge thank-you to my family: Mom, Dad, Baird, Cole, Alexa, and Martine. I love you all so much. I'm so lucky to have you.

Endless, eternal thanks to my wonderful friends, many of whom have offered me a lot of support and love over the past year. Maia Sacca-Schaeffer and Hannah Koerner: thank you for making every single week better. Elizabeth Keto, our conversations always make the world seem a little brighter. Special thank-yous to Rachael Morris; Jax Gill, my lifting buddy; Irene Bunnell, my almost running buddy (hey, we went once!); Meghan McCarthy, my hiking and deep chats buddy; Lauren Heirigs, my theater consultant for this book; Shannon Cox; Laura Harshberger; Rose Pleuler; Maria Messick; Kinza Baad; Sarah Manhardt; Hewitt (you don't get a first name, sorry); and Stuart Yandell. A special shout-out to Crescendo, the world's best softball team—I love you all.

Thank you to all of the wonderful booksellers and librarians who supported my debut. Thank you to all of the readers who have reached out to let me know how *Just as You Are* affected you—your notes mean more to me than I can say. And a special shout-out to anyone who identifies with this book: figuring yourself out is a long journey with multiple steps. You're doing great.

THE NEXT CHAPTER

CAMILLE KELLOGG

Dial Delights

*Love Stories
for the
Open-Hearted*

*Hey cutie.
Hope you don't mind—
I added some notes in
the margins of your copy.
Happy six-month anniversary!
Love, Jude*

AN EXCERPT FROM

Curled Around Your Finger

by Eileen Styles

Sam sat hunched over on the locker room bench, breathing hard. The door burst open, hitting the wall behind it, and Ella stormed into the locker room.

"What the hell was that?" she demanded.

"I'm sorry." Sam put her head in her hands.

"You're lucky we didn't get disqualified!" Ella shouted, pacing around the tight space. "I haven't seen curling that bad since the juniors."

You know, I'm not sure Eileen did any actual research on the intricacies of curling strategy...

"We won, didn't we?" Sam said into her hands. "We made it to the finals."

"Barely. I was sweeping my heart out. But you were totally distracted."

"It's just . . ." Sam swallowed. "You were sweeping so hard. But all I could think was that I want you to sweep something else."

"What are you talking about?" Ella stopped in front of where Sam was sitting. "What else would I sweep?"

"Me," Sam whispered. "Off my feet."

This is so cheesy!! Why do I love it so much??

Ella's mouth opened. "But we said . . . We promised

when we became teammates that we wouldn't do that again."

"I know," Sam said. "And I know that teammates dating is totally against the curling code of ethics. My whole life, all I've ever cared about has been proving I'm as good of a curler as my mother. But I don't dream about curling my way to the top anymore. I dream about curling around you every night."

"Do you really mean that?" Ella asked, her voice barely above a whisper.

Sam nodded. "I used to love this sport. But now, when I throw the curling stone, my heart is colder than the ice." It's impressive how many curling puns Eileen managed to fit in one book

Ella knelt on the ground in front of Sam's bench, putting her just below Sam's eye level.

"You have no idea how much I want you."

"But—but after the quarterfinals, you said we couldn't—"

"I'm our team's skip, Sam," Ella said. "And you're our vice-skip. Our teammates are counting on us. And our community is counting on us, to win the tournament prize money and save the local-bakery-slash-animal-rescue that our town loves so much."

"I know," Sam whispered. "Old Mr. Jenkins will have to close up shop without the prize money. And where will our town get our baked goods and adoptable pets then?"

"Exactly." Ella stood up and paced around the locker room. "We can't be together. Because of the curling code of ethics, but also because I've sworn off dating,*" she said. "But if our sexual chemistry is distracting us on

*Due to her emotional intimacy issues that definitely won't be hurriedly resolved right at the end of the tournament

---

Margin notes:

The curling what???

TBH, this is how I feel about you. Curling up next to you is the best part of every day

I looked this up and I guess the skip is, like, the captain of a curling team? And I guess a vice-skip is like the deputy captain? In case the skip dies in the line of curling duty?? Who knew!

the ice . . . then maybe we need to find a way to clear our heads."

Sam looked up. "You mean . . ." she said, a question in her voice.

"I *mean* get over here, Daniels."

Sam stood up and crossed the locker room. She paused a few steps before Ella. "So just sex? To clear our heads?"

"Right," Ella said. "Just sex." *This plan definitely won't backfire*

"Just sex," Sam echoed. Then she was kissing Ella with all the passion she'd been saving up for weeks. She would have liked to savor the moment she'd been dreaming about for so long, but she couldn't make herself slow down. Her lips were on Ella's lips, her hands were in Ella's hair, her body was pressed against Ella's as if she couldn't bear to have a single inch of them apart. *This sex scene always makes me think about you* ☺

Ella seemed to feel the same way: she pressed against Sam, her hands grasping hungrily at Sam's back, neck, arms, body. Ella pushed her against the wall and Sam's elbow banged into the locker behind her, but she didn't care. She only kissed harder, pulling Ella's bottom lip between her teeth until Ella moaned. Ella ran a hand through Sam's hair, then tugged, and Sam whimpered, tilting her head to give Ella better access, begging Ella with her eyes to pull harder.

"You still like that, then, do you?" Ella said huskily into her ear.

"Yes," Sam moaned, nodding so her scalp tugged against Ella's fistful of hair. "I really do."

Ella's hands grew bolder, moving more firmly down Sam's sides. She dug her nails into the sensitive back of Sam's arm and squeezed, sending a dizzying wave of pleasure and pain running through Sam's body. "Do you like that?"

"Yes," Sam panted. "So much. I—I want you to hurt me."

Ella dug her nails in even harder, making Sam gasp. "Say please," Ella crooned into her ear.

"Please," Sam said, moaning the word so it stretched out, long and desperate. "Please hurt me, Ella."

"Turn around."

Sam turned. Ella pushed the back of her head downward until Sam was bent over, and positioned her hands on the wooden bench that ran in front of the lockers, palms down. Sam waited, breathing hard with anticipation. Then Ella's hand came down hard on her ass. The fabric of her curling pants cut the sting, and the thuddy blow seemed to travel directly to Sam's clit.

Wait, weren't they just leaning up against the lockers? Where did this bench come from?

"Yes," she moaned. "Please. Please, Ella. More."

Ella brought her hand down again and again. Sam moaned. She could feel her underwear getting soaked under Ella's hands. Then the blows stopped and she heard Ella cross the room and pick something up.

"Do you need more, Sam? Do you need me to hurt you more?"

"Yes," Sam said. "I want you to push me to my limits."

"Do you want me to push you to your limits with this?"

Sam turned her head to look at the object Ella was holding out. She held the handle of a curling stone in her hand. Sam's breath stuttered in her throat. She nodded, wordless with desire and a little bit of fear.

"I'm going to hit you five times," Ella said. "Count for me."

I looked it up and you're right: curling stones are wayyyy too heavy for this scene to make any sense. Oh, Eileen.

Sam nodded desperately, and then Ella swung the stone. Sam cried out as it slammed into her, sending her body rocking forward over the bench. The pain was so intense it washed away all the thoughts that usually overfilled Sam's brain: The expectation that she would carry on her mother's curling legacy; the conflict she'd been having with her best friend;* the bitterness of her lifelong curling rivalry with Ella. They all drifted away, leaving her brain peacefully quiet, until all that mattered was this moment right here with Ella, bent over in the locker room.

*a necessary subplot for any rom-com

"One," Sam moaned.

Ella swung the stone again and Sam put a fist against her mouth to muffle the scream she wanted to let loose. When she could trust her voice again, she gasped, "Two."

The third hit set Sam moaning, the pain turning into a deep, bruising pleasure that flushed through her, leaving her aching. She loved this. Feeling fully present, every nerve in her body painfully alert, every part of her yearning for Ella's touch. She wanted Ella to hit her again and again, until she lost all sense of reality.

This scene is so hot, but now that I know curling stones are 42 pounds, I am a little worried about Sam's safety. Don't try this at home, folks!

"Are you ready?" Ella panted in Sam's ear. "These last two are going to hurt."

Sam nodded desperately. The stone came down in quick succession on each cheek, much harder than before. Sam screamed into her fist, unable to stop herself. Ella grabbed Sam, holding on to her as the wave of pain rose and then crested, grounding Sam with her body and her soothing touch.

"You did so well," Ella crooned softly in Sam's ear. "You took that so well for me."

Sam could barely speak. She moaned out words between gasps. "Please. I need . . . Please."

Ella's hands moved down Sam's body and lifted her shirt. "Is this what you need?

"I—*yes*," Sam groaned as Ella's hands closed around her.

Ella tugged Sam off the bench. They pressed against the lockers again, tugging at each other's clothes, until they were fully undressed. <u>Then her mouth was on her tits, sucking and teasing with her tongue.</u>

[margin note: Wait, whose mouth is on whose tits?? It's so hard to keep track when both pronouns are "her"... This might be the hardest part about being gay]

Sam ran Sam's fingers down Ella's body, watching Ella's head tip back as Sam's hand got closer and closer to Ella's center.

Then Sam sank to her knees. She lifted one of Ella's legs and rested it on her shoulder as Ella leaned back against the lockers. Sam ran her tongue over Ella's thighs, teasing her, until a sharp tug on her hair directed her to where Ella really wanted her. Then she let herself go, licking eagerly, every gasp and moan from above urging her on.

Faster than Sam would have thought possible, Ella's grip on her hair tightened and her thighs shook as she came. Then she was back on her feet, bending Sam over the bench. Her breath was hot on the back of Sam's neck as her hands found the exact right spot and began to thrust. Sam moaned, enjoying the pain from her sore ass mixed with the pleasure from Ella's hands. She'd been dreaming about feeling Ella inside her again for weeks—it was hard to believe that it was finally happening. She wanted to savor the experience, but it felt too incredible: the pleasure crested until she cried out and collapsed onto the bench beneath her.

DIAL DELIGHTS

Ella's hands caught her and slowly lowered her to the carpeted floor. They lay there, their arms around each other, until their breathing slowed. They didn't say a word. Not even when they heard a noise in the hallway that sent them scrambling for their clothes, or when they paused to share one last, lingering kiss in the locker room before pushing through the door back toward the ice. But even without speaking, Sam was pretty sure that they were thinking the exact same thing:

Having sex with each other hadn't gotten it out of their systems. <u>In fact, it had done the exact opposite.</u>

Whaaat! Who could possibly have seen that coming!!!

And here's the other solution to the pronoun problem... Nothing says sexy like repeating a character's name three times in one sentence

CAMILLE KELLOGG is the author of *Just as You Are* and *The Next Chapter*. She's based in New York City, where she works as an editor for children's and young adult books. She's passionate about queer stories, cute dogs, and bad puns.

camillekellogg.com
Instagram: @kellogg_camille

ABOUT THE TYPE

This book was set in Fairfield, the first typeface from the hand of the distinguished American artist and engraver Rudolph Ruzicka (1883–1978). Ruzicka was born in Bohemia (in the present-day Czech Republic) and came to America in 1894. He set up his own shop, devoted to wood engraving and printing, in New York in 1913 after a varied career working as a wood engraver, in photoengraving and banknote printing plants, and as an art director and freelance artist. He designed and illustrated many books, and was the creator of a considerable list of individual prints—wood engravings, line engravings on copper, and aquatints.

DIAL DELIGHTS

Love Stories for the Open-Hearted

Discover more joyful romances that celebrate all kinds of happily-ever-afters:

dialdelights.com

🅾 @THEDIALPRESS

▶ @THEDIALPRESS

Penguin Random House collects and processes your personal information. See our Notice at Collection and Privacy Policy at prh.com/notice.